THE
FARAWAY
WAR

★

Enrique Clio

★

THE FARAWAY WAR

★

A NOVEL

THOMAS DUNNE BOOKS

St. Martin's Press ≋ New York

This is a work of fiction.
All of the characters, organizations, and events portrayed in this novel
are either products of the author's imagination
or are used fictitiously.

THOMAS DUNNE BOOKS.
An imprint of St. Martin's Press.

www.thomasdunnebooks.com
www.stmartins.com

Design by Kathryn Parise

LIBRARY OF CONGRESS CATALOGING-IN-PUBLICATION DATA

Clio, Enrique.
    The faraway war / Enrique Clio.—1st ed.
        p. cm.
    ISBN-13: 978-0-312-37958-2
    ISBN-10: 0-312-37958-7
    1. Reeve, Henry M., 1850–1876—Fiction.   2. Revolutionaries—
Cuba—Fiction.   3. Cuba—History—Insurrection, 1868–1878—
Fiction.   I. Title.
    PS3603.L5658F37 2009
    813'.6—dc22

                                                            2008037675

First Edition: April 2009

10   9   8   7   6   5   4   3   2   1

I dedicate this work to all Americans, in particular Brooklynites, who should be proud of the contribution that this novel's real-life main character made to the birth of a nation.

Acknowledgments

★

While conducting the research required for this novel, two dear friends provided invaluable help and assistance. I will reveal their names when the time is right.

QUESTION: What's the difference between a historian writing history and a novelist?

ANSWER: The historian will tell you what happened. The novelist will tell you what it felt like.

—E. L. DOCTOROW
Time magazine, March 6, 2006, Canadian edition

THE
FARAWAY
WAR

★

ONE

May 28, 1869

The corpses of eleven white males lay strewn in a wide clearing bathed by the pale light of a full moon. Stars twinkled above the unseeing eyes of those supine; dozens of ants explored facial orifices. The stained clothing the men wore evidenced that bodily fluids had flowed abundantly, and even though the soil had absorbed nearly all, the immediate surroundings glistened with traces of blood and urine, globs of vomit and droplets of sweat, saliva and tears. A few bodies were in close physical contact—legs overlapping, shoulders brushing—but most lay by themselves.

The dense primeval forest encircling the glade had very large canopy trees, royal palms, fruit trees, and undergrowth. Bats were squeaking and owls hooting. Daytime birds slept in their nests or in the holes of old trees. Far away a wild dog howled. A deer raised his head and ears, stopped chewing the cud. The stench of death discouraged rodents from entering the area, where they customarily feasted on worms and insects.

A night for fruits, they had decided hours earlier, then took to the forest, minding out for reptiles.

A human sneeze brought animal life to a standstill.

Henry Reeve opened his eyes to dark greenness and knit his brow in complete bafflement. After a moment, it came to him that he was facing blades of grass. He tried to scratch his itching nose but found that his hands were tied behind him. A second sneeze dislodged the remaining two ants from his left nostril. Lifting his head, Reeve looked around; the hairs at the back of his neck stood on end. He retched twice before vomiting a mouthful of bile. Memories returned while he spat out the bitterness in his mouth.

He and his brothers in arms had been arranged in a single line, standing side by side. They had faced twenty-odd Spanish infantrymen wearing white-and-blue-striped drill uniforms and panama hats, aligned in two rows. Those in the front had had their right knees and left feet firmly planted on the ground; the second row had stood a step behind their kneeling comrades. Their commanding officer had barked out orders at the top of his lungs. As they took aim, their faces had been partially concealed by the brims of their hats and the Berdan rifles on their shoulders. A blinding volley was the last thing he remembered.

Reeve wondered whether he was dead or alive, dreaming or awake. Had he fainted after the fusillade? He turned over on his back and intense pain shot through his left arm and the right side of his rib cage. He was alive and awake, for sure. It seemed he had caught a slug, maybe two. Grimacing, he managed to sit up. With blurred vision, he inspected himself. The bloodstain on his long-sleeved shirt started five or six inches below his left shoulder and ran down to the cuff. There was another one below his right armpit. Oh Lord, how it hurt.

Next, he glanced at the corpses to his right, then to his left. Had anyone else survived?

"Hello?"

Eager crickets calling out to the females of the species were the only respondents.

All his comrades appeared to be dead; none moved. How could he be alive? "'Yea, though I walk through the valley of the shadow of death, I will fear no evil: for thou art with me; thy rod and thy staff they comfort me,'" he muttered, his gaze roving about the corpses.

Staring at the edge of the clearing, recollections dissolved reality. St. Paul's Lutheran Church on a cold Sunday morning. His father, in his dark blue frock coat, delivering one of his fire-and-brimstone sermons from the pulpit. His mother, in her black velvet bonnet and brown overcoat, sitting in the front pew, eyes fixed on his dad, making it appear she was listening for the first time ever to what she had lent an ear to on innumerable occasions over twenty years. His sisters alongside mom, daydreaming to conceal their boredom and occasionally blowing on their cupped hands and rubbing them.

The sight of a black-crowned night heron taking flight, signaling that animal life had resumed, brought Reeve back to the present.

Now, near death, he was wishing he had said good-bye personally, rather than leaving a letter on the kitchen cupboard. But he had dreaded that they would have moved heaven and earth to prevent him from joining the expedition, arguing he was a kid. That's what they had done four years earlier when, at fifteen, he joined the New York Volunteers as a drummer. In hindsight, he *had* been a kid then.

Well, here he was: still a kid, a stupid kid at that, dying merely two weeks after landing. A fellow who drops and loses his revolver in the middle of the battle is stupid. He had been searching frantically in the tall grass when the Spaniard had rushed him into surrendering. Butt under his armpit, finger on the trigger, the soldier had moved his rifle's muzzle up and down several times, excitedly shouting in Spanish. Reeve had sensed there was nothing he could do and had thrown his arms up, more in despair than to concede defeat.

Twelve in all: ten Cubans and two Americans. Eighty-five Americans had joined the two-hundred-man expedition, and he had met most of them, including the other Yankee taken prisoner. Tough-looking old chap in his thirties, dark hair, Union army officer's hat. Reeve had addressed him respectfully aboard ship—"Glad to make your acquaintance, sir"—trying to be polite with a stranger on account of the fact he was much older, had seen action, and came from where Reeve did, but he had forgotten his name.

Helping himself with the heels of his ankle-jacks, Reeve turned on his buttocks, sniffled back mucus, and spat. Moving his gaze from one corpse to the next, he spotted a body lying prone, eight or nine feet away. In the dead of night, he couldn't be sure if it was his fellow countryman, but it certainly looked like him. His hat was nowhere to be seen, though. Reeve caught sight of what appeared to be four exit wounds on the man's back, so the Yank had presumably taken the .54-caliber flat-based bullets in his chest and belly. He felt proud of his compatriot; the man hadn't whined, despaired, or asked to be pardoned.

Then Reeve realized he hadn't either, nor had any of the Cubans. Well, maybe all had been too scared to implore forgiveness—or had assumed retribution sensible, under the circumstances. Two days earlier, General Jordan had put to death four Cuban prisoners who fought for Spain. The general had set the rules of engagement on board while haranguing his men. Cubans who peaceably campaigned for self-determination, Jordan had made known, were exiled. But should one who took up arms against the Spanish Crown surrender or be captured, regardless of his nationality, he was shot on the spot. Consequently, Jordan had gone on, Spanish regular soldiers or Cuban volunteers captured by the Liberation Army would be given identical treatment.

Fair enough, Reeve had concluded at the time. You live by the sword, you die by the sword.

But it hadn't seemed fair enough at all when his wrists had been tied behind his back, the enemy platoon retreated twenty or so paces, and cartridges were loaded into the rifles' breeches. The colonialists had noticed right away that he was a foreigner because he hadn't understood a word of their patois. And if those with Spanish blood in their veins were executed without ceremony, an alien couldn't expect better treatment.

The young American concluded that the Lord God, in His wisdom, had spared him. So he should start doing something. He tried to stand up by tucking his legs underneath him and bending forward. Each of the first three unsuccessful attempts sent waves of pain sweeping through his body. Breathing hard, recovering for his next try, his father's voice resonated in his head: *"Fear thou not; for I am with thee: be not dismayed; for I am thy God: I will strengthen thee; yea, I will help thee; yea, I will uphold thee with the right hand of my righteousness."*

On the seventh attempt, Reeve got to his feet. No sooner had the throbbing decreased than his bladder emitted a distress signal. For an instant, he pondered what to do; then it registered that he had no choice. He let urine flow and breathed a sigh of relief, then was filled with disgust as it ran down his leg, soaking the trouser and the sock, seeping into his boot. Blood was trickling down his arm and rib cage as well, the result of his attempts to get on his feet. His mouth was parched.

After the long piss, Reeve turned his head left and right to catch a glimpse of what kept him bound. He clucked his tongue in frustration. How idiotic of him. He couldn't see behind his back. He needed a knife. No, wait. He ran the risk of slashing his wrists. Then what?

Reeve mulled things over for a few minutes while the first day birds trilled tentatively to herald dawn. God Almighty had reserved a blessing for him: to be the sole survivor among twelve men executed by firing squad. He was under His protection. He would not die. The Lord wanted Henry Reeve to perform work for Him. Here in Cuba, maybe. It was foolish to stand here doing nothing. His comrades wouldn't revive if he stood by their side. It had not been the Lord's will to spare anyone else.

Henry Reeve took a deep breath and started wending his way to the southern edge of the glade as a ray of sunlight broke over the horizon.

A little after eight o'clock in the morning, three rebels were steering their mounts around teaks, mahoganies, cedars, and oaks; *granadillos* and *guayacans*; mango, tamarind, and mamey trees—all smaller than a few gigantic ceibas. From the humus-covered soil, lianas climbed over trunks and branches. Several types of ferns prospered at spots hardly ever touched by the rays of sun streaming through the canopy. Cardinals, humming-birds, parrots, and other songbirds were warbling as wood-peckers pecked holes and reptiles slithered slowly toward nests where defenseless young pigeons were waiting for their parents to feed them. The fragrances and odors emanating from thousands of plants and herbs and fruits and flowers combined with the myriad smells the wild fauna exuded to create the tropical forest's inimitable perfume. The temperature was already high.

The men—a white twenty-nine-year-old lieutenant and two Cuban Yorubas in their thirties who a year earlier had been slaves—had departed from their base camp at dawn under orders to look for survivors and search corpses for documents. The officer's horse, a fine fourteen-hand gray Andalusian stallion, was tacked up from head to back in fine calfskin leather. The Yorubas rode smaller Creole horses bareback—an old emaciated gelding and a very tired mare—which they steered by pulling pieces of rope circling the bridge of the animals' noses. The white man's feet were shod in fine boots that had spurs affixed to the heels; his barefoot companions carried torn-off twigs to whip the flanks of their mounts when necessary.

The officer was wearing a fairly new straw hat with a four-inch brim and a narrow black cotton hatband, a white collarless dress shirt, and trousers. The rifle holster on the saddle's right side nestled a Model 1859 Sharp carbine. The holster hanging from the right side of his belt stored an 1851 Colt navy revolver. On his left, inside leather sheaths, hung a sword and a hunting knife.

His shirtless companions were wearing stained, frayed straw hats and soiled and ragged mid-calf pantaloons. They gripped long narrow-bladed machetes, the sort used to cut thick vegetation, now turned into offensive weapons by those destitute insurgents who hadn't been able to steal, snatch from the enemy, or recover from the battlefield a cavalry saber, a sword, or the ultimate luxury, a firearm.

Born in Santiago de Cuba to wealthy Cuban landowners,

Martín Herrera had set foot in the northern coast of Oriente a week earlier. The Yorubas had been born and raised nearby, at the slaves' living quarters of a sugarcane plantation and mill near the town of Bijarú, and knew the territory like the back of their hands. The officer rode behind Bartolomé, the youngest of the scouts. His livelier stallion appeared resigned to the relaxed walk of the much older gelding.

They were wasting their time, Herrera thought. The expeditionary force had been resoundingly defeated at the battle of Las Calabazas. General Jordan had fled, leaving behind a tiny pocket of resistance, fifteen or twenty men covering the retreat. They had either died fighting or been shot after surrendering. Rumor had it that when the captain general appointed Count Valmaseda chief of military operations in Camagüey and Oriente, he had made clear he wanted no prisoners.

They would be stumbling on corpses covered with flies. He was supposed to frisk them, yet at no time had he touched a cadaver. The officer was hoping against hope that the battlefield wouldn't be located. Absorbed in his thoughts, it took him a moment to notice that Bartolomé had stopped his horse dead in his tracks. The lieutenant reined in his mount. Francisco, the older slave in the rear, did the same.

Bartolomé turned, directed a meaningful glance at the white man, and, by tilting his head to his right, indicated that someone was straight ahead; then he bent over the neck of his horse to get out of the way. Staring intently, Herrera drew the carbine, cocked its hammer. Yep, between the tree trunks and lianas, someone was staggering along. An enemy scout? No, he was on foot and moved at right angles to their course, westbound. The officer gently squeezed his mount's sides with his calves and pulled slightly on the left rein. Bartolomé and Francisco followed. They were fewer than forty feet from the stranger when Herrera reined back the horse and took aim.

"Who goes there?" he boomed.

Reeve froze, swung left toward the scouts, and squinted. Herrera took in the young pale face, the labored breathing, the bloodstains. Had the lad lost both arms? He lowered the carbine, uncocked it, reholstered it. A wounded and disoriented Spaniard?

"Who goes there?" he asked again, curious now, drawing the revolver and steering his horse closer to the stranger.

Reeve grasped that if two shirtless blacks rode with an armed white man, all three had to be revolutionaries; the Spanish army provided uniforms to black and mulatto volunteers. He tried to speak, but nothing audible came from his lips.

"What?" Herrera shouted in Spanish.

"Viva Cuba Libre," whispered Reeve, almost exhausting his knowledge of Spanish.

"What?"

"Viva Cuba Libre," Reeve repeated in a normal tone as he leaned on the trunk of a *granadillo*.

Herrera dismounted, put his gun away, handed over the reins to Francisco, and hurried to the wounded man. The foreign accent made the lieutenant realize he had stumbled on an American expeditionary. Herrera didn't know a word of English.

"You came in the expedition?" he asked.

"Viva Cuba Libre."

"General Jordan?" the lieutenant asked, trying to overcome the language barrier.

"Yes, General Jordan. I am his adjunct. Please, untie me."

"What?"

Reeve turned. Herrera cast a quick glance at him, extracted

his knife, and got to work on the piece of rope, minding Reeve's wrists. It took him almost a minute. When the American felt his hands free, he clutched at the trunk of the tree, closed his eyes, and slid to the ground.

"*Agua*," he said.

With a few paces, the lieutenant reached his horse and removed a tin-lined copper canteen from the saddlebag. He pulled out the stopper, strode back to Reeve. The American drank avidly.

"*Gracias*," he said, wiping his mouth, then stared at his bruised wrists.

Herrera recapped the canteen and reflected on what to do next, gazing at his find. The young man required medical care at once, and his commanding officer, Brigadier General Figueredo, had set up a three-hammock infirmary staffed with a male nurse. Taking his find back to camp immediately was the right thing to do; it would temporarily excuse him from turning corpses over. He beckoned his subordinates to join him. Both Afro-Cubans dismounted and, pulling the horses behind them, reached the white men.

"This man, patriot. We go back camp now. He rides my saddle. I ride pillion. Get him to mount."

Francisco and Bartolomé grunted and nodded to signify their understanding. Herrera held the ropes of the Creole horses and the lead of his mount as a groaning Reeve was lifted to the lieutenant's saddle. Francisco ripped open the left sleeve of the American's shirt and quickly inspected a superficial bullet wound. Walking around the horse, he lifted the shirt and stared at a gash in Reeve's rib cage. The freed slave swiftly glanced at his surroundings, then hurried to a nearby thicket. Bartolomé gently made Reeve seize the pommel, rested and placed his feet into the stirrups. Francisco came back with a handful of leaves in the crown of his hat, tore off two long strips of cloth from the right leg of his dirty pantaloon, and covered the rib cage wound with leaves, keeping them in place with one of the strips.

"*Gracias,*" said Reeve to Francisco. "*Muchas gracias,*" he repeated, glancing next at Bartolomé.

The arm wound was treated in the same manner. After tying the second knot, Francisco's eyes went to the lieutenant.

"Good. Let's get going," the white Cuban said.

The Yorubas simply nodded.

Bartolomé helped the lieutenant mount pillion on his stallion and handed him the reins. Both blacks jumped up onto their mounts; Herrera waited for Bartolomé to take the lead, then giddyap. By closing his eyes and biting his lips, Reeve suppressed the scream of pain he wanted to let out. But having been rescued filled him with joy. All was not lost. Even better, all would be fine, God willing. The Cuban war was starting; he hoped the patriots wouldn't kick out the Spaniards before he had the chance to fight a few battles and show them what a chap from Flatlands could do.

June 1

Capt. Emilio Battle was staring at the dozing patient with a furrowed brow. How old was this kid? He struck Battle as being sixteen at the most. It was an act of desperation on the part of the Cuban revolutionary junta in New York to ship American teenagers to wage war in Cuba. Did they figure there were not enough Cubans willing to fight for liberty? The thin adolescent had sickly white skin, brownish hair, and an unlined, beardless face. Well, he was a lucky son of a gun, Battle thought.

Not ever had he heard about anyone surviving an execution by firing squad.

The thirty-one-year-old lean and fair-headed Cuban stood five seven, sported a reddish beard, and was wearing reasonably clean civilian clothes. A Remington revolver hung from his belt. Friends fluent in English never tired of teasing the captain about the inappropriateness of his last name. A peace-loving family man and patriot, Battle had taken up arms seven months earlier and greatly missed his wife and two daughters.

What was pretentiously called "the infirmary" consisted of a fairly new *bohío*. Its walls were made up of dry *yaguas*—the name given the fibrous tissue atop royal palms—superimposed and tied to a structure of branches and twigs set crosswise; the roof was a sloping frame covered with dry *pencas*—palm fronds. Sunlight was coming in through the openings that served as door and window and through spaces between the walls and the roof.

Three coarse-cloth hammocks were suspended from hardwood posts whose ends rested on thick, eight-foot-long, Y-shaped branches of *majagua* that had been driven into a packed-earth floor from which sprouted short stumps of recently cleared undergrowth. Reeve had been assigned the left hammock. Next to him, a sergeant with a chest bullet wound seemed to be at death's door; the other patient suffered from acute dysentery. All three were oblivious of their surroundings. Battle disliked waking up a wounded man, but Figueredo wanted to find out everything concerning the youngster.

According to Oropesa, the male nurse who had sewn up Reeve, the lad's wounds were not serious; in a couple of weeks, he'd be moving around, as good as new in a month or so. But he had lost much blood, Oropesa had said; the unnatural paleness of Reeve's face confirmed this. Battle sighed and tapped the patient on the shoulder. The young man opened his eyes.

"Hello, how are you feeling?" Battle asked.

Reeve frowned. "Hello yourself, sir. You speak English?"

"I do."

"My goodness! I'm feeling much better, thank you. Are you American?"

"No, I'm Cuban."

"Dead earnest?"

"Deadwood earnest."

Henry Reeve chuckled for the first time in days. "And where did you learn English?"

"University of Virginia."

Taken aback by the officer's educational credentials, Reeve tried to stand up, grimaced in pain, then lay down again.

"There's no need for you to get up," Battle said. "Take it easy."

Reeve nodded. "What time is it?"

From his waistline watch pocket Battle extracted a Vacheron Constantin, opened its lid, and glanced at the dial. "Five minutes to three," he said, then restored the timepiece to its place.

"Sakes alive! I've been sleeping since lunchtime. Are you a surgeon, sir?" Reeve asked.

"No, I'm a civil engineer. But I'm the only one around here who speaks English, and Brigadier General Figueredo—he's the regional commanding officer—asked me to find out who you are, how you came to Cuba, where you were wounded, and so forth and so on. You reckon you can answer a few questions now?"

"Gladly, sir."

Battle extracted a notebook and a pencil. "Very good. What's your name?"

"Henry Reeve."

"Double *e, v, e*?"

"Exactly, sir."

"How old are you?"

"Nineteen."

Battle frowned and stared at the patient. "You look between hay and grass," he observed.

"I know. But I'm nineteen, honest."

"Where are you from?"

"Flatlands—that's in Brooklyn, New York."

Battle wrote that down, too. "All right. How did you end up in Cuba?"

Reeve heaved a deep sigh and stared at the brownish vegetal ceiling, considering where to begin, then moved his eyes back to Battle. "Well, sir, at my place of work—a branch of the bank in Manhattan; I was a bookkeeper—I befriended two young Cuban clients, Federico Zenea and Ricardo Piñeira. By and by, we got to talking about Cuba. I had no idea Cuba existed, never heard of it. Federico and Ricardo told me that Cuban patriots had tried, by peaceful means, to make the Spanish government understand Cuba wanted to be free but that the Spaniards didn't want to let go. They said that a few months earlier, Spanish volunteers had killed Cubans outside a Havana theater . . . Vi something."

"Teatro Villanueva."

"Yeah, sounds familiar. They also said the only way to gain self-government was to wage war. One evening, they told me they were getting ready to join an expedition that would sail to Cuba. I thought that was a very brave thing to do and I said,

'Looky here, I want to go with you; I want to fight for Cuba Libre."

"Just like that."

"Well, yes, just like that. You see, our Civil War ended before I came of age and I wanted to . . . How I should put this? . . ."

"Go to war? Any war?"

"No, sir, not any war. A war of independence, a war to end slavery."

"I see. So, how did these Cubans react when you said you wanted to fight for Cuba Libre?"

"Well, in the beginning they thought I didn't mean it. They warned me that the Spaniards outnumbered the insurgents and were better armed, that rebels weren't paid a penny, that I wouldn't eat the meals I was used to. I said I didn't mind all that. As time went by, I kept insisting, so they took me to a meeting of the Cuban revolutionary junta at Delmonico's. That's a Manhattan restaurant on—"

"Beaver Street. I've been there. Go on."

"You've been to New York?"

"Yes, I have. Listen, lad, I don't mind talking to you for hours on end, but you've lost a lot of blood. You need to rest. Let's try to . . . stick to the point. We'll chat when you get well. So, go on. What happened at Delmonico's?"

"I was introduced to other young Cubans, but not to the older men, the leaders: Mr. Cisneros, Mr. Morales, and Mr. Aldama. I hadn't heard about General Jordan until that night. But he was American, so I approached him when the meeting ended and said I wanted to volunteer. He said I was too young. I begged, said he wouldn't regret it. In the end, he accepted me as errand boy. I took letters from Brooklyn to Manhattan and back so many times, I got to know hands on the ferries on a first-name basis. By and by, I came to be his adjunct. I begged him to let me join the expedition that sailed in the *Mary Lowell* last January, but he refused. I got lucky. The British intercepted that ship in the Bahamas and turned it over to the Spaniards. Then preparations for the *Perrit* expedition got under way. I tried hard to become indispensable. . . ."

Half an hour later, inside a smaller *bohío*, Captain Battle was making an oral report to Brig. Gen. Luis Figueredo. They sat in *taburetes*, rustic chairs with backs and seats of goatskin; between them stood a small three-legged stool that had two gourds containing dregs of coffee and a snuffed tallow dip smeared with tallow drippings. A hammock was suspended at the back of the hut. In a corner, on the packed-earth floor, a horse's harness rested on sackcloth. Clean garments on wooden hangers hung from a string. A bluish haze from cigar smoke pervaded the hut. Every once in awhile, Figueredo spat a stream of brown saliva on the ground.

A self-made, semiliterate, courageous man with a short temper and a large fortune, the forty-four-year-old general reckoned he owned around seven thousand head of cattle, give or take a few dozen. Believing that nearly all Spanish cattle ranchers would be selling off their herds and going back to their homeland once Cuba achieved sovereignty, he had taken up arms in mid-November 1868, six weeks after other well-to-do Cubans of the Eastern Department had freed their slaves and declared war on the metropolis. Despite his strong profit motive, Figueredo loved good fights, and for him war was just a multitudinous brawl. As a rule, he practiced what he preached and used to lead into combat his hundred-horsemen squadron.

Deeply religious, he believed he would die when and where and how God wished. Should it be the Lord's will to make him the richest cattleman in Cuba, no Spanish bullet would be standing in His way.

"Maybe General Jordan judged him a born adventurer with a romantic streak, appointed him his adjunct, and let him sail in the *Perrit*," Battle said, concluding his report. "He says he lost his gun and was captured at Las Calabazas. All the prisoners were executed. Herrera came back around two, says he found eleven bodies. Ten Cubans and one American, as the lad said. It's a miracle."

"Miracle it is," Figueredo said, then spat. "Ten to one he shit in his pants, threw away his gun, ran for cover, and was captured. I don't believe he's nineteen; he's just a shaver. Well, I hope he gets well. I'll make a man out of him. I've got younger soldiers. And you know what? I'd enjoy having a Yankee subordinate, rather than getting ordered around by this General Jordan. Why did Cisneros sign him up? I hate taking orders from foreigners. I know the terrain; Jordan doesn't. I don't need anybody to show me how to fight the Spaniards."

Battle believed Figueredo dead wrong, but he thought it unwise to say so. Most Cuban insurgents had little, if any, knowledge of military strategy and tactics; they had been appointed colonels and generals on the bases of social standing, political ideas, and personal wealth, not combat experience.

"I don't reckon the junta recruited anyone to teach us how to fight," Battle said instead. "Some experienced American officers volunteered to lend us a hand and Cisneros accepted their offer. Jordan is a professional soldier. He resigned from the Union army, joined the Confederate army as a lieutenant colonel, and made brigadier general. He could be very useful."

"The Confederacy lost. And you don't appoint a foreigner chief of staff," countered Figueredo. "Maybe Cisneros wants to annex Cuba to the United States; having an American general leading the insurrection would facilitate that."

"Maybe," Battle said soothingly. "But most of us stand for nothing else than full independence. However, a number of our high-ranking officers are foreigners. Ryan is Canadian; Gómez is Dominican; Inclán is Mexican; Castillo is Colombian—"

"No Cuban I know wants Cuba to be part of Canada, Santo Domingo, Mexico, or Colombia," Figueredo said, waving aside Battle's observation. "Yet, I know many who want Cuba to become part of the so-called United States. Pretty disunited, you ask me."

"Yeah, I know some Cubans want that. They believe the colonies fought hard against the British, gained autonomy, drafted and enacted a great constitution—"

"I know. Spare me the history lesson. You graduated from an American university, right?

"Right."

"Are you an annexationist?"

"I am not."

"Oh, no?"

"No."

Pleasingly surprised, Figueredo closed his smile around the wet, chewed end of his stogie, took a drag, blew the smoke out, and spat on the floor.

"How come?"

While pondering the best way to explain his rationale to the uncultured general, Battle lifted his gourd, sipped the last drop of coffee, and placed the receptacle on the table. He dragged on his cigar, stared out the window, then locked gazes with his commanding officer.

"Once we beat the Spaniards, I believe we should adopt a democracy. I don't want a king here, or a dictator, which is what the French have ended up with. Emperor Napoleon suppressed the greatest revolution ever; now it's Napoleon III. That's not what I want for my country. I want Cubans to elect their president and senators and representatives, three branches of government, independent judiciary, a free press, the end of slavery—in three words, the American model. But I want our own government, our own laws, because we are a different people with a different culture, different language, and different values."

"Makes me glad to learn that," Figueredo said. "We've been together for . . . how long?"

"Two months."

"And have never sat and talked politics. I thought that, well, having spent a few years there, you were an annexationist."

"Well, now you know, sir."

"Yeah. Let's move on. Jordan is in Jiguaní, with Donato Mármol's troops. The rumor is he will look for greener pastures in Camagüey. How will Jordan haul twenty-four-inch bronze cannons fifty leagues across the jungle? I haven't got a clue. But you say he's an experienced Confederate general. Well, the good news is that the *Perrit* brought thousands of guns and tons of ammunition, and I want to get some for me and my men before it all goes to Camagüey. Take ten men and five burros, go see General Mármol, and ask him to send me fifty Springfield rifles, ten revolvers for noncoms, and ammunition to boot. How soon can you leave?"

"Is tomorrow morning acceptable to you, sir?"

"Perfect. Send in my adjunct. I'll dictate the letter you'll take to General Mármol. See you later."

June 13

With an easy stride, Battle and Reeve approached the captain's sixteen-hand palomino charger. The captain seized the rope that tethered the horse to a tree. The animal lifted his head, twitched his mane, and waved his tail. He had no tack on, and the rope was long enough to allow him to eat grass within a ten-foot radius.

"Meet my best friend, Henry," Battle said to the young American. "He doesn't argue with me, does what I order him to do, is not aware that a bullet may kill him, and unhesitatingly gallops into combat. He won't accidentally shoot me in the back, as some of my partners in this outfit could; I don't pay him a wage and he gets to cover a mare only when I let him. But I take good care of him. Oh yes. I care for him like I care for family. If you are serious about fighting for Cuba Libre, you'll need a horse, so you'd better start learning about horses and how to take care of them."

For three consecutive mornings Reeve had felt well enough to wander around the base camp, shake hands with dozens of insurgents, learn words in Spanish, and smile when others laughed—albeit he had no clue what caused their hilarity. His gaze kept being drawn to wives and concubines of rebels, the women having followed their men's footsteps and encamped there, some with their offspring, too. They made campfires with top-quality hardwood, which released fragrant smoke, to cook for their families. On sunny days, wet clothes hung from clotheslines. Reeve was getting accustomed to the high humidity and temperature, the daily schedule, the smells and the sounds. He patted the heads of tame dogs, watched species of birds, butterflies, and beetles unknown to him, marveled at *jutías*—the big rodents that lived on trees and fed on fruits. Having already sampled mango, guava, red mamey, and cherimoya, Reeve regarded *jutías* as the connoisseurs of the woods.

That morning, he had bumped into Battle and started conversing. Reeve had acknowledged he knew next to nothing concerning horses. Then Battle had walked him to one of the four clearings where equines and two cows were kept.

"Shoulder, forearm, knee," Battle said, tapping the front left leg of his horse. He forced it up and bent it back; the horse snorted. "This is the hoof, *casco* in Spanish. This is the shoe, *herradura* in Spanish. The timely and proper shoeing of a horse is extremely important. In normal times, finding a good farrier is of the essence. In wartime, it's even more important. The general has forbidden our farrier to join in battle. Repeat after me: *casco, herradura*," he said, his finger moving from the hoof to the shoe.

"*Casco, herradura.*"

"Very good."

Battle released the leg of his horse, reached for the rope, and patted the animal's neck.

"Horses are not dumb, you know. They either like you or dislike you, according to how you treat them. So, it's important to treat them well. I wear spurs constantly; see if you find spur marks on his flanks."

Reeve leaned forward and peered. "No."

"It's because I trained him to respond to the pressure of my calves and boots. If he doesn't respond to that, you spur him gently, trying not to harm him. Understand?"

"I . . . reckon so, yeah."

"The best horse for you is the one you broke, meaning you trained him when he was a colt or a young mare. We don't ride mares into combat, though."

"Why not?"

"Well, primarily on account of the fact that they perpetuate the species. A slew of horses die in combat. But apart from that, mares fear gunfire more than stallions; they shy when it comes to combat and charges. Mares are kinder, gentler than stallions."

"Like women are gentler than we are."

"Yeah. Females aren't violent or destructive. Makes you wonder. But we're talking horses. You get to know the animal and the animal gets to know you, too. He knows if you are angry, happy, sad; he knows if you've made love or taken a bath. It's their sense of smell, I suppose. But you won't have time for that. You'll get a horse trained by someone else. Just make sure you don't get one that's crow bait."

"Crow bait?"

"Lousy horse. *Penco* in Spanish. Now, a horse needs grooming. You free him of ticks, lice, and botflies. The stomach of a horse is delicate, and parasites do him great harm; that's why you have to have him wormed periodically—remind me to give you the recipe of the purgative I use. Brush him every time you get a chance; bathe him when a river or a lagoon is nearby. After a strenuous ride, you cool him down."

"What do you mean, 'cool him down'?"

"You dismount, take off the saddle, the bridle, the bit, and walk him for a couple of minutes. You pat him, talk to him, let him know he's done a good job and the day is over. Then you tie him up."

"I see."

"Now, observe his ears. How are they?"

"What do you mean, 'How are they?'"

"Are they up?"

"No. This one's droopy. I can't see the other."

"It's limp, too. Means the horse is wondering what's going on."

"Is that so?"

"Yep. If both ears are up and together, he's fine. If both are back, he's mad."

"Is it in fun or earnest?"

"Deadly earnest. He knows what he should eat and what he shouldn't even smell. You can give him a little sugar, as a reward, after a very hard day. Leal loves maize. Sometimes I feed him a handful of grain before sundown."

"His name is Leal?"

"Yeah. Means 'loyal' in Spanish."

"He has beautiful brown eyes. And I like how he smells."

Battle smiled. "C'mon. Let me show you my tack. The bridle goes around a horse's head and serves to control the animal. . . ."

The captain was showing Reeve how to adjust the stirrups to the length of a rider's leg when Figueredo's adjunct approached them and said the general wanted Battle and "the Yankee" to report to his *bohío*.

Months earlier, when General Figueredo had delimited his private theater of operations, he had made sure its confines, on all points of the compass, were within a two-hour riding distance—at a horse's walking speed—of the house where his famously beautiful twenty-two-year-old mulatto mistress dwelled. His bivouac was within a league from the love nest, and one or two nights a week, escorted by his security detail,

Figueredo rode to the secluded place and spent several hours in the arms of the half-breed. Enemy forces entering his theater of operations would most surely be challenged by his cavalry squadron; conversely, Figueredo wouldn't chase after the king of Spain if doing so would place his paramour beyond accessible distance.

The chief of the Liberation Army, Manuel de Quesada, had had a dual purpose in mind when he appointed Battle chief of staff of Figueredo's squadron. The captain would gain combat experience serving under the general and would provide the superior intellect and education the unit needed. Yet, soon after reporting for duty, Battle detected rumbles of annoyance among the men. Some complained that by no means did the general take advice, and he demanded unquestioning obedience from subordinates.

But Battle knew there was nothing he could do. Figueredo was El Jefe, owned most of the territory where he waged war, had contributed a lot of money to the cause, and was fond of fraternizing and bending an elbow with the boys. Practically all those under him seemed to believe those facts more than compensated for his failings.

Having made love the previous night, the general was in a fine mood. Battle and Reeve found him sitting in his rustic chair alongside the stool. He had on a collarless white cotton dress shirt, trousers with side-seam pockets, single front suspenders with an X-patterned back, well-polished ankle-high boots, and leather leggings. Battle guessed the mistress washed and ironed Figueredo's several changes of clothes, maybe blacked his boots, as well. Reeve wondered if the middle of the jungle was the right place for the general to wear his best bib and tucker.

It was the American's first time ever inside the *bohío* and he took in the hammock, the stool with the candle, the saddle, and the clean garments. Battle saluted; Reeve imitated him. Figueredo plucked a burning cigar out of his mouth, spat, smiled, and returned the salutes by distractedly waving the stogie.

"Would you translate for me, Captain Battle?"

"With pleasure, sir."

Figueredo addressed Reeve.

"I informed General Mármol what happened and that you were here, lad," he said. "He broke the news to General Jordan. They both send their good wishes. General Jordan has promoted you to sergeant."

The dumbfounded Reeve shook his head and cast a glance at the general's feet. "Oh, shucks. That's very . . . good. Thank you," he said as his eyes went back to Figueredo.

"Now, I want you to learn Spanish. Can you do that?"

"I'll try my best, sir."

"Good. As soon as you feel well, you must start riding with us. I want to teach you how to trounce Spaniards. In three months, I'll make a fine soldier out of you."

Reeve smiled awkwardly. Battle sensed something was amiss.

"Well, sir, that's mighty kind of you. But I reckon I should report to General Jordan and follow his orders."

Figueredo frowned, his fine mood evaporating fast. "Mind and behave yourself, young man. I offer you the opportunity to serve with the finest cavalrymen in Cuba, and you turn me down?"

Reeve smiled in confusion. "No, sir, I'm not turning you down. But I came to Cuba as an adjunct to General Jordan. It occurred to me I should report to him as soon as I get well enough to ride."

"You came here to fight for Cuba Libre or to fight for General Jordan?" Figueredo asked.

Again Reeve smiled and bowed his head, trying to avoid a confrontation. "For Cuba Libre, so help me God, sir. I had many a time heard about your plight and wanted to lend a hand. But I reckon I should report to my commanding officer before anything else."

Figueredo moved his gaze to Battle and leaned forward in his seat. "See what I mean? We save his damn life and the bastard doesn't want to serve under me. Americans believe they are the best. They reckon we are all Negroes, born fools who can teach them nothing."

Battle scratched his beard while pondering how to calm the general down. "You could be right, sir," he said tactfully, "concerning most Americans. I don't know. But that's not the case with this young man. He knows little about war, horses, and firearms; he's been asking me questions, wants to learn from us. It appears to me that all he wants is to report to the man who brought him to Cuba, give his version of what happened at Las Calabazas, then do whatever he is ordered to do."

Unable to understand the exchange in Spanish, Reeve kept shifting his intent stare from one man to the other. Their facial expressions intimated that Figueredo was mad at him and Battle was trying to placate the general.

"If he wants to go, good riddance," the general said, and waved a hand dismissively. "Don't translate that. Tell him he should think it over, because this is the finest cavalry squadron in all of Cuba. No, wait. On second thought, I don't want a damn Yankee in my unit. Tell him he's free to go. Today, right now."

Battle fought back the impulse to rebuke his commanding officer. "A wise decision, sir. But wouldn't it be better to let him recover more? Oropesa applies sugar ointment to this man's wounds twice daily; he says they haven't healed completely yet. You know General Jordan may move to Camagüey. He may have departed already. A three- or four-day ride would be too trying for someone who has recently lost a lot of blood. Besides, somebody has to take him there and—"

"What?" exploded Figueredo. "Are you suggesting I provide an escort to this Yankee from here to . . . wherever Jordan is? A nineteen-year-old ass-kisser escorted by *my* men?" he shouted, pointing at his chest with his thumb.

Battle managed a smile. "No, sir, that's not what I meant. I apologize. What I was trying to say is that a guide has to take him to the nearest base camp, maybe General Mármol's. The lad can't ride unaccompanied; he doesn't know how to get there. He could bump into a Spanish patrol or encampment. I guess nobody survives an execution two times in a row. General Mármol and General Jordan would be extremely disappointed should that happen."

Figueredo took the cigar to his mouth, dragged on it, found it had stopped burning, plucked it out, and spat disgustedly. He had a clear understanding of exactly how much he could get away with. Battle was right. Ordering Reeve to leave immediately would be pronounced maltreatment. Denying him a guide would be tantamount to sentencing him to death.

"Once at General Mármol's," Battle continued, "if General Jordan is already in Camagüey, when there's a message for him, the lad may ride with the dispatch rider."

"That's fine by me. Tell the shaver I withdraw my offer; he won't serve under me. He can't hold a candle to the least courageous of my Negroes. He must let you know when he feels fit to ride; then a guide will take him to Mármol's camp. Tell him he will take a letter to General Mármol. From then on, his reunion with his beloved General Jordan is not in my hands. But tell him this outside. Dismissed."

As dusk fell, after supper, Battle was tutoring Reeve in cavalry charges. The American's wounds had healed enough for him to sit cross-legged on the ground, arms around his knees, hands clasped. The captain was sitting in his hammock. The inverted V above him—a rectangular piece of cotton cloth treated with linseed oil and hanging from a cord, its four corners tied to branches—protected Battle from raindrops and dewdrops. A soft breeze dissipated the heat and made leaves rustle.

"Have you ever fenced?" Battle asked.

"No."

"You know something about fencing?"

"I've listened to men talking about duels. I know you say 'on guard' before attacking. I've seen drawings of positions, too."

"Forget positions. Fencing instructors tell you, 'Stretch out and balance on your right leg. Bend and raise your left arm above your head. Turn the hand back. Bend your wrist.' But war is not a fencing competition. At university, I exercised with foil, saber, and broadsword. I find it useful to have learned that, of course. But in war? Ha. In war, you don't need to know shit about fencing. Nobody says 'on guard.' Nobody wastes a second thinking about the position of his free hand. Cavalrymen charge, brandishing their sabers or swords or machetes. . . . Are you right-handed?"

"Yes."

"The thing is, you try to crack open the skull of the first man you run into, or slash his neck so he bleeds to death in a blink of an eye, or cut his arm. Our Negroes haven't heard about fencing, and they kill and maim as many Spaniards as the best white fencer. In fencing, your blade's cutting edge is blunt; here you grind and sharpen your blade daily, keep it as sharp as your razor's edge. You don't shave yet, do you?"

"I do, Captain, sir. I shaved last month, on board; a friend loaned me his razor," Reeve said, and stroked fuzz on his upper lip and under his chin. "I need to buy a razor, though," he added with embarrassment.

"By and by you'll reach an age when you'll loathe having to shave. Tomorrow I'll show you how I grind and sharpen my sword."

"Wonderful! But I wonder, what about firearms? The *Perrit* brought over two thousand Springfield rifles, fifty Remingtons, fifty Spencer carbines, three hundred Colt revolvers, and lots of ammunition. I know because General Jordan asked me to write down the bill of lading in his diary. We brought machetes, too, but the firearms were deemed critical."

Battle nodded in understanding. "Sure, firearms are essential. You set an ambush, wait for the enemy to get near. Both the infantry and the cavalry tote rifles. After the commanding officer fires the initial shot, the rest open fire. The enemy regroups. Spaniards form squares—four lines of men at right angles. Then the cavalry charges, to break the squares. Firearms are hardly useful then, as it's nearly impossible to take aim from a galloping horse. So what I do is pull out my sword, bend over Leal's neck, and then, when I'm within a few yards from the enemy, straighten up and start swinging right and left. We call that '*carga al machete.*'"

"*Carga al machete?*"

"Yeah, it means 'machete charge.'"

"But you use a sword."

"Right. But most of our men have machetes."

Reeve slapped a mosquito that was biting his earlobe.

"Your gun is useful," the captain went on, "once you break the square, at short range. At full gallop? Forget it."

Battle took out a cigar from the breast pocket of his shirt, bit its end, and clenched it between his teeth.

"I can go to the kitchen and fetch you a glowing ember," Reeve volunteered.

"Would you?"

"Gladly," he said, scrambling to his feet. He went away, dusting the seat of his pants.

Within minutes, Battle was puffing contentedly. Reeve sat on his haunches.

"Captain, this morning," the American began hesitantly, "the general was huffed at me. Is it because I want to report to General Jordan, or is something going on I know nothing about?"

Bending forward, Battle unfastened his spurs, inspected the soles and heels of his boots for mud, and, judging them reasonably clean, lay down in the hammock. He dragged on the cigar, blew smoke toward a few mosquitoes.

"To put in plain words the general's reaction, we have to get into the politics of this war, Henry. I suppose you know little about politics, right?"

"Well, I'm a Republican. I'm against slavery because liberty is a God-given right. And let me see. . . ." Reeve gazed into the bushes, contemplating what else would prove he was very adept at politics. "Yeah, I love democracy and hate monarchies."

"Good enough. Are you aware that when the colonies declared independence, many Americans thought it better to remain under British rule?"

"I know that."

"Same here. Spaniards, of course, are for the status quo.

Creoles, the sons and grandsons and great-grandsons of Spaniards, are divided. Those who want Spain to keep governing the island forever are of two minds: the reformists, also called separatists, demand special laws for Cuba, representation in the Spanish legislature, and other things. Creole Hispanophiles say everything is fine, that nothing is to be changed.

"Then there are pro-independence Creoles. A minority hopes to achieve self-rule by peaceable means. The majority believes Spain will never yield and will opt for war. Most Negroes and mixed-blood Creoles waging war are freed slaves who joined us; others joined the Spaniards. But most didn't take sides—can't blame them. Well-educated Creoles admire your democracy, but some admire it so much, they want to annex Cuba to the United States; they are called annexationists. Most annexationists have taken up arms, but many believe we can't win this war without help from a foreign power and thus advocate U.S. intervention in Cuba.

"It's why pro-independence patriots are divided on this issue. Some opine that we should ask President Grant to send your troops to fight on our side. Others strongly oppose that. General Figueredo opposes intervention and he seems to reckon that—Well, I shouldn't speculate on what my commanding officer reckons. Let's change the subject. My impression is that the general was angry with you because he believes his squadron is the best in the world and it's an honor to serve in it. So when you said you wanted to report to General Jordan, he very likely felt . . . belittled."

Battle dragged on his stogie once again. Staring at the ground, Reeve was turning over in his mind what he had just learned. If Figueredo had felt only belittled, why had Battle said that to explain the general's reaction he had to get into the politics of the war? Something was missing. Neither while in

Gotham nor aboard the *Perrit* had he learned there were factions. He had assumed all Cubans were united in their quest for freedom; it was news to him that some hoped the island would become U.S. territory, and that others wanted the U.S. Army to lend a hand. He didn't find that a bad idea. He waited until Battle finished a big yawn.

"Captain, would you like it if our army helped you kick out the Spaniards?" he asked, waving his hand alongside his ears to shoo away mosquitoes.

Battle smiled. "I would welcome anything that shortens the war, including your army, for it would save lives and we could go back home and pursue our professions sooner. But I have reservations. At the beginning of this century, you bought Louisiana from France, and later Spain transferred Florida to you.

"Spain transferred Florida to us? I didn't know that."

"Well, it did. Florida was colonized by Spaniards; last century, they exchanged it for Havana, then under British occupation. Spain recovered Florida after you defeated the redcoats. But during the 1812 war, Spain let England use a naval base in Florida. After you folks won, an agreement was reached and Florida was transferred to the United States. Later, Floridians rooted for slavery and joined the Confederacy."

"I know that."

"Of course you do. Sorry. You may also know that twenty years ago, your country waged war against Mexico and annexed the area from Texas to California. Recently, in 1867, you purchased Alaska from Russia. Lots of Cubans reckon that American politicians and the big bugs in business, too, are intent on expanding hither and yon; they want your country to become a power—leastways it looks so. What these Cubans fear is that if the United States helps us expel the Spaniards, they might want to annex us. Now, in my opinion, that wouldn't be catastrophic. You are a democracy; you cherish liberty. Rather than Madrid appointing Spanish officials, we would be electing Cubans to all positions, from the governor to the local sheriffs, have a much bigger say in all matters. But we wouldn't be independent. We would be subject to your laws, your regulations, just as now we are subject to Spanish laws and regulations. And that's not what I want, nor what most Cubans I know want."

"So?"

"So, if I could be certain your troops would go back home once the Cuban Liberation Army and your army, acting together, defeat the Spanish army and you let us build our independent republic the way we deem best, I would say yes, send your men. But as nobody can give such assurance, I reckon we better slog on by ourselves."

"But . . . eighty-five American volunteers sailed on the *Perrit,* and General Jordan is American."

"It's different. You are volunteers, all of you. You are not acting on behalf of your government—I hope."

"You hope? You are not sure?"

"How could I be sure, Henry? In politics, you are sure of nothing. That you haven't hung up your fiddle despite having come out at the little end of the horn makes me feel sure you are on the level. But I don't know if your Department of State has designs concerning Cuba. Among those eighty-five men, one or two or three bad eggs could be covert agents. It's a possibility."

Reeve mulled things over. Battle had obviously taken a liking to him, was as smart as a steel trap, and talked like a Philadelphia lawyer. Everything the captain had said was probably true. Well, what he wanted was to fight for Cuba Libre. Divergences of opinion among Cubans were not his concern. As a foreigner, he shouldn't take sides. The Lord had spared him so he could help these people get rid of Spanish rule. Once that was achieved, maybe he would help liberate Puerto Rico. He stole a peep at Battle, who had his eyes closed.

"I guess it's possible," Reeve said.

Battle turned his head, opened his eyes, and smiled at Reeve.

"Well, sir, it's been a long day. I set great store by your teachings, honest I do. They put me in the way of fighting better for Cuba Libre."

"Sleep well, Sergeant."

"You, too, sir," he replied, rising to his feet. "Mind your cigar."

June 28

In midafternoon, two leagues from the town of Las Tunas, under the shade provided by a huge mahogany tree, Sergeant Reeve was standing opposite Donato Mármol. The thirty-one-year-old general, one of the first Cubans to take up arms and commander of the two-thousand-strong Jiguaní Brigade, was reading a letter the American had surrendered to him moments earlier:

Camp of El Mijial
June 27, 1869
General Donato Mármol
Holguín Division

Dear Friend:
The bearer of this letter, Sgt. Henry Reeve, came in the Perrit *with General Jordan. He is the sole survivor of the execution at Las Calabazas.*

Although he claims he wants to fight for Cuba Libre, he refused to serve in my squadron and wants to reunite with General Jordan. I most gladly agree to his petition, as I find him inept and useless for military activities.

Yours faithfully,

Brig. Gen. Luis Figueredo Cisneros

Mármol folded the letter, put it in the envelope, and slipped it into the interior left breast pocket of his coat. Trimmed black hair parted on the left side presided over the Cuban's wide, unlined forehead and thin eyebrows. There was a marked contrast between his deep-set brown eyes and clean-shaven pale cheeks. The tips of his thick waxed mustache had been twisted and pulled up.

The general gazed reflectively at Reeve. At five five or six, weighing around 110 pounds, looking sixteen or seventeen years old, ears bent down by a too-big straw hat, the American certainly came across as fragile and pathetic, the general concurred. But it was unwise of Figueredo to term him inept and unfit. Battlefield experience had made Mármol realize that height and build provided no indication of a man's courage. And the lad was a foreigner and a volunteer, an idealist, in all probability. He liked the way the American was staring back at him, unimpressed by his rank.

"No English," Mármol made known.

"*Poquito español,*" the American said, hoping to hide his discomfiture behind a smile.

"Wait."

Mármol beckoned a middle-aged black orderly ten yards away to join them. The man hurried to the general's side, listened for a moment, gave a quick nod, and then flew past Reeve, who noticed he was barefoot—the American had yet to see a man of African descent wearing footwear. The general clasped his hands behind his back and, gazing at the treetops, thought things over. He wouldn't show Figueredo's letter to Jordan; it would serve no good purpose, he reasoned. Reeve guessed they were waiting for a translator, and so he kept respectfully quiet and silent, looking around. He noticed an identical mix of white, mulatto, and blacks; women, children, and dogs populated this bivouac, too.

The aide returned with a tall white man hot on his heels. Reeve recognized him from a distance: a Cuban who had sailed on the *Perrit*. They had exchanged greetings on board and his English was understandable. Still at a distance, the man identified Reeve, gave a broad grin, and raised his hand in salutation. Reeve imitated him. The newly arrived addressed General Mármol.

"At your service, General," he said.

"You know this lad, Ventura?"

"Yes, sir, he's General Jordan's adjunct. He came in the *Perrit*. But I don't remember his name."

"Henry Reeve," Mármol said.

"Oh."

"Are you aware what he's been through?"

"Who isn't, sir? It's the talk of the town. The camp, I should say."

"Shake hands with him."

A smiling Ventura turned and did as told. "Welcome, Reeve."

"Thanks."

The orderly, a freed slave, kept a respectful distance and an ear to the ground, as he always did when white men conversed. With few exceptions, upper-class Cubans addressed black people in the simplest terms. Illiteracy and mispronunciation were marks of ignorance; blacks were deemed intellectually inferior. From the fact that almost all slaves and freed slaves were illiterate *and* black, the conclusion followed they were stupid, as well. Adult Africans taught their children that such misconception worked in their favor, so, despite the fact that scores of them knew the literal and figurative senses of numerous words in Spanish, few laid bare their fluency.

"Ask him how old he is," Mármol said to Ventura.

"Nineteen," replied Reeve.

"Looks younger," the general observed.

"He sure does," Ventura said.

"Tell him he is very welcome here. That we are relieved he survived."

Ventura translated.

"Thank you," Reeve said. "I'm proud to make your acquaintance, General."

"Me, too, young man. General Jordan is conducting operations nearby. As soon as he comes back, report to him."

"I most certainly will, sir."

"Show him around, Ventura. General Jordan's *bohío*, the kitchen, the comfort area. Give him a hammock, a plate, and a spoon. And a hat that fits him, for God's sake."

Gen. Thomas Jordan was experiencing difficulty in concealing his satisfaction. At West Point, he had been taught the importance of keeping emotions in check in the presence of subordinates, and even in the most trying moments of his military career, as during the final days of the defense of Charleston, he had seemed emotionless despite the dark thoughts crossing his mind. But seeing this young man in apple-pie order made him extremely pleased. For several weeks after learning the news, he had remained skeptical. In his years of active duty—all through the war against the Seminoles, the Mexican War, and the Civil War—only once had he heard of someone who had survived a summary execution by firing squad.

But it wasn't only that. During the battle of Las Calabazas, Jordan had caught glimpses of Reeve standing fearlessly, with complete disregard for his safety, firing his .32-caliber revolver at enemy riflemen, shouting encouragement at his brothers in arms above the noise of the battle. The lad had fought like a Kilkenny cat. A few seemingly curly wolves had taken cover at the first gunshot and then retreated soon after. Reeve couldn't have displayed more gallantry during his baptism of fire.

Jordan regretted having misjudged his adjunct. He had considered the young man too romantic and slim for the unwritten rules and rigors of war. Reeve's persistence and enthusiasm in New York, his pledge that Jordan wouldn't be lamenting his decision to let him join the expedition and fight for Cuba Libre, repeated over and over, should have served as warnings that the lad was game as a bantam rooster. He had cheerfully taken dictation, delivered messages, run errands, and so forth. The general, however, had failed to provide the most basic military training to his adjunct. He had given Reeve a revolver so he wouldn't feel defenseless.

And now the kid, as though he didn't care a continental, had reaffirmed his intense desire to participate in this war, then proceeded to recount, head bowed and eyes on the floor, how he had dropped the gun as he was reloading it. Reeve swore that would never happen to him again, because a new friend of his, a certain Captain Battle, had taught him that a leather string tightly tied in the metal bucket under the butt of most revolvers, its other end fastened to a buttonhole or an epaulette, would prevent the gun from hitting the ground should the shooter drop it.

Well, Jordan thought, Reeve had gone through the mill; he was someone you could ride the river with. No more secretarial duties for him. The boy was a soldier to the manner born.

Reeve was extremely pleased at reuniting with the man he admired most, and he showed it by talking and smiling cheerily most of the time, including the half-minute he had devoted to telling the general about his attempted execution. He had turned grave and beet red when recounting how he had lost his revolver.

They were inside the general's hut, sitting in rustic chairs. The only indications of Jordan's rank were a hanging tin candleholder with a glass chimney suspended above the three-legged table and an antique rope bed with feather ticking. His riding tack lay in a corner, next to the old metal cabin trunk that, Reeve knew, stored the general's clothes and documents.

From the very night he had met Jordan at Delmonico's, Reeve suspected the general had cut a swell figure with the ladies as a young man. Even now, at forty-nine, with half the energy and enthusiasm of younger men and a graying full beard, his flaming green eyes, serious yet noble countenance, and tall, imposing figure attracted the attention of New York women of all ages. Without trying, he won the respect of subordinates and created a sense of togetherness among them.

"Do you like Cuba?" the general asked, to leave behind the execution and its aftermath.

"I do, sir, I do. Except for the heat. But even if I didn't, I still would be willing to fight for it. This reminds me. My new friend, Captain Battle? He's a pretty intelligent man. Civil engineer, perfect English, a graduate of the University of Virginia. He says rebel Cubans are split down the middle concerning the participation of American volunteers in this war. Some don't want us here, says he."

"What exactly did he say?"

It took Reeve a minute to sketch Battle's version of contemporaneous Cuban politics. When he finished, Jordan fixed his eyes on the tabletop, considering whether to voice what he had been musing about for weeks and deciding if Reeve was the right person to take into his confidence. The general had no doubt the lad would keep mum if asked to, but, on the other hand, Reeve lacked the maturity and culture required to understand his misgivings. He opted for an indirect approach.

"The first Cuban I met was Ambrosio González," said Jordan after a moment. "He joined the Confederate army, made it to colonel, and was in command of the artillery in the defense of Charleston."

Reeve managed to click his mouth shut. "A Cuban colonel in the Confederate army?"

"Yep. There were other, lower-rank Cubans fighting for the Confederacy, captains, lieutenants. A few Cubans fought for the Union."

"How did they get involved in our war?"

"Well, I guess every man weighed different issues when taking sides. But if I were asked to find a common denominator, I would say slavery. Slaves are as important to Cuban sugarcane plantations as they were to cotton, tobacco, and rice plantations in the South. Perhaps Confederate Cubans were against abolition; whereas those who served in the Union army were in favor."

"But Cuba is under Spain. And Spain hasn't abolished slavery."

"Cubans thought that if the United States abolished slavery, Spain eventually would yield. Whatever his reasons, Ambrosio was courageous—very much so, I would say—but . . . unpredictable. He rejected strict discipline, wanted to do things his way. Maybe it's a common trait to Creoles; maybe they can't see they must first win this war, then discuss if they prefer self-government or statehood."

"You reckon so, sir?"

"No. I'm guessing. I don't speak Spanish; I see them arguing a lot, but I don't understand a word of what they are saying. When a Cuban translates for me, I don't know if he's honey-fuggling around me. But I have the full support of General de Quesada and President Céspedes."

Reeve solemnly nodded in agreement. Jordan smiled inwardly.

"Tomorrow you will join the cavalry squadron under William Ryan. He's Canadian, so language won't be a problem. Ryan was with the Union army and has substantial experience."

The general paused. Overwhelming joy made Reeve's face suffuse with color.

"You have a horse?" asked Jordan.

"No, sir."

"I'll get you one tomorrow. And a firearm and a machete. But now I have to write a letter. Report here at sunup. Good night, Sergeant."

"Good night, sir," Reeve said, jumping to his feet.

TWO

January 1, 1870

★

On horseback, shivering, Reeve ran the tip of his tongue over parched lips. Despite a brilliant sun shining in a clear blue sky, there was a slight chill in the air and he was coatless. Ryan said humidity was to blame for them feeling like thirty-two degrees when the thermometer registered seventy-five. The American's clammy hands were holding the reins tightly. A Spencer carbine in a rifle holster hung on the left side of his saddle's skirt; a sheathed machete dangled from the seat's right rear housing. With his stomach in knots and his pulse racing, Reeve was squinting at the long serpent of Spanish troops winding its way along the narrow pass.

The enemy column, reportedly, was made up of four infantry battalions, three cavalry squadrons, an artillery company, and a company of army engineers, about two thousand men. Six-horse teams hauled four artillery pieces. Jordan would join the battle, counting on a 548-strong task force, a six-pound field gun, positional advantage, and the element of surprise.

It had been a long wait. In the small hours, Cuban infantrymen had excavated a five-hundred-yard-long trench, where
they now hid, rifles at the ready. Jordan's light cavalry stood
on higher, densely wooded terrain. Ten men from Squadron A
were out scouting the flanks; the rest of the unit stood in reserve. If the enemy formation broke, Squadrons B and C would
charge.

Ignacio Agramonte was to be credited for choosing the best
place for the ambush; hunting for insurgents, the Spaniards
unavoidably had to come this way. Around ten in the morning,
scouts had reported that the Spaniards were getting close. A
few minutes later, officers had ordered men to kill their cigars,
talk in low tones, and detach bayonets from rifles to prevent
sunlight reflecting on steel and revealing the position. At 11:15,
the scouts had said their opposite numbers were three hundred
varas away.

Now the enemy vanguard was fully exposed; the column's
main body was entering Reeve's field of vision. Spanish regi-
mental flags, guidons, and streamers caught his eyes: red, yellow,
blue, black, orange. They seemed so out of place, such a contrast to the omnipresent green, he thought. His mount snorted
and bowed his head twice. Reeve clapped the animal's neck
and shushed him.

The Cuban field gun opened fire. Horses bucked, many riders were startled, and a loud flutter of wings arose from the
treetops. Reeve restrained his charger and observed the enemy's reaction. The shell landed short, but the formation stopped
in confusion. Mounted Spaniards turned their horses back,
foot soldiers crouched and manipulated their rifles, and officers pulled out their revolvers and sabers, all trying to identify
where the cannon shot had come from. The initial volley of
Cuban rifle fire followed and hundreds of colonialists dropped

to the ground, taking cover; rooky rebels cheered, thinking all had been wounded or killed. In fact, the salvo merely killed two Spaniards and wounded nine.

The enemy vanguard regrouped fast, faced the entrenched Cubans, and started firing back. Cuban snipers concentrated on the artillerymen; when two were felled, others sought shelter behind their pieces as a few tried to position the howitzers. Reeve noticed that the right flank of the column's main body appeared to be in great confusion. Men were shouting and running in one direction, then backtracking, as if orders were being reversed. The formation was on the verge of breaking. The Cuban piece fired again.

Reeve bent forward, turned, and gazed past a few riders, in search of William Ryan, the twenty-six-year-old Canadian in command of the Camagüey cavalry. Because the two men shared a mother tongue, ideals, a fighting unit, a taste for adventure, and a distaste for hot weather, their friendship seemed to be preordained. A dozen yards away, Ryan was surveying the action through his 5×50 military binoculars.

Drawing upon his combat experience during the Civil War—Battalion 192, Union army—Ryan had told those under him that cavalry proved particularly useful when an enemy formation was on the point of breaking. Infantrymen could be cut to pieces, smashed by the horses' hooves. Moments later, Ryan put the binoculars into their leather case, turned to General Jordan, and asked permission to charge. Jordan considered things for a few moments, then nodded. Reeve saw Ryan unsheathe his blade, and he knew what was about to happen.

"Men! Draw machetes, walk, march!" hollered Ryan in Spanish.

Having been promoted to lieutenant two months earlier, Reeve joined other officers in repeating the order down the lines.

Reins were gripped tighter, horses goaded on. Eventually, Companies B and C emerged from the woods.

"¡*Al machete! ¡Que viva Cuba Libre, carajoooo!*" Ryan yelled next, and led the charge at a full gallop.

Bending over his horse's neck, machete raised at shoulder level, Reeve surprised himself as he listened to the rhythmic sound of hooves on the ground. Over it, suddenly, his father's voice intoned a biblical verse:

"*When thou goest forth to battle against thine enemies, and seest horses, and chariots, and a people more than thou, be not afraid of them: for the Lord thy God is with thee, which brought thee up out of the land of Egypt.*"

Spanish infantrymen were growing increasingly discernible. He was spotting expressions of anger, courage, or panic. He could make out the green rosettes pinned to their shirts, see their mustaches and sideburns. They were shouting at one another. Reeve took leave of his senses.

Instinct told him that the apparently unconcerned enemy to his left was the most dangerous man in proximity. The Spaniard took the butt of his rifle to his shoulder, aimed, and fired. The horse next to Reeve's caught the slug in his chest, stumbled, and fell; his rider rolled over and over and lost his blade. At no time taking his eyes from the nonchalant adversary, Reeve jerked the reins left, to have the man on his right side, then jerked them back. The horse swerved and, to avoid the pressure of the bit, jumped upward and arched his back. The Spaniard stopped the blow of Reeve's machete with the barrel of his rifle. As the animal's front legs hit the ground, the American feinted to the right of the infantryman. Tricked into it, the soldier shifted the Berdan to his right. Then Reeve swung at the left side of his head.

The man's skull stopped the momentum of the blow, but even so, the blade reached the white and gray matters, stopping vital functions. Astonished at the force of the recoil in his arm, Reeve yanked his machete out and watched the slashed panama hat fall and the deep gash redden as the man crumbled, an amazed expression on his face. The horse neighed and bucked wildly, and the American lost sight of the first casualty. Following an instant of confusion, Reeve realized he was spurring on his mount and pulling the reins back at the same time. He spread his calves and feet apart and made the animal turn around.

An infantryman, his back to Reeve, was his next target. He went for the man's neck, but a sudden movement of the frantic stallion made him hack the Spaniard's right collarbone instead. Not having seen his foe, the man reeled sideways with the impact, dropped his rifle, took his left hand to the wound, then stared in total bewilderment at the blood dripping from his fingers. Reeve lost interest in that opponent. According to Ryan, wounded soldiers created more problems for their army than dead ones.

Glancing about, Reeve registered appalling confusion: scores of men fighting it out, inert bodies, wounded men writhing and screaming in pain, orders shouted in Spanish, the strong odor of gunpowder, riderless horses trotting away from the carnage. Judging by his cassock, a Roman Catholic priest was running for his life. Reeve's nose-flaring horse tripped on the dead body of a Cuban cavalryman and Reeve had to hang on tightly to the pommel to not fall. The American sheathed his machete, extracted his revolver, and glared at his immediate surroundings. Ten yards away, a Spaniard was trying to reload his rifle and keep an eye on Reeve, who fired two shots at him and missed both times. He spurred his mount and drew closer. The Spaniard brought his rifle up and fired once. Reeve felt the bullet whiz by his ear before firing two more shots at point-blank range. The infantryman froze, and his eyes glazed over; he coughed and choked on the blood filling his mouth, then collapsed.

A saber-wielding Spanish lieutenant, who had spent all his rounds, lunged at Reeve. The man aimed at his midriff, but the frightened horse bucked and the point stuck into Reeve's left thigh. The American fired his last two rounds at the lieutenant's face. The wave of pain that engulfed him and his raging fury made him keep pulling the trigger again and again, hammer clicking on spent cartridges. The Spaniard crumbled after the bullet that had pierced his right eye and wreaked havoc in his brain exited through the back of his head.

The boom from a Spanish artillery piece made Reeve come to his senses. His duties as a platoon commander included looking after his men, but the melee was so tumultuous and violent, he couldn't distinguish his subordinates from other insurgents. Another Spanish howitzer roared. He glimpsed fleetingly at his bleeding thigh, holstered his revolver, unsheathed his machete, and then sought out the nearest enemy.

"Retreat! Retreat!" a mounted rebel captain yelled. Far away, a bugler was insistently sounding the notes that confirmed the order.

"Retreat," Reeve shouted in Spanish.

Forcing his horse to go around in a circle, the American watched as other cavalrymen obeyed the order.

"*¡Inglesito, Inglesitoooo!*" a wounded Cuban bawled.

For reasons that Reeve failed to understand, the rank and file had dubbed him "the young Englishman," El Inglesito. Everybody knew he was an American—no confusion about that—yet the nickname had stuck. Jordan, Ryan, and most Cuban officers called him Reeve, Henry, or Enrique; for the rest, he was El Inglesito.

Having lost his horse, the insurgent was holding his bleeding right arm with his left hand. Reeve sheathed his machete,
spurred his charger, and approached him.

"*Monta*," Reeve said.

"I can't."

Reeve stretched out his arm. The man reached for it, jumped,
trying to ride pillion on Reeve's horse, and failed. The Spaniards were recovering fast and bullets were whizzing by. On
the third try, the wounded rebel managed to lie prone behind
the saddle, his head dangling to one side, his feet to the other,
his hands grasping Reeve's right foot. Reeve half-turned and
took hold of the man's left leg, then steered his mount back to
the woods and spurred him. The horse seemed to be going mad
now, cantering, neighing, and kicking all at once. The wounded
Cuban slipped and fell; as he tumbled down, the stallion kicked
him in the chest.

Reeve reined in the horse and turned in his saddle in time to
see the man stand up. As he was rushing back to his rescuer, a
rifle shot pierced the Cuban's spinal cord and heart; his body
convulsed in pain, then tumbled over and landed on the grass.
Reeve shook his head in dismay and spurred the animal back
to the Cuban positions.

He was among the last few to reach the partial protection
of the forest. Pain made him grind his teeth when dismounting.
He drew the reins over the horse's head and tethered him to
the thin trunk of a young teak tree. Blood trickling down his
leg made Reeve remember his long piss the night of his attempted
execution.

Ignoring appeals to take care of his wound right away, raising his voice to make himself heard over the shooting and oc-
casional cannon fire, Reeve spent a few minutes determining his

casualty toll. Two rebels were positive Feliciano had died from a head wound; a cattleman, he had joined the cavalry because he was a good rider. Blas, a superb scout who had cast his lot with the insurgents the day he was granted freedom from slavery, had been rescued after sustaining a nasty chest wound. Three horses had been lost, too. The soldier Reeve had tried to rescue had not been his subordinate.

Someone presented a canteen to the American. He removed the stopper, took a long pull, recapped the canteen, and gave it back.

Then Reeve approached his horse and inspected its left flank; it had cuts and scratches that were bleeding; he felt sure the other flank was in bad condition, too. Patting the animal's neck, he began talking to him.

"Oh, shucks, I hurt you bad, pard. I'm sorry. You were the best horse in the battlefield, but I daresay, I was a little scared, you know, on account I'd never charged before."

"What the dickens are you telling the horse?" asked a smiling William Ryan in English.

He rode his black seventeen-hand Spanish-Norman stallion, a mighty charger famous among all Cuban cavalrymen. Both mount and rider were drenched in sweat.

"See?" Reeve replied, pointing at his mount's flank. "I hurt him."

"Is that so? What about your leg?"

"It's nothing."

Ryan's glance swept over the men surrounding Reeve. "You and you," he said in Spanish to two rebels standing side by side. "Take the lieutenant to the infirmary."

"No," Reeve said.

"That's an order, Lieutenant."

The American pressed his lips and hung his head. The designated men positioned themselves at Reeve's sides, took hold of his wrists, and lifted his arms, putting them around their shoulders.

"How is it going?" Reeve asked Ryan.

"So far, so good. Go take care of your wound. Men, off with him."

Ryan giddyapped his horse and departed.

January 2-January 15

Despite having repelled three consecutive assaults launched by the Spanish infantry, the Liberation Army had to retreat due to a shortage of ammunition. The Spanish casualty toll was three hundred, the rebels' fourteen. The battle of Tana was the most important Cuban victory to date and a feather in General Jordan's cap.

The insurgents retreated to the Najasa Highlands, a half-league-long string of small hills amid the vast plains of Camagüey. Ignacio Agramonte, a Cuban lawyer who was acquiring a reputation as a born military genius, had chosen this secluded region to grow plantains, beans, cassava, and sweet potato, raise chicken and pigs, and keep a few heads of cattle. Recently erected *bohíos* housed farmhands, artisans, and their families; other huts served as workshops for repairing firearms, making and repairing shoes and tack, weaving baskets to transport munitions and provisions by mule train, making rope from agave fiber, and producing slaked lime for tanning leather. In a distant hut, off-limits to everyone except Agramonte, a trained pharmacist made gunpowder by mixing and cooking sulfur, charcoal, and saltpeter. An old married couple, assisted by three camp followers, ran the communal kitchen.

Rosa la Bayamesa, a thirty-six-year-old daughter of slaves, was in charge of a field infirmary located in a nearby cavern in the one-thousand-foot-high Cerro del Chorrillo.

Reeve was admitted to Rosa's domain in the late afternoon. She made him lie down on a cot, took his boots off, and started pulling his pantaloons down. Since the woman took no notice of his protestations, the American covered his privates with both hands. Rosa chuckled that bigger reptiles had not scared her, but the blushing Reeve failed to see the joke, because both nurse and patient spoke deficient Spanish, her African accent was too strong, and he had no clue what *majá* meant.

Neither chloroform nor ether was available; anesthetics were supplied only to the two field hospitals staffed with physicians who amputated limbs or operated on the most seriously wounded rebels. What made Rosa realize the young foreigner possessed real grit was seeing that he just held his breath and ground his teeth as she sewed his thigh with cotton thread. She had seen taller, stronger, and reputedly very courageous men wail in anguish as she sutured their wounds. He even had the nerve to thank her when she finished covering the wound with mold.

Five days went by. On the sixth, after breakfast, Reeve removed the blanket covering him, wiped off the mold Rosa had spread on his wound every evening, seized the pantaloons she had ordered washed and sewn, and sat on the cot to put them on. Rosa would not allow a fully recovered patient to linger on, but this was quite the opposite. She stormed over to the patient and snatched away the garment.

"Lie down," Rosa ordered.

"I'm feeling fine, Rosa. I merely want to take a stroll."

"Lie down."

"But Rosa—"

"Lie down."

Reeve sighed and did as he was told.

"This mold I put? Hard to find; don't waste. Now I put again. Take hand off white little thing; don't mean nothing to me."

On his tenth morning in the hospital, Rosa carefully inspected the wound before addressing her very embarrassed patient.

"Stand up. Put pantaloon. I give you cane. Go outside, take fresh air, and come back in. Just little moment."

Therefore, twelve days after the battle of Tana, Reeve was freely, albeit carefully, hobbling around. He explored the entire camp, made sure his men were doing all right, asked them to clean their guns, sharpen their machetes, wash their clothes, beware of head lice, and free their mounts of ticks. He located his tack, recovered his guns, cleaned them, and took care of his horse. He assured Jordan, Ryan, Agramonte, and many others, when they passed one another on the footpaths, that his health was improving from hour to hour.

The forest, not as impressive as in Oriente, had trees that were new to him: crabwood, carob, and *yagruma*. There were ferns and orchids galore. He discovered *zunzún*—reputedly the smallest of hummingbirds—kingbirds, and *tocororos*. *Almique* and *jutía*, two species of mammals, also roamed the Najasa Highlands. Reptiles were a common sight; two-yard-long *majáes* made most women scream.

Adults and children alike yanked twigs from certain shrubs and positioned them between their ears and skull. Reeve asked why folks did that, and a rebel told him they served as good-luck charms. The name of the shrub was *albahaca*—basil—the man said, then presented him with a twig. He loved the fragrance, learned to identify the plant, and from that day on, before his early-morning strolls, he approached a shrub of basil, yanked a twig, and set it in place. He took a liking to the many species of lilies, too.

"'I am a rose of Sharon, and a lily of the valley,'" he would intone.

One day, he decided to explore in a new direction, but a black soldier stopped him.

"Don't go that way, Inglesito."

"Why?"

"Witchcraft. Stone trees."

This, of course, made him curious. About six hundred varas away, he found a small forest of felled stone trees. Knocking on the light gray trunks sounded similar to knocking on marble. There were branches, twigs, and leaves of stone, as well. Encountering a complete mystery, his education led him to seek a religious explanation. Had this place been cursed? Sort of a Sodom or Gomorrah the Lord God had destroyed? Turned trees into stone so men wouldn't forget His fierce wrath? When Reeve returned to the mouth of the cavern, he found a cluster of staring people waiting for him.

"What?" he asked in complete confusion.

Without a word, a black woman ran a recently uprooted shrub of basil all over his body, from head to toes, front and back, as she mumbled African incantations. As soon as she was finished, a white woman unfolded a yellowish page and read a prayer to Saint Mauritius, patron saint of the military, followed by devotions to the Virgin of Perpetual Succor. Lastly, she made the sign of the cross over his forehead, lips, and chest. Only then did the gathering dissolve and the confused Reeve enter the cave.

★   ★   ★

That afternoon, Reeve took his first bath in nearly three weeks and donned a fresh change of clothes supplied by Rosa. In the evening, he was sitting on his cot, scraping up a plateful of red beans and boiled sweet potato, when a soldier entered the cave and said something to Rosa. She nodded and then, after the soldier left, reached for a candleholder with a burning tallow dip and approached the American patient's cot.

"You lutenan, boy?"

Reeve smiled. "Yes, I am, Rosa."

"General Jordan want see you. Now."

Reeve jumped to his feet and handed the plate to Rosa.

"No hurry, boy. You fall, break leg, two more months in cot."

Since it was dark already, Reeve took Rosa's advice and carefully threaded his way to Jordan's *bohío*. He yearned for active duty and hoped that was the reason the general had sent for him.

"Lieutenant Reeve reporting for duty, sir," he said in a loud voice to the coarse-cloth sack covering the hut's entrance.

"Come in."

Under the tallow dip's poor illumination, Jordan appeared somber, maybe even a little sad. Reeve hadn't seen the general wearing gold-rimmed spectacles before.

"Take a seat, Henry. How are you feeling?"

"I'm feeling fine, sir. My wound has completely healed over. I'm ready to rejoin my unit," he said as he sat in a *taburete*.

Jordan scratched his beard and raised his eyebrows. "Yeah, well, let's consider that."

"Yes, sir."

"I want you to listen very carefully to what I have to say. I'll talk to you like a Dutch uncle because you are the youngest member of the expedition, because you were my adjunct, and because you have behaved gallantly in the battlefield. So, hark."

Jordan moved his eyes to his hat, which lay on the four-legged small table where the tallow dip burned. Suddenly, Reeve felt on tenterhooks.

"I am at loggerheads with Agramonte," Jordan began. "He is a bright and courageous man. He admires our country and wants Cuba to become a democracy. But his notions on how to conduct this war clash with mine. I have tried to make him see he's wrong, but to no avail. The language barrier complicates things, but it's not a problem of languages. Our tactical ideas and our strategies on the conduct of the war differ. In a nutshell, I think Cuban forces ought to concentrate, form strong columns, and keep on the offensive; Agramonte and his officers disagree. I am totally in opposition to soldiers' families hanging around the camps; he doesn't share my view. I want to enforce stronger discipline; he has an aversion to authority and argues for minimal discipline."

Jordan paused. Reeve was perplexed. That the man he admired most had such profound differences of opinion with the man the Cubans revered confounded him. He had assumed there was perfect harmony between them.

"To complicate matters further," Jordan went on, "I received a letter from a friend. It says President Grant is strictly enforcing the neutrality proclamation. Rawlins, the only advocate of Cuban autonomy in the cabinet, died last September; he had been actively promoting the recognition of Cuban insurgency. The president doesn't want the United States to get involved."

"Who was this Rawlins, sir?"

"The secretary of war. The end result will be that our government will step up efforts to intercept shipments of ordnance.

By and by, our vital supply route will dry up. It will be nearly impossible to win this war without American weapons and ammunition. In this age, sabers and machetes are no match for cannons, rifles, and revolvers. We are already running low on ammunition.

"The straw that broke the camel's back is that Cubans are divided over the conduct of the war—leastways I think so. That is a very serious matter. Unity is indispensable; yet, unity among Cubans isn't what it's cracked up to be, I daresay. It transpires that Agramonte is at odds with President Céspedes. I am not sure—certain things they don't discuss in my presence—but I believe Agramonte opposes the president's policy of going whole hog and torching sugarcane and coffee plantations, sugar mills, warehouses, stables, slaves' living quarters, everything. Céspedes is wrong; Agramonte is right. Such policy will make rich Cubans oppose the war and tighten the purse strings."

For an awkward moment, Reeve felt compassion for the old warrior. Staring at the tallow dip's flame, absently stroking his mustache, he seemed lost in contemplation. Eventually, the general moved his eyes to the lieutenant.

"I hope you realize the sort of fix I'm in. We came here to lend a hand. I can't give Agramonte a good going-over, nor can I impose my views. It's their country. So I have tendered my resignation to the government of the Republic in Arms. I will inform the Americans who sailed in the *Perrit,* so they can make up their own minds. You are the first; Colonel Warren will be next. Those who want to go back home with me will be welcome. Those who want to stay are free to do so. But in your case, Henry, given your age and lack of experience, it would make me awful glad if you would go back home with me."

The length of the ensuing silence made clear that Jordan had nothing more to say. Dumbfounded, Reeve had his eyes on the packed-earth floor. Twice he opened his mouth, but no sound came, and he closed it again.

"Think it over, Henry. You don't have to make a decision now. I am still second in command of the Liberation Army. Weeks will go by before I will transfer this responsibility to whoever is appointed. But I ask you to mull over everything I've said tonight, since the day will come when I will ask you what you want to do. And let's keep this conversation private."

"Of course, sir. I must admit I'm pretty confused. I had no idea these differences existed. I'll think it over and let you know. Honest I will."

"Good. Tomorrow we will decamp, your platoon included, but not you."

"But sir!"

"You are still convalescing. Don't argue with me. I hope to ambush Marshal Puello near the village of Imías. Two reserve platoons, one infantry, the other cavalry, will guard the people here. I'll be back in a week or so. Meanwhile, take good care of your wound. That's all. Go to sleep now, lad."

Reeve stood. "Yes, sir. Sleep well."

"You too, son."

January 19

Three days had gone by when, at the crack of dawn, the insurgent stronghold in the Najasa Highlands was awakened by heavy artillery fire. Unbeknownst to its dwellers, a Spanish force under Brig. Gen. Zacarías González—six battalions, a cavalry squadron, a squadron of volunteers, and four field guns—was launching a determined effort to wipe out insurgent bases.

Inside the shadowy cavern, Henry Reeve jumped from his cot and started dressing at top speed. Two other patients imitated him. As though getting shelled were a daily occurrence, Rosa remained seated by the cot of the sole rebel still lying on his back, a delirious mulatto in his thirties, who was dying from peritonitis due to a burst appendix. She was doing the only thing practical: whispering words of comfort and holding one of his hands. After lacing up his boots, Reeve adjusted the cowhide belt around his waist, made certain his revolver was fully loaded before holstering it, loaded his Sharp carbine, sheathed his machete in the scabbard dangling from his belt, put his straw hat on, and sprinted to the mouth of the cave.

Unsure of what was going on, astonished women and children, a few in nightgowns and nightshirts, were exiting their huts. Several held tin cups or redware mugs of milk and coffee; others rubbed the sleep out of their eyes. Half-naked, disconcerted soldiers were going around in circles, trying to figure out where the enemy fire had come from. Eighty yards from where Reeve stood, a twelve-pound howitzer shell exploded in the treetops. Women woke to reality and screamed in terror; children began trembling and weeping. Dozens of alarmed fowl cackled and ran in circles; dogs sprinted and barked alongside their masters.

Clutching a machete and a rifle, a pair of binoculars dangling from his neck, a rebel captain ran past the American, hollering the names of his soldiers. "¡Jacinto! ¡Miguel! ¡José María!" he cried, trying to round them up. A panting rebel soldier was swiftly coming down the crest of the hill, his eyes nearly popping out.

"There're a million Spaniards coming up the other side," he shouted to nobody in particular at the top of his lungs.

From this, Reeve assumed the man had seen two or three

hundred enemy soldiers, maybe more, ascending. Artillery fire confirmed it was a major force; small units lacked cannons. Forty or fifty men with small arms and probably short of ammunition were no match for such a contingent; they would be overrun in a matter of minutes. Retreat was the only option, the American concluded. He hobbled to the glade where equines grazed. His horse was nervous.

"Don't be afeared, boy. We'll vamoose."

Reeve untied the animal, led him to the hut where tack was kept, bridled and saddled him up, and then mounted. Another shell exploded nearby. The artillery fire's precision made Reeve realize the Spaniards knew exactly where the rebel base was. He trotted his horse along a footpath to the mouth of the cave.

The captain who had been trying to find his men minutes earlier reappeared. Seven scared-looking insurgents followed him.

"Inglesito, what are you going to do?"

The tone of his voice denoted it was a question, not a reproach; thrilling versions of Reeve's feats at the battle of Tana had reached him.

Another volley of artillery fire blew up two huts and felled several trees fifty yards to their right. Reeve had to employ all his amateurish skills at riding to control his mount. Piercing shrieks of dying or wounded people reached them seconds later.

"Captain," Reeve bellowed, "have you climbed to the top, used your binoculars?"

The rebel nodded.

"How many men?"

"More than a thousand. Four field guns."

"We should retreat," Reeve said.

The captain nodded again.

"All right. Let's save as many people as we can," Reeve said. It dawned on him that he was about to give orders to a superior; he didn't feel at fault, though. "Round up all available horses, mules, and donkeys; make women and children ride bareback on them, two on each animal. I'll be waiting for you at the base of the hill."

"Yeah, let's do that," the captain yelled. "Men, follow me."

The group sprinted to where the equines were tethered.

At the mouth of the cave, arms akimbo, Rosa was calmly contemplating the course of events.

"Rosa, bring a stool from inside, stand on it, and ride pillion with me," Reeve shouted.

"Ain't you gonna fight?"

"No. There're too many Spaniards."

Rosa squinched in disapproval. "Sick man here."

"Bring him out. He'll ride my horse, you sit astride behind him, and I'll lead on foot."

Rosa shook her head energetically. "He can't. He die soon," she blurted.

For a few moments, Reeve weighed his words. Two shells exploded nearby. The horse neighed and bucked.

"If he'll die soon, your staying with him won't save him. The Spaniards will capture you," Reeve observed.

Rosa's coal black eyes gave Reeve a hard stare as she pondered something.

"Gimme gun."

Reeve considered it for a moment, then drew the revolver from the holster and surrendered it to Rosa, who went back into the cavern. Fewer than fifteen seconds went by before a gunshot reverberated from inside the infirmary. After awhile, the black woman stepped outside, the smoking gun in her right hand, a stool in her left. Wiping tears from her cheeks, she surrendered the revolver, then mounted astride behind him and put her arms around his waist.

"*Vamo*," she ordered.

Reeve pressed his legs against the flanks of his horse. "Let's go, boy."

The plan to ambush Puello near Imías failed because the Spanish marshal took another route, so by noon that same day, as the rebel column was heading back to Najasa, scouts came across the fleeing survivors. Jordan learned of the disaster from Reeve; Agramonte from the Cubans. The Spanish force, meanwhile, razed the insurgent camp to the ground, executed nine prisoners by firing squad, and released the women and children who, for various reasons, had stayed behind.

Once the rebel column camped in a wooded area, senior officers discussed what to do next. In the evening, General Jordan, lying down in a hammock, listened to Reeve's second, more detailed, and less emotional report. Dreading it might be misconstrued, Reeve did not mention Rosa's merciful act. The younger man sat on the ground, on the oilskin William Ryan kept rolled up and tied to the back of his saddle. The Torontonian used it to brave tropical downpours, but that evening he had loaned it to Reeve so he could wrap it around himself for warmth and also sleep on it.

The young American finished the account and both men fell silent. Crickets were performing the first movement of nature's nocturne, accompanied by the hoot of an owl or the neigh of a horse. Since two- and four-legged beasts were trampling all over their world, most insects deemed it prudent to call a truce for the night and stayed in their caves. The exceptions were hundreds of fireflies, their shining tails turning on and off. In the wood's canopy, twinkling stars appeared and disappeared as branches swayed and thousands of leaves softly rustled in the light breeze, carrying the fragrances of butterfly jasmine and wild gardenias.

"My father would've cowhided me till I was black-and-blue," Jordan said.

"Sir?"

"What he used to do when I anticipated something would go awry and did."

"You saw it coming?"

"So help me God. The concept is strategically correct; it's important to establish an operations base to stock supplies, evacuate the wounded, and so forth. Yet I was not in favor of it, because once you set it up, you have to defend it. But we lacked then, and do now, enough men, weapons, and ordnance to seize the initiative throughout the whole territory *and* maintain a strong garrison at Najasa. Allowing all those women and children to live there was wrong, too."

"And you told Agramonte?"

"I did. He paid no heed."

"Then I reckon you shouldn't blame yourself."

"I don't blame myself. But I feel I did right by resigning. The load is not on my shoulders. What we've got to do now is make the Spaniards pay a high price for attacking Najasa."

"We sure will, sir."

"You bet. Let's call it a day, Henry. I'm tired."

"Yes, sir. Sleep well."

"Thanks. You, too."

Reeve laid out the oilskin on the ground before turning over. Gradually, human voices trailed off, fires died, and right on cue a loud snore joined the nocturne.

January 20

The rebels felt sure that from Najasa the enemy would retreat to Puerto Príncipe to replenish stocks and take a rest. Such a decision inevitably involved going across a place known as El Clueco, so the next morning the column force-marched to the spot, dug trenches, and set an ambush. The terrain did not lend itself to cavalry charges, so with the sole exception of scouts, men on horseback tied their mounts to trees and resigned themselves to double as riflemen. Ryan situated Reeve's platoon to his right to idle away the hours chatting.

The day the American, as recompense for his bravery, was made a lieutenant, Jordan had presented him with a .50-caliber Spencer carbine, reputedly the best firearm a soldier could have. A tubular magazine at the end of the butt stored seven copper-rim cartridges, making it possible, according to Jordan, to fire fourteen rounds per minute. The *Perrit* had brought a mere fifty of the coveted carbines. Agramonte had one, Ryan another, but the Canadian wondered if his friend was worthy of such an excellent weapon.

"You know all there is to know about rifle shooting, Henry?"

Reeve tilted his head left and right, his body language for "So-so." The lieutenant's reputation as an unassuming man made Ryan press on.

"Tell me exactly what you know."

It turned out that Captain Battle had taught the basics of rifle shooting to Reeve, who, additionally, had taken apart and cleaned his Spencer a dozen times and was familiar with the weapon. Ryan considered it convenient to add that to shoot accurately, it was of the essence not to hurry as you loaded your gun, not even when the rushing enemy was within ten yards, to aim carefully at the midsection, and to save ammunition.

Too respectful of his elders and superiors to say he knew that, Reeve nodded occasionally, making it appear he was listening attentively, drinking from the fountain of wisdom. Like his mother at his dad's sermons, he thought.

For three or four minutes, nothing was said. The morning was cool, partly cloudy. Once humans finished excavating and quieted down, animal life resumed cautiously. Songbirds trilled and flew from branch to branch, butterflies fluttered about, spiders spun their webs, buzzards circled overhead, and reptiles renewed their hunting.

"It's a beautiful country," Reeve said, gazing around.

"It is, it is."

"Free of venomous snakes, lions, tigers, and panthers. No elephants or rhinoceros, either. No gorillas, no grizzlies, no monkeys—"

"Hey, I like monkeys!" Ryan objected.

"Oh, you do. Well, I don't. The drawback is temperature. Between December and March is all right; the rest of the year is hot as hell."

"Where I come from, winter is not nice. And we have grizzlies. From time to time a grizzly kills someone."

"That figures. We have grizzlies in New York, too. Tell me about Toronto, Colonel."

Ryan chuckled. "There ain't much to tell. It used to be called 'Muddy York,' on account it sits over marshy ground by Lake Ontario; imagine the mosquitoes. Big city, maybe thirty thousand people. It has—"

"Big city? Thirty thousand?"

"Well, I reckon by New York standards it's not big. It has two impressive new buildings, though: the General Hospital and the Rossin House Hotel. The railway must be completed by now; couple of factories were under construction last time I was there."

"You had slavery in Canada?"

"Yep. It wasn't until this century—the 1830s, I think—that legal emancipation took place."

"Say, you were probably the first to abolish slavery!"

"Reckon we were. In this continent at least."

"When did you win independence from Britain?"

"We haven't. We are still a colony. Not on paper, though. On paper, we are a dominion."

"But don't you people want to become independent?"

It took Ryan about five minutes to explain that Canadians were greatly concerned about their southern neighbor and wanted the British military to defend them should the United States invade. For that to happen, colonial status, in fact, if not on paper, was inescapable.

Reeve mulled this over. He wanted to ask Ryan why he was not fighting for Canadian liberty, but it was not his concern. He found it surprising that the man who had fought against the South was now trying to liberate Cuba from the colonial yoke, and seemed not to mind that his country was under British rule.

"You miss your folks, pard?" asked Ryan, searching for a fresh topic.

"A little, yeah. My mom, my two sisters, and my old man, too."

"Any cherry?"

Reeve blushed, and Ryan knew he had found a chink in the armor.

"C'mon. Acknowledge the corn," a smiling Ryan insisted.

"Well, there's this gal I sort of cotton to."

"From Flatlands?"

Reeve shook his head.

"Manhattan?"

Same head movement.

"Well, where's she from?"

"She's from Havana."

For an instant, Ryan was taken aback. Then a wide smile opened parentheses at the corners of his mouth.

"Well, well. That caps the climax. Are you here because you hope to ride victorious into Havana and ask for her hand in marriage?"

"Of course not, Colonel!" said a vexed Reeve.

"All right. Don't pitch a fit. I'm joking. You met her here?"

Reeve struggled to keep calm; it took him a moment. "No, I met her in Manhattan. Her dad had a checking account at my branch. But she moved to New Orleans a few months before I sailed to Cuba."

"Oh."

"Can we change the subject, sir?"

"By all means."

After a minute, Reeve felt that the embarrassing silence was his fault. Reflecting on a fresh topic, he remembered the disagreements between Agramonte and Jordan. Surely, Ryan had an opinion, but how could he raise the problem without revealing what Jordan had told him?

"What do you think of Ignacio Agramonte?" was what he came up with.

Ryan grew serious and pondered his reply. "He's . . . different."

"What do you mean?"

Again, Ryan weighed his words. "I don't know."

"You don't know?"

Ryan sighed. "Listen, lad. I've been to war with hundreds of men. Agramonte is like no one I know . . . or knew. He is courageous . . . smart . . . but I've met lots of men with guts and brains. Something makes him stand apart. Trust, maybe. His soldiers trust him. Even if common sense says he's wrong, they follow him full chisel across lots. I've seen folks twenty years their senior hang their heads if he scolds them. As if he were their father."

Reeve nodded, considered what to ask next. "Before rising up in arms, did he do military service?"

"Not to my knowledge. He's a lawyer."

"So how come he's such a great soldier?"

"I don't know. Maybe he's a born soldier, just as some are born musicians or inventors. This Mr. Morse who invented the telegraph? He was a professional painter; painted pictures, for Lord's sake!"

"Don't swear, Colonel, please."

"Sorry for that. What I mean is, Morse invented this dot-dash system, and now you can send a message from New York to London within minutes—some say within seconds, but that's impossible—through this underwater cable. What does that have in common with painting pictures? You tell me."

"Nothing, I reckon."

"Exactly. What happened was, this Morse was a born inventor and didn't know it. Well, I suppose Agramonte didn't know he was a born soldier, either, and chose to study law."

The topic of inventions sidetracked Reeve. "What I can't figure out, Colonel, is this cable beneath the sea. Whales or sharks can bite it to pieces. Why don't they?"

"Beats me."

"Whales are big hungry fish; one swallowed Jonah," Reeve observed.

Ryan wiped the hint of a smile off his face and thought it best to remain silent.

"I've noticed there are telegraph poles here," Reeve said next.

"Sure."

"I had no idea Cuba was so advanced."

"Cubans brag they had railways before Spain did."

"You don't say."

"It's true. And Havana is perhaps the biggest city in the Caribbean. Busiest port in the American continent after New York."

"Really? How many people live in Havana?"

"Well, I don't know for sure, but some say two hundred thousand."

"I guess New York City has ten times more."

"No, four times more, less than a million."

A courier trotted to Ryan. "Colonel, General Jordan says scouts report the enemy is close and he wants your men to get ready."

"Thank you."

The courier sprinted away.

"You heard him, Henry. Warn your boys."

Although no hand-to-hand combat took place, the battle was bloody and both sides suffered heavy losses. Intent on saving ammunition, Cuban riflemen tried to achieve sharpshooter effectiveness. Reeve and Ryan selected a target and aimed carefully, squeezing the trigger only when the chosen adversary was fully exposed. Reeve spent thirteen cartridges and felt sure he had killed or wounded two enemies; he guessed he might have taken down one more. Ryan figured that with a mere nine shots, he had hit four foes, two of whom he had no doubt about whatsoever.

The combat had been going on for an hour and a half when Jordan called for a casualty toll. Finding out that thirty-nine Cubans were dead or wounded made him order a retreat. Agramonte disagreed and asked permission to charge, but Jordan pulled rank and prevailed.

The battle of El Clueco was the starting point for a successful Spanish army counteroffensive. Once he wiped out all rebel camps near Puerto Príncipe, Gen. Zacarías González expanded the war zone to Caonao and the Cubitas range. The Spanish general also created units of counterinsurgency riders, who from new, strategically dispersed garrisons, combed forests and hills, hunting for insurgents and their supporters. Communications with the most important cities to the east were secured.

That state of affairs aggravated the disagreements over tactics and the conduct of the war between Jordan and Agramonte. The American general was persuaded he couldn't postpone his departure any longer. For that reason, on February 27, he summoned Reeve to the hammock that marked his space where the column was bivouacking.

"Let's take a walk, Henry," the general suggested, then nailed the cigar with his teeth, snatched his hat, put it on, and ambled along. As soon as he felt certain they were out of earshot, Jordan stopped and faced his compatriot.

"The word is that your men hold you in high regard."

"I hope so, sir," Reeve replied, respectfully removing his hat.

"I must apologize, Henry. I believed you were too young for this. Fact is, your maturity is beyond your years."

"No apology is required, sir, please."

Staring at Reeve, the general dragged on his cigar, blew smoke out. The thought crossing his mind made him smile and nod appreciatively.

"Inglesito. So strange. El Muerto Vivo would've been more appropriate."

"The Living Dead?"

"Exactly."

"Ah."

"But no, these people wouldn't call you that. It goes against the national character. They try hard to overlook bad times and unpleasant realities to see if they'll go away by magic. Not many would use a nickname that reminds them you survived an execution by firing squad. Mexican Indians would call you El Muerto Vivo for sure."

Reeve gave a chuckle.

"Cubans have a just cause, all the same," Jordan went on. "A just cause whose time has not come."

"What do you mean, sir?"

"I mean they won't achieve independence anytime soon because, first, they don't have the men, weapons, and ordnance required to win this war. Second, they lack military experience and ignore the advice of those who do. Third, they are divided: The leaders of Oriente, Camagüey, and Las Villas can't agree on what time it is; to the west of Las Villas, peace reigns. To make matters worse, the Chamber of Representatives wants to tell its inexpert generals and colonels how to wage war. And fourth, this neutrality agreement of ours has severed their main supply line. No, Henry, the time for Cuban sovereignty has not yet arrived. This war is already lost."

Reeve took a deep breath and gazed west, studying the setting sun. Was this what Ryan called "defeatism"? Jordan dragged on his cigar.

"My resignation has been accepted, Henry. I will head back home tomorrow. What will you do?"

Reeve swung right and made eye contact with Jordan.

"I will stay, General. I shall always remember that I am here thanks to you. Have a safe journey."

"It's what I expected you to say. You will be much more valuable to the cause alive than dead, so be careful."

"I will, sir."

"If you want me to mail a letter for you, write it tonight. God bless you."

Jordan turned on his heels. Suddenly feeling a tinge of sadness, Reeve put on his hat and followed the general.

On March 28, the Star Hunters cavalry squadron, under Col. William Ryan, conducted a surprise attack against a Spanish infantry battalion camped at the Cercado sugar mill.

Riding Tiger—Jordan's parting gift, a sixteen-hand sorrel Creole charger that galloped up to combat as if a mare in estrus awaited him—Reeve spearheaded the attack. The light breeze blowing carried the smells of sugarcane juice, sugar, and burning firewood typical of harvest time. The astonished expressions of the Spaniards when they saw a hundred centaurs brandishing machetes coming down on them made him smile. The onset of the battle decides its outcome, Ryan had preached time and again. The hands of enemy soldiers tremble when trying to open the breech; rounds fall to the ground; the staccato from four hundred horses' hooves heralds doom for them. Yeah, Ryan was right; surprise was of the essence, Reeve decided.

His first *machetazo* cut the right arm of a sergeant and broke the man's humerus. Mindful not to spur his mount, Reeve yanked the reins left and aimed at the head of a soldier, but the man raised his arms defensively and the frightened stallion stood on his hindquarters.

"Fuck!" Reeve mumbled when he missed delivering the blow. He had never cursed before.

The instant the animal's forelegs thumped the ground, he swung the blade again. As on his debut charge three months earlier, the recoil when it hit the cranium shocked him. He tugged the blade out now and took his eyes off the crumpling enemy to hunt for another opponent. None was near, so he sheathed the blade, drew the carbine, and fired it at such close range that, despite the horse leaping and revolving, he did not miss one shot. Having felled seven men, he drew his revolver and emptied the cylinder on two more. Reeve glanced around, looking for a place to take cover while reloading. A hundred or so varas away, a rather big sugar warehouse seemed suitable. He galloped to the rear of the building. The fired-up animal kept neighing and moving, so reloading the carbine took him almost a minute. By the time he had finished, the rebel bugler sounded retreat. Reeve trotted back to the battlefield and, firing the Spencer at a hastily formed enemy square, made sure all mounted rebels retreated before he galloped away.

The Spanish battalion suffered seventy-five casualties, thirty fatal. Ryan's squadron sustained eleven casualties, five dead—three who were taken prisoner and executed on the spot and two who died in combat—and six wounded.

Ignacio Agramonte strenuously argued for hit-and-run tactics. He said it was how small bands of Spanish soldiers had fought the French army when Napoleon invaded Spain. The minute he learned about the Cercado sugar-mill combat, he said its outcome corroborated that guerrilla warfare was the kind of campaign Cuban insurgents should conduct.

Jordan's departure notwithstanding, owing to his disagreements with President Céspedes concerning strategy and tactics,

Agramonte resigned as military chief of Camagüey in late April. Unofficially, though, he kept a prominent position in the rebel military hierarchy because he did not lay down arms; escorted by a few adjuncts and his security detail, he joined other units and engaged in battle when the occasion arose.

Agramonte belonged to the select category of individuals who inspired extreme feelings, either of admiration and devotion or of censure and contempt. Those who rooted for the twenty-eight-year-old lawyer proclaimed he had immense courage, was cultivated yet unassuming, came from an old and rich Cuban family, shared with his men the rigors of life in the open, and had joined the insurgents a mere three months after marrying his childhood sweetheart. His detractors judged him to be power-hungry, a know-it-all, arrogant, inflexible, and prone to fits of violence.

Word reached Agramonte that the young American he had passed the time of the day with a few times, at present serving under Colonel Ryan, was consistently proving exceptional valor. After the Cercado sugar-mill charge, Reeve was promoted to captain and given the most dangerous of missions: chief of a scouts unit that would act as the vanguard and rear guard of Ryan's squadron. He distinguished himself at the battles of Puente Carrasco on June 18, where the Spaniards tallied up twenty-one dead and 121 wounded, at La Gloria and Santa María on June 24, and at Santa Brianda de Altamira on July 5. Rumor had it the young man was mastering Spanish. He had allegedly found a copy of *Don Quijote de la Mancha,* lost by a fleeing Spaniard, and spent all his free time reading the thick volume and asking about the sense of words.

Soon after promoting William Ryan to brigadier general, President Céspedes needed someone fluent in English to send to New York on a fact-finding mission, and he chose the Canadian. Ryan surrendered his command and departed on August 6. Reeve got reassigned to the First Cavalry Squadron, Southern Camagüey Brigade. There he reunited with Cristóbal Acosta, a Venezuelan who had sailed in the *Perrit* and was a general in the rebel army. Nonetheless, by late September, stocks of ammunition had decreased so much that every bullet counted. Cavalry charges were the preferred form of combat. The judicious observations of General Jordan frequently came to Reeve's mind. Maybe he was a realist, not a defeatist.

The Spanish colonel Montaner was infamous for implacably murdering helpless Cubans and maltreating guiltless families. Therefore, when, on November 13, General Acosta learned that Montaner was bivouacking around Jobabo and purchasing cattle, he immediately put on the march the First Cavalry Squadron, a company of the Fourth Infantry Battalion, fifty soldiers of the Riflemen Battalion, and his adjuncts, orderlies, and security detail. The first ambush failed, but the next, with the Spaniards herding five hundred head of cattle, was successful. The rebels spent all their ammunition before ordering a cavalry charge. The cattle dispersed and the colonialists registered eighty-one casualties, of whom nineteen were fatal. Montaner, the hated adversary, was unharmed. Four rebels were wounded, Reeve one of them, shot in his left foot. Only one insurgent died.

The young captain saw himself confined to an infirmary for the second time in a year, on this occasion near a village named La Gertrudis. The big *bohío* could admit twelve patients, but only three hammocks were in use when Reeve and the other wounded rebels arrived. One patient had malaria, another suffered from typhoid fever, and the third was ill with something nobody could diagnose but was wasting away by the hour.

Six smaller huts housed the families of the veterinarian

serving as general practitioner, of the cook, and of four rebels too old for active duty who performed as sentries, messengers, growers, grave diggers, and whatnot. Crutches were available, and Reeve was hobbling all over the place two days later. It was how he came to chance on Ramona.

"Hey, take off those dirty pantaloons and shirt and I'll wash them for you," she shouted. The woman was hanging the family's laundry on a clothesline. "You have socks, make sure you throw them in. I bet they stink."

Then she burst out laughing.

Bad move—the worst. Reeve was a virgin and his vague sexual notions derived from biblical verses: "A widow, or a divorced woman, or profane, or an harlot, these shall he not take: but he shall take a virgin of his own people to wife." Or, "The woman also with whom man shall lie with seed of copulation, they shall both bathe themselves in water, and be unclean until the evening." The present his father had made him on his fourteenth birthday had been a warning against touching his penis when not urinating; so every time Reeve masturbated, guilt gnawed at his conscience. He knew nothing about female genitalia and imagined that lovemaking consisted of a man embracing and kissing the woman he loved. Besides, he *knew* his pantaloon was caked with nightly emissions. As a result, he shambled away as fast as he could.

But the twenty-six-year-old brunette with brown-black eyes and wide hips was not easily discouraged. One week after her eighteen-year-old cousin deflowered her, when she was fifteen, she began enjoying sex very much. Regrettably, at no time had her cousin made a proposal of marriage; in the end, he moved to Las Villas. Five years and four neighbors later, Ramona started wondering if she was infertile. The only way to find out was to have sex with lots of virile-looking chaps. Eventually, she was dubbed "Ramona la Regalona"—roughly, "Ramona Giveaway"—since she did it for free, but by the time she reached twelve sexual partners, Ramona felt sure she was barren. Her father, a true-blue patriot, never figured out why villagers repressed smiles and turned their head when he came to buy provisions. He moved his wife and two daughters to the infirmary, ignorant of the fact that soldiers drove Ramona wild, especially young and brave soldiers.

When Reeve awoke the next morning, he fumbled for his sole change of clothes. It had disappeared, socks included. After a moment of total disbelief and reflection, he felt certain the woman with the hair plaited into two long tails was the culprit, but lacking proof, he refrained from voicing his suspicions. Clothing was scarce, and the only male who could spare a pair of pantaloons and a shirt was the cook, who had a forty-two-inch waist and an eighteen-inch neck; Reeve's waist measured twenty-eight, his neck fourteen. Nobody had seen anything, and he had to stay in the hammock all day long, mealtimes included, fuming at his immobility.

The following sunrise, the American found his laundered clothes in a *taburete* near his hammock. The bullet hole in his sock had been mended, too. Again, nobody knew anything. Reeve smiled and shook his head in wonder. He got dressed and, after breakfast, headed directly to the clothesline. As sure as eggs are eggs, Ramona was there, hanging wet clothes. Getting closer, Reeve did what he always did when confronted with a woman: He compared her to the beautiful Cuban teenager he had been infatuated with in New York. He found Ramona plain.

"You shouldn't have done this" was his opening line as he gestured to his shirt.

"Oh, you speak Spanish?"

"A little. Thank you very much."

"You are very welcome. You know what? I'd love to get to know you better. When you heal, I mean."

"I am all right. I can talk."

"No, I meant— Never mind. You a soldier?"

"I'm a captain."

"A captain! Oh my God!"

"Don't take the name of the Lord in vain. What's your name?"

Ramona sensed she had to bide her time, and the brief early-morning chats progressed matter-of-factly for a week or so. Reeve learned that her education had concluded in elementary school because no secondary schools were to be found within a ten-league radius, that her parents had lost two boys to yellow fever, that she loved red mamey and blue dresses, that the most delicious fish in the world came from the seaside village of Santa Cruz del Sur, and other things of similar nature.

She considered him an inveterate liar trying to impress her with fantastic stories. With a straight face, he had said that Niu Yor, the city where he used to live, had five-story buildings. Five stories! In the same godforsaken place, he claimed, flakes of frozen water fell from the sky in wintertime (the nerve of the guy) and grown-up men played a game called beis-bol, in which they hit a ball with a wooden stick and ran in circles. Did the lean, fair-headed captain think she would swallow that guava? Everybody knew that everywhere grown-up men did only four things: work, get drunk, fight, and fuck. She was further supposed to believe that a machine produced a thing called tintypes, faithful reproductions of people's faces, better than portraits, albeit lacking color. To top it all, he had said that men flew aboard baskets suspended from big balloons full of hot air, with the purpose of observing the movements of enemy armies. Such impudence; balloons that fly indeed. Well, the time would come when *she* would impress *him*—with the real thing, not bla-bla-bla.

The rebel who was wasting away died and was buried. Reeve said a prayer at the internment. He was limping less and using one crutch when she suggested chatting in the evenings, after supper. Later that same afternoon he felt well enough to leave the crutch by his hammock. She took his hand, drew him into the forest, and set off a kissing spree. After three or four minutes of this, she half-forced him, half-helped him to lie down prone on the soil, unbuttoned his fly, extracted a hard regular-size penis, lifted her skirt, crouched down, filled herself with him, and switched her hips on. A mere sixty seconds later, Reeve was experiencing supreme physical pleasure. Due to her loving ministrations, soon after he was hard again and she enjoyed her orgasm.

During the next five days, they were insatiable. Because one of Ramona's lovers had told her that copulating during digestion killed men, and the thought of a man dying while fornicating terrified her, Reeve hobbled to the woods before breakfast, before lunch, and two hours after dinner. She taught him every position she knew and made him forget that a war was going on. Resting in his hammock postcoitus, however, Reeve kept asking himself why Ramona, when pressing his head against her bare breasts, always said, "Fly these balloons, honey." Fly? When he was inside her, what she asked bordered on "You like my *jom pleit*?" Home plate? Maybe the problem was his insufficient Spanish, and he feared offending her should he ask what she meant. He merely mumbled simple words in her language—*Sure, yeah,* and *fine*—in conformity with what he supposed she had meant or asked.

Ramona had tallied eighty-four copulations when Ignacio

Agramonte visited the infirmary and, unknowingly, ruined Reeve's sex festival.

In December, President Céspedes reconsidered and on January 13 restored Major General Agramonte to the position of military chief of Camagüey. Forewarned that his designation was a sure thing, the Cuban lawyer set about visiting all units in early January to assess combat preparedness, weaponry, stocks of ammunition and supplies, lines of communication, and morale. When he was told that Captain Reeve was recuperating within two leagues of General Acosta's camp, Agramonte resolved to sound the man out personally and decide if the young American had the guts and brains required to lead the vanguard of the Camagüey Cavalry.

Agramonte entered the *bohío* followed by two men, one of whom walked unevenly. The lawyer was six feet tall but looked taller. His dark hair made a stark contrast to the paleness of his wide forehead, straight nose, and cheeks. His big droopy brown eyes could reflect a wide range of emotions, from steely resolve to platonic romanticism. A sparse mustache and an unkempt goatee encircled slim lips.

Left speechless by the unexpected visitors, by how gaunt all three were, and by the dirty and tattered clothes they had on, Reeve rose to his feet. Agramonte's pantaloons had been cut off four or five inches below his knees, but buckskin leggings covered his calves. His shirt was torn in several places, maybe from riding too close to the thorny bush named *marabou*, Reeve figured. His companions had fared no better.

"Major," he managed to say. Rookies excepted, every rebel in Camagüey knew that Agramonte detested the word *general*. Having noticed how he struggled to repress a grimace of dis-

gust when a subordinate called him "Major General," his inti-
mates spread the word: Agramonte was to be called "Major"
or "sir."

"Sit down, Enrique. It's Enrique in Spanish, right?" His vel-
vety voice and clear enunciation failed to conceal the ruthless
determination of a man with a cause.

"Yes, sir."

"Sit down, please."

"Not while you are standing, sir," Reeve replied, offering
Agramonte the *taburete* by his hammock. The major smiled.

"You know these two gentlemen, Enrique?"

"I don't have the pleasure, sir."

"Colonel Julio Sanguily." Agramonte gestured with his hand
in the lame man's direction. The twenty-four-year-old colonel
was of average height, had brown hair and eyes, a straight nose,
and a five-day-old beard.

"Glad to meet you, sir," Reeve said, shaking hands. The
rebel colonel nodded.

"And his brother, Lieutenant Colonel Manuel Sanguily."

The word *brother* made Reeve realize that what he found
intriguing in the major's associates was the clear family resem-
blance. Manuel came across as a tad younger.

"Glad to meet you, too, sir." Again handshakes were exchanged.

"Take the *taburete,* Julio," Agramonte said.

"No, Ignacio, you take it."

Agramonte turned his head and shot a pleading glance at
Julio Sanguily, who hobbled to the rustic chair and sat.

"When were you wounded, Enrique?"

"November 18."

"Well, it's January fifth. Let's see . . . twelve, plus thirty-one,
plus five, it's—"

"Forty-eight days," contributed Julio Sanguily.

"Are you not yet feeling well?" Agramonte said.

"Oh, no, sir, I'm as good as new."

"Then . . . something keeping you here?" Agramonte asked suspiciously.

"No, sir," replied Reeve, swallowing hard.

Two patients took the initiative and fetched chairs for Agramonte and Manuel Sanguily. Reeve sat in his hammock. The next few minutes were spent on introductions and a question-and-answer session. Agramonte wanted to know in what battle each of the patients had been wounded, if the men were married or single, when they had joined the Liberation Army, the most recent time they had seen their families, and so forth and so on. When the exchange dried up, Manuel Sanguily repeatedly moved his head sideways and glanced at the door. The patients understood that the visitors and Reeve were to be left alone and had the good sense to go out and strike up conversations with Agramonte's ten-man security detail. One of them swaggered to the kitchen to see whether the cook would brew fresh coffee for the visitors.

"So, if you are feeling fine," Agramonte, settling back in the chair and crossing his legs, "are you wondering if the time has come for you to piss on the fire and head back home?"

"I am not, sir." Reeve thought the man had a piercing stare.

"Let me put my cards on the table, Enrique. Nowadays we are short on ammunition and all sorts of supplies. We are not capable of doing battle. All we can do is fire a few rifle shots from afar and gallop away. Deserters abound, and when one is caught, I have him hanged. In short, the enemy has the upper hand right now. In spite of that, we are not giving up.

"But we are Cubans; this is our homeland. That's not the

case with you. You've made a contribution we appreciate, but we wouldn't hold it against you if you wish to follow General Jordan's steps."

"Major Agramonte hopes to turn the war around in six months," said Manuel Sanguily, interrupting. Agramonte silenced him with a glance. The man blushed.

"I might or might not achieve what I hope," Agramonte went on after a short pause. "Your conduct in battle has won you the right to be told the truth. I want you to make a decision based on the current circumstances, not on what I hope."

Reeve understood the gravity of the situation, but three reasons determined his decision: a sense of adventure, his belief that the cause was just, and a character trait most humans possess—a refusal to acknowledge their own mistakes.

"Major, I'm ready to rejoin my unit. If you don't need me in Cuba, I'll fight for the liberation of Puerto Rico," he said.

Agramonte smiled widely. "I need you here."

"Makes me glad to learn that. How can I help?"

"I want you to take charge of the vanguard of the Camagüey Cavalry. Can you do that?"

"I'd give it my best shot, sir. Honest I would."

"All right. I'll tell you what I want to do. I want to unify all disperse units and form a strong division. The backbone of that division will be the cavalry, especially its exploration unit. I want a very mobile and effective cavalry. Listen, Enrique. Past experience shows . . ."

Agramonte rattled on for fifteen minutes. In subsequent weeks, months, and years, each and every time Reeve remembered Agramonte's impassioned exposition that day at the infirmary, he would try to find the word that might better define

how he had felt. Eventually, he settled for *persuadido*—
"persuaded" in English. The Major's persuasiveness was the
consequence of two qualities he possessed in vast quantities:
First, he worded his opinions so brilliantly that common
folks came to view them as incontrovertible. Second, implicitly he made individuals sincerely believe that his or her
contribution was crucial, for without it the supreme goal—
independence—would be unattainable. Reeve had *felt* he was
not one of many fighters, but the most important fighter in
the Liberation Army. He would recall that he had perceived
the glaring contradiction between what Agramonte advo-
cated and what Jordan thought, yet he was won over by the
Cuban lawyer. Suddenly, Jordan's notions had seemed mistaken: too conservative, defeatist, lacking in fervor and patriotism.

When Agramonte finished speaking, Reeve stood up.

"Major, I'll go bridle and saddle my horse and leave with
you."

"You sure you can ride, Enrique?"

"I'm sure, Major."

"All right, saddle up."

Later, leading his horse by the bridle, Reeve waved good-bye
to an apparently sad Ramona. As he approached Agramonte's
party, he saw a rebel inserting the lame man's foot into the stirrup, helping him mount, and then encircling his waist with a
strange leather contraption that was next secured to the saddle.
Reeve's admiration for the older Sanguily was born then and
there.

All others were savoring gourds of freshly brewed coffee,
and the newest convert to Agramontismo was handed over a
container. He took three quick sips and returned it empty.

Then he clutched the pommel of the saddle, placed his left foot in the stirrup, experienced a dull ache, and pulled himself up. Agramonte glanced around, making sure every man had finished his coffee.

"Forward!" he ordered.

Reeve rode away without looking back.

THREE

February 20, 1871

★

The Pinto optical tower, within four leagues from Puerto Príncipe, Camagüey's most important city, was a wooden two-story Spanish military construction with battlements. Its operation and defense were the responsibility of a second lieutenant, a sergeant, three corporals, and twenty soldiers. To enter or exit the outpost, a drawbridge was lowered over the ditch encircling it.

Many similar towers dotted the Cuban countryside, elements of a communication network employing optical telegraphy. Numerous marks, each representing a phrase, were posted on a huge board. Roughly two leagues away, at the next tower, a telescope-bearing soldier made out the symbols, reproduced them on his board, and relayed the information to the adjacent tower. A dictionary of phrases with the meaning of each mark made decoding possible. The system was not luminous, so it worked only in daytime.

Such a device, invented by a Frenchman in the final years of the eighteenth century, improved upon by a Spaniard in the 1840s, and then made obsolete by the electric telegraph, was still in operation in Cuba for economic and military reasons. A main telegraph line connected all provincial capitals to Havana, but linking up dozens of garrisons scattered all over the island was too expensive; the exception to this was the fortified line of defense from the port of Júcaro, on the southern coast, to the town of Morón, nearby the northern shoreline. Wires could be cut, but blocking the view between two towers was a physical impossibility.

A hamlet consisting of four *bohíos* had sprouted up near the outpost. The first who commissioned a hut built a hundred or so yards from the tower was a whore. A cook, who wound up preparing three square meals a day for the platoon, his wife, and the whore, had been the next settler. A laundress moved in a few weeks after the cook; she had two school-age daughters. The fourth hut was erected by a Galician barber who made a living trimming sideburns, beards, and mustaches, giving haircuts, and extracting teeth. A widow and her two boys moved in with the barber.

Ignacio Agramonte decided to launch an attack on the tower to show that the rebel army, like the phoenix, had risen from its ashes. The secondary goal was to disrupt enemy communications. In a little over a month, he had reorganized both the cavalry and the infantry, but short of firearms and ammunition, he deemed the poorly defended tower a good place to restock. Therefore, around midday on February 19, he positioned four infantry companies and a cavalry squadron, a total of three hundred men, half a league away from the Spanish outpost.

In the afternoon, however, the colonialists spotted two Cuban scouts. The lieutenant placed the garrison on full alert and had the bridge drawn. The night was sleepless yet uneventful. At sunrise, the Spaniards felt like sipping what they half-jokingly termed "the black nectar of the white gods" and pleaded with the lieutenant to lower the bridge and send a man to fetch freshly brewed coffee. Surely the small party of rebels had fled, they argued. The decision maker botched it, and the assault began.

As it turned out, Agramonte's decision was even worse. The bridge was speedily lifted the moment the tower echoed with the sound of gunfire. The initial wave of besiegers, carrying hastily assembled ladders and torches, had to beat a retreat carrying two dead and five wounded. The defenders managed to put out three fires. The ditch prevented the cavalry from charging. Insurgent sharpshooters took down several defenders by getting their bullets through the parapet's crenels, but a number of colonialists were pretty good shots and felled several Cubans crouching behind trunks at a grove of royal palms.

The Spaniards fought so bravely that only four men were unharmed; five died and sixteen were wounded. When ammunition was running low, those still firing searched the bodies of the dead and the wounded for rounds. Thirty-five rebels were injured, five fatally. Before ordering the bugler to sound retreat, Agramonte had the hamlet burned to the ground. Seeing their huts in flames, the whore and the laundress started shouting curses at the rebels and calling them names. They threw in acclamations to Spain and its king for good measure. The cook and the barber, well aware that men were not given the degree of latitude women got, considered it better to keep their mouths shut.

That night, after burying the dead and providing emergency care to the wounded, a somber Agramonte held a war council with his officers. The column had camped outdoors at Sabana

Nueva, the place where they had stayed overnight two days earlier. That three hundred rebels had not been able to take a stronghold defended by twenty-five Spaniards had discouraged many insurgents.

"I'm fully responsible for what happened today," Agramonte began, reaching for the heart of the matter.

Reeve's right arm shot up, as in his primary school classroom.

"You want to say something, Captain Reeve?"

"Yes, sir. You are not responsible. The Spaniards were alerted by the carelessness of two of my men. If that hadn't happened, the attack would've succeeded."

Agramonte gave an emphatic nod. "Even if that hadn't happened, I doubt we would've taken the tower. Well-fortified adversaries, even if outnumbered ten to one, can repel an attack. It was wrong to send men across an open space; they couldn't take cover. It was wrong to attack the tower when lacking artillery; one piece at least was required. And in war, mistakes cost lives.

"We must learn the lesson and stick to the tactic of finding out where the enemy is headed, set an ambush, let the vanguard show itself, entice the Spaniards into chasing what looks like an isolated, fleeing platoon, and draw them to the ambush. Then the infantry catches them in cross fire and, once they are in disarray, the cavalry charges. I want all of you to remember that. We've opted for mobility over firepower, so we lack howitzers. As long as that remains our tactic, we don't attack fortified outposts, however isolated and poorly defended they may seem. Had we fired two cannon shots at the tower, the very same men who repelled us today would've surrendered. Overwhelming force makes a difference. When the enemy comes at us with overwhelming force, the intelligent thing to do is to retreat.

"The obverse, as our struggle proves, is not true. We have defeated the enemy time and again with fewer men, even at great disadvantage. Why? Because we are fighting for the liberation of our country and they are fighting to keep us under oppression. They understand that, believe me. From the captain general to the illiterate soldier, they all know we are right and they are wrong. They know they were defeated by Bolívar and Sucre and San Martín not because those patriots were military geniuses, even though they *were* military geniuses, but because Spain was oppressing and plundering Venezuela, Colombia, Peru, Chile, and the rest of their colonies. It's why they lost South America. It's why, by and by, they will lose Cuba and Puerto Rico and the Philippines and all their colonies in Africa. Because the people born and raised in those countries want to be independent and are willing to fight and die to achieve self-determination. I have nothing more to say. I would appreciate your comments now."

Several officers shifted their weight from one foot to the other and exchanged glances. Two took off their hats and scratched their heads.

"Major?" Julio Sanguily said.

"Yes, Colonel."

"As far as I'm concerned, you've done the first thing that needs to be done to correct a mistake: to admit one erred. It's all I wanted to hear from you."

"Thank you, Colonel. Next, please."

"Major?"

"Yes, General Boza."

"I opine it was also mistaken to torch the huts of people living near the tower. We need allies, not adversaries, especially among Cubans. When we torch the homes of Cubans, we make enemies."

Agramonte clasped his hands behind his back, rocked on his heels, and glanced at the branches above him.

"I understand the viewpoint of the barber living there; he's a Spaniard," Agramonte said, lowering his eyes and giving Boza a hard look. "But the Cubans, General Boza, sided with the enemy long ago, the day they decided to fuck, feed, and wash and iron the clothes of Spanish soldiers."

The ensuing pause lasted a mere second.

"You know, Major," Boza carried on, undeterred, "that folks in the countryside are starving. Those who sell things to the Spaniards, or cook for them, or wash their clothes, or fuck them, do it to survive, not to side with the enemy. And a few spy for us. Thanks to some of those folks, we occasionally find out where the enemy is headed before they decamp."

"Did you listen to those women? Cheering for Spain and its bastard king?"

"I did."

"You think they are spying for us?"

"If they are, Major, and I'm not saying they are, but if they are, they should cheer for Spain and Amadeo de Saboya to place themselves beyond suspicion."

For a moment, Agramonte was taken aback.

"Those who share General Boza's opinion, please say so," he said, recovering fast.

Most men hovered between speaking their mind or keeping mum.

"Maybe what General Boza objects to," Manuel Sanguily said, "is indiscriminate torching. Today I would've torched the *bohíos* of the whore and the Spaniard. But I would've spared the laundress and the cook."

"Quite Solomonic," Agramonte replied ironically.

"Major?" Reeve said.

"Yes, Captain."

"I'm not Cuban, so maybe this is no business of mine—"

"On the contrary," Agramonte said, interrupting. "You are fighting for Cuba Libre. Many Cubans are not doing that, so you are entitled to speak your mind. So please, Captain Reeve, go on."

Reeve nodded and swallowed. "Thank you, sir. I ain't a learned man like you gentlemen, but it appears to me you, Major, and General Boza, are both right. Collaborators should be punished, and these people were so. But only the whore was by herself. Two small girls live with the laundress—her daughters, I figure. The woman living at the cook's is pregnant. The woman living with the Spaniard has two small boys. Now, these are civilians. And, dash it all, I'd rather see a collaborator go unpunished than torch the diggings where innocent children and women live."

Agramonte took a deep breath. Boza and the Sanguily brothers gave Reeve an approving look.

"You may be right, Captain Reeve," Agramonte conceded. "Gentlemen, I shall carefully mull over your opinions. Now let's call it a day. Dismissed."

February 21-November 27

On May 28, during a skirmish at Hato Potrero, Reeve was shot in the right shoulder and sent back to the infirmary. As soon as he had regained a little movement in his arm, he started taking care of Tiger. Every morning he asked another patient, who was convalescing from malaria, to help him bridle and saddle the charger, then rode it for a few minutes.

Three weeks after Reeve's arrival, Ramona was feeling sorely disappointed in him. She had washed and mended his clothes the very day he got there. She had had sex with him when he intimated, somewhat shyly, that he felt like it. She had forborne letting loose all her passion until he had fully recovered. Nonetheless, early on Ramona had intuited that the American captain was no longer spellbound by her lovemaking, as he had been five months earlier. Having sex three times a day was all he had dwelled on; the consummate liar had not at all showed a longing for the battlefield. Then a so-and-so general had shown up and taken him away. And Enrique had changed.

These days, all he talked about was rejoining his cavalry squadron, and he spent most daylight hours reading *Don Quijote,* a book that, according to her sixth-grade teacher, told the adventures of a madman who covered his head with a piss pot and charged at windmills. Now, what man in his right mind would prefer reading *that* shit, or any other book, to screwing? Ramona asked herself. Enrique seemed quite satisfied with making love once a day, in the evening. He even seemed relieved the few nights she told him they had to abstain because she had her period. Ramona had practice in identifying the symptoms of male boredom and lack of interest. And there was this Cuban sergeant recovering from a saber wound in his calf. . . .

Reeve rejoined the squadron on June 30 and took part in shootings, ambushes, and skirmishes all through July, August, and September. On October 7, Agramonte and seventy cavalrymen camped at the Consuegra savanna, to the south of Puerto Príncipe, the provincial capital. Soldiers and noncoms were dressed in tatters, which they would have to keep wearing until a Spanish supply caravan with uniforms was seized, or until prisoners were taken and stripped naked. Officers fared a little better, but after weeks riding under the scorching sun, sleeping outdoors, and crossing marshlands, lumped together with the smelly horses and dogs that followed them, they found their ragged, dirty, stinking clothes clamored for washing and mending. Having in mind to make himself more presentable, Julio Sanguily asked for Agramonte's permission to visit Cirila López next morning. The young woman ran an infirmary at a *bohío* not too far from where they were.

Agramonte had several reasons to feel special affection for the handicapped man, especially since he had devised a leather contraption to strap himself to the saddle and ride and fight as though able-bodied. Sanguily's lameness was the result of war wounds; his bravery and perseverance in the face of adversity was an example to those in the ranks and to all officers. Despite all that, Agramonte would have denied Sanguily the permission to wash his clothes had all other subordinates been in good health. But three of them, suffering from typhoid fever probably, were in need of rest and whatever herbal remedies Cirila could give them to mitigate their suffering. So he consented.

The next morning, Sanguily, Captain Palomino (his adjunct), Luciano (his orderly), and the three sick men rode to the infirmary. As luck would have it, Palomino fell behind. He was approaching the place when he saw the strangest thing: Sanguily riding on the back of his fleeing orderly! The adjunct reined in his horse, froze, and frowned in confusion. Then he spotted a group of Spanish soldiers in hot pursuit.

Realizing that he stood no chance, Sanguily reached for the branch of a tree and, hanging from it, ordered Luciano to run and save himself. An instant later, a Spanish sergeant aimed his rifle at Sanguily and bawled, "Surrender, rebel, or I'll shoot you." The lame man didn't say a word, merely stared.

Captain Palomino turned his mount around and fled to Agramonte's camp.

The minute the Major found out what had happened, he sent for El Inglesito.

"At your orders, Major," Reeve said upon arriving.

"Enrique, Colonel Sanguily has been taken prisoner. I want you to follow the trail to Cirila's place, spot where the enemy is headed, and come back without being seen."

"Yes, sir."

Reeve made the round-trip within fifteen minutes. Agramonte, standing next to his horse, was waiting for him, surrounded by the cream of the crop, thirty-odd riders. All those on Reeve's vanguard were there.

Reeve reined back Tiger. "Major, the enemy column has halted at a well five minutes from here. They are drinking water and seem in no hurry. A hundred cavalrymen, give or take a few."

Agramonte nodded, reached for the pommel, inserted his foot in the stirrup, and heaved himself up. In the tense silence, the leather's creaking was audible.

"Major, if we are to rescue my chief, I ask you to please assign me the most dangerous post," Palomino pleaded.

"Then ride alongside Captain Reeve. Men, forward."

It was a short ride to the edge of a clearing. The Spaniards were still milling about the well. Agramonte turned in the saddle.

"Commander Aguero, inform your men that their commanding officer, Colonel Sanguily, has been taken prisoner by that Spanish force over there. We are to rescue him, dead or alive, or perish at the attempt."

Agramonte had spoken loudly enough for all rebels to hear him, but Aguero addressed Sanguily's direct subordinates with the same words. When he finished, Agramonte turned to the bugler, who always was near him.

"Bugler, sound beheading!"

And as the few shorts notes played, Agramonte roared, "CHARGE!"

In theory, rescuing Sanguily was highly improbable. The time-tested tactic for cavalry units confronting enemy charges was to counterattack with all men riding their mounts. Such response had proven particularly successful when the assailants, as was the case this time, were fewer than the assailed. But the Spanish officer, Commander Matos, made a fatal mistake the instant he heard the rebel bugle.

"Guerrilla. Dismount! Entrench!" he ranted.

Spaniards on horseback jumped to the ground and joined their comrades on foot firing at the galloping posse of seminude, reeking, and vociferous men headed by Reeve and Palomino. Sane people are terrified of armed madmen, and the rebels came across as a bunch of crazy centaurs excreted by the bowels of the earth, flanked by barking dogs foaming at the mouth. The American captain and Sanguily's adjunct spearheaded the V-shaped formation and were the first to slash limbs and shoulders and ears and heads. The full impact of the charge was felt a split second later: Blood began flowing abundantly; the air vibrated with screams of pain. A dozen or so Spaniards ran away, but a stampede took place within a minute, when those trying to put up resistance saw Commander Matos mount and flee from the battleground.

Dumped by his captors, Julio Sanguily was sitting on the ground, joyously shouting "*Que Viva Cuba Libre*" again and again.

Agramonte ordered his men not to chase the escapees, but to make off with the weapons and horses that had been seized. The bodies of eleven dead Spaniards were left alone; a dead Cuban was strapped to a horse; six wounded rebels were carried back to camp.

Two hours later, back at the Consuegra savanna, Agramonte was sitting in his hammock when he was given a list of the booty and began reading it. All officers and many sergeants, corporals, and regular soldiers had spontaneously gathered around him. They were whispering, chuckling, and making jokes in low tones, as schoolchildren do when the teacher is absorbed in something unrelated to the class. Dogs were wagging their tails and tongues.

"Well, not bad," the Major said. "Listen, gentlemen," he continued, raising his voice and reading from the paper. "We collected nine rifles, two boxes of rounds, three revolvers, two swords, a saber, a tent, and forty tacked horses. Not bad, hey?"

A chorus of voices expressed delight at this.

"No clothes, Major?" asked a tall mulatto in his late twenties.

"No, Nicolás, no clothes, I regret to say."

"Then I'm going back home, Major."

Most men smiled, and a few burst out laughing in anticipation of a joke. Nicolás, one of Reeve's explorers, was the son of a white planter and a black housemaid. Famous for his tracking abilities, sense of humor, and military exploits, he had become sort of a camp joker.

"Oh, really? Give me a good cause or I'll order you hanged from the tallest cedar around here," Agramonte said, pretending to be dead serious.

"Well, you see, Major, the thing my woman values most is this." Nicolás signaled at the glans of his penis and the scrotum sticking out from what long ago had been the crotch of a pantaloon.

"And with all due respect, sir, if my cock and balls keep swinging madly back and forth in the open every time we charge, I won't be able no more to show my woman how much I love her, and she'll kick me out."

Agramonte's reply came after laughter subsided.

"Tell you what, Nicolás. I'll give you a special dispensation from combat duty if you start screwing all the mares in our herd. For every foal-boy they beget, I'll present you with a pair of new trousers."

All roared. Only smiles survived by the time Julio Sanguily hobbled to the crowd.

"Major, I would like to say a few words," he said.

"Go ahead."

"Today many of you risked your lives to rescue me. I don't know how to suitably express my eternal gratitude to all you men, and especially to Major Agramonte." Sanguily kept moving his gaze from one face to the next. "A soldier died during my rescue. I've been told he was bringing the horse I was supposed to ride. We are ready to inter him now, and I ask you to please accompany me to say the final good-bye to this soldier who gave his life for me."

Agramonte stood from the hammock. "Lead the way, Julio," he said.

As chief of scouts, Reeve used to leave a fifty- to eighty-foot gap between him, at center, and the subordinates to the left and right. With each passing day, he enjoyed more unaccompanied riding, for in solitude he could dissect past events and think ahead. Steering Tiger along wooded areas, clearings where tall grass presided, or as the horse sloshed through a brook, Reeve was doing two things at a time: exploring and trying to realize why his present standing among his brothers in arms was not to his liking.

After his promotion to captain, subordinates had begun treating him differently. Respect, never lacking, had increased in a way he failed to welcome. When the men looked at him, a vague sense of uneasiness shone in their eyes; a little admiration, a desire to please him, even a touch of alarm were evident in a few. This last response—he wanted to believe—was caused by nothing more serious than angry reprimands. In some he perceived one of those reactions, in others two; the rest rolled all three into one: undeserved deference. One morning, as he was observing the unmistakable imprints of Spanish horseshoes, it dawned on him that he had witnessed something similar, albeit less intense, in the attitude of parishioners toward his father. They gazed at his dad a trifle too respectfully, as though the grace of God was upon him, as if the pastor were beyond sin, or hierarchically above them.

Well, Henry Reeve thought, he had killed and severed the limbs of Spaniards, so the grace of God was not upon him anymore, if it ever had been. He wasn't beyond sin, either, as he had fornicated with a woman far removed from being a virgin, and not one of his own people at that. (The recollection made his scrotum contract dissolutely.) So, it had to be pecking order that made his men look at him that way.

He didn't like no longer being one of the boys. Nowadays, folks didn't put their arms around his shoulders and hug him, a frequent Cuban display of affection; nor did they make jokes about his leanness or youthfulness. Many had stopped calling him El Inglesito and now addressed him as "Captain" or "sir."

After hours of reflection, he realized he was getting a crumb of what the Major received by the wagonload: adoration. Agramonte's case bordered on deification, a response that Reeve felt certain he didn't want for himself, not that he deserved it, either. Does admiration grow as people elevate in rank? he asked himself. If Agramonte were a plain soldier; would his men idolize him? He wasn't sure, but he thought not. When the Major addressed the rank and file, Reeve had seen fear in the eyes of several soldiers. Were they thinking Agramonte could order them hanged should they abscond?

Fellow bookkeepers had respected and unquestioningly obeyed the New York branch manager because he was authorized to promote and give notice. At school, boys and girls had learned that teachers loved and patronized their favorite students; they also had struck, suspended, and even expelled those who infuriated them. Parents punished and commended, too. Was this what both the Old and the New Testament recurringly referred to as "power"? The Good Book mentioned not only the supreme power of the Lord but also that of men. "Then saith Pilate unto him, Speakest thou not unto me? Knowest thou not that I have power to crucify thee, and have power to release thee?"

Maybe he had a little power now, Reeve reflected. Being a foreigner, he should use it sparingly. No matter how hard he tried, there would always be issues setting him apart, as certain things Cubans did seemed somewhat odd to him. You aren't a native, he thought, language and customs and traditions and other things, too, will make you stand out, a lot or a little, depending on how much time and effort you devote to adapting. That was the Lord's truth. Whatever power he had acquired, he should use it to make Cuba an independent nation, not for anything else.

Approaching the edge of a clearing, Reeve reined in Tiger, dismounted, and tied the horse to a teak tree. Getting closer to the edge, he extracted the binoculars and scanned the horizon.

A quarter of a league away, moving along one of the immense savannas of Camagüey dotted with cattle, a column of no fewer than three hundred Spaniards was wending its way. Reeve was all eyes for almost two minutes, taking rudimentary bearings, counting, making mental notes. He lowered the optical device, turned left, and saw Pascual peering at the enemy; to his right, Nicolás was staring intently, hand on his forehead, visorlike. Reeve knew Agramonte would want to learn it from him, because he had the binoculars; when the enemy was much closer, the Major trusted the locals more.

Reeve's whistle was a lousy imitation of the *tomeguín*, a Cuban birdsong, but it got the job done: Pascual and Nicolás glanced at him. Reeve made the sign to return to the column; both men nodded.

That afternoon, during the skirmish at Sitio Potrero, Reeve sustained another wound, this time on his left arm. He thought he wouldn't mind spending a few days at Ramona's infirmary, and, even in pain, his scrotum contracted dissolutely.

1872

Since medical records were nonexistent, few realized that the infirmary near La Gertrudis had a lower mortality rate than others. The lifelong ambition of the veterinarian acting as general practitioner had been to cure humans, but his family hadn't been able to afford the cost of a bachelor of medicine degree at the University of Havana, and so he became a self-taught and well-read animal doctor. The war presented him the opportunity to heal humans, and he seized it with both hands. He administered time-honored remedies for diarrhea, malaria, and typhoid fever. By a process of trial and error, he learned to remove bullets from limbs surgically, to immobilize, and to apply ointments and mold. Insurgents with chest and abdominal no-exit gunshot wounds were referred to a field hospital near a village named Génova, which was staffed by a young surgeon. But the less seriously injured, who were transferred to La Gertrudis, almost always got well. Erotic feelings inspired by a certain young woman may have positively influenced the healing of a number of convalescents.

Therefore, on January 13, Reeve and three other officers departed from the infirmary and started roaming the countryside in search of Agramonte. To confound the enemy, the Major marched and countermarched, a tactic that had yielded fine results. Therefore, it was on the evening of January 15 when Agramonte's sentinels gruffly ordered the four riders to halt, dismount, and lay their weapons on the ground. Warned about the new arrivals, Julio Sanguily embraced the reinforcements.

"Let's awaken the Major. He'll be delighted to see you," the lame man said.

"No, Colonel. Absolutely not," Reeve objected. "Let him sleep. I'll tell the chief of the guard to awake me the minute he gets up; still around four, I presume?"

"When the rooster crows. Now, let's get you some food. I suppose there's horse meat left over. I'm sure there is boiled sweet potato, plus a gourd of coffee."

A little earlier than five the next morning Reeve learned from Agramonte that he had been promoted to commander and made chief of the Second Cavalry Squadron, First Regiment, First Brigade, Camagüey Army Corps.

"But . . . but . . . Major. I don't deserve this honor. I haven't fired a shot for over a month and a half. I—"

"Enrique, are you refusing the promotion and the command?" Agramonte asked.

"I . . . no, sir. But maybe the men would prefer to be led by a Cuban."

Agramonte clasped his hands behind his back, rocked on his heels, and looked up before addressing Reeve—his body language when suppressing impatience or irritation.

"I wish you'd understand, once and for all, that you, Ryan, Gómez, Acosta, and all other foreigners fighting for Cuba Libre are as Cuban as you are American, Canadian, Dominican, Venezuelan, or Mexican. I won't ask you to forgo your nationality if you don't want to. But the greatest sacrifice a man can make for his country of birth is to fight for its sovereignty, and you are fighting for the sovereignty of this nation. You have thrice spilled your blood on Cuban soil, for God's sake. Me? I've never been wounded."

"But, sir—"

"Case closed, Commander. We'll order the squadron to fall in after breakfast, and introduce you."

The men hoorayed when told who their newly minted commander was, and Reeve started meeting and shaking hands with those officers and soldiers he knew only by name or by sight. Under him were eighty-five insurgents: a captain (vacant), a lieutenant, two second lieutenants, a major sergeant, two sergeants, eight corporals, two buglers, and sixty-six soldiers, two of whom doubled as cooks. Two others were a marshal—to feed and water the horses when the squadron camped and to stock horse supplies—and a saddler to repair saddles, bridles, and other leather objects. The squadron had two sections, each section two platoons.

Afterward, Reeve approached Agramonte.

"Major, am I supposed to choose a second in command, or will you appoint one?"

Reeve had noticed Agramonte's eyelids drooped a little more when he suppressed a smile, as right now.

"I'm considering candidates. I know of no English-speaking captain, so I'll try to find someone who understands your half-African, half-Cuban accent."

Near midday on January 18, as Reeve was checking the stocks of horseshoes and nails, an adjunct told him the Major wanted to see him. Soon after, he was shaking hands with Capt. Emilio Battle, slapping his back, and getting his shoulder slapped in return.

"Very well, gentlemen," Agramonte said, amusedly contemplating them. "I suppose you want to reminisce for a while and then discuss your next moves. I have to write a report to the Chamber of Representatives, so if you'll excuse me . . ."

After midday, Reeve introduced his second in command to all officers and soldiers. They ambled across the camp, the American showing the ropes to Battle and recounting brief anecdotes about military actions in imperfect, although quite good Spanish. Battle listened attentively and occasionally cut sideways looks at the commander from beneath his hat. It came to him that Reeve had gone through a striking transformation from the time they parted ways thirty months earlier. The innocent, wide-eyed teenager had vanished into the acrid smoke of gunpowder, the wailing of dying men, the pain of his wounds, the nightmares where dead enemies were resurrected, the sweat, the hunger, the filth, the downpours, and the blistering heat. From that maelstrom, El Inglesito had emerged. However, it seemed fear had not played a role in the psychological maturing of this young man so sure of himself. In fact, Reeve described combats in a way that made it appear he . . . enjoyed them? Was *enjoyed* the right word? Liked? Relished? Could anyone derive pleasure from war? Battle asked himself. What-ever Reeve felt, he gave the impression of never having done what Battle was proficient at: suppressing fear.

In the evening, they had a long conversation. Reeve learned that Battle had requested a transfer on the grounds of not get-ting along with Brigadier General Figueredo. By serendipity, he'd been assigned to the Camagüey Corps, where he'd learned of Reeve's exploits. He'd written a letter to the Major, men-tioning when and where he had met the American and asking whether it would be possible to join the unit where Reeve served. Later, with moist eyes, Battle admitted that living es-tranged from his wife and daughters was the greatest sacrifice he made for Cuba.

Even though the captain kept to himself that before each charge he had to overcome panic, Reeve grasped that Battle must have had to pluck up courage to serve his homeland. Like Agramonte, a lawyer, and Julio Sanguily, a schoolteacher, Battle was a trained professional. Those men could have remained in their comfortable homes, safely cursing the Spaniards, loving their wives, watching their children grow up, making money, and peace-ably waiting for someone else to win self-rule for them and their offspring. Yet, they had relinquished the bed of roses.

Before coming to Cuba, Reeve thought, he had honestly believed he knew the meaning of *patriot* and *patriotism,* but only after meeting these men had he come to understand the full sense of both nouns. Apart from their lives, slaves had nothing to lose and everything to gain when they took up arms; desti-tute and landless whites and mulattos risked next to nothing. But the equation changed drastically for the likes of Agra-monte, Sanguily, and Battle; they had everything to lose to gain a single thing: freedom. Washington, Jefferson, Adams, and the others must've been as these folks were, he supposed.

It was almost midnight when Reeve, lying in his hammock, hands clasped beneath his head, reflected on what he had learned about Agramonte's wife and children from the Sanguily brothers. The Major had been madly in love with Amalia Simoni ever since both were children. Soon after taking up arms, he had her moved to a ranch in the Cubitas range that he named El Idilio (the Idyll.) In May 1870, when Amalia was three months pregnant and dwelled there with her one-year-old son, her parents, her sister, and her brother-in-law, all were captured. The colonialists had the decency to deport her to New York, where she gave birth to a girl and currently resided. Nobody had seen the major approach another woman, and in his few spare moments he wrote long letters to his wife.

So, how did he compare with those heroes? Reeve asked himself. What had he left behind? His parents and sisters, yes, but all men, at certain point in their lives, break new ground. He also had quit a job at a bank branch, and missed baseball games. That was all. What force had dragged him to Cuba? Had the Lord chosen him to do His work here? But he was not preaching the Gospel, nor did he demand that black soldiers forgo the amulets they carried and the witchcraft they practiced. All he did was kill and fornicate.

"Lord, would you please show me the way?" he whispered. And waiting for His guidance, contemplating two stars through the foliage above the hammock, Henry Reeve fell asleep.

Between February and April, the Second Squadron, as part of Agramonte's column, engaged the enemy on five occasions. On May 10, at Jimaguayú, they drove back a concentration of Spanish forces that threatened to cut them off. Unbeknownst to the Major, on that day the rebel government appointed him military chief in Las Villas, while allowing him to retain his present position in Camagüey.

After learning this, it dawned on Agramonte that having to divide his time between two territories made delegation inevitable. Concerning military issues, he had no doubt whatsoever; in Camagüey, Julio Sanguily was unbeatable. But who among his subordinates was better prepared to oversee the new shoe and tack shops? Who would supervise the raising of produce and farm animals? Who should deal with civilians? He grew more withdrawn and pensive than his customary self.

Ever since the optical-tower fiasco, the Major had been mulling over the objections of subordinates concerning the torching of huts where Cubans lived. He concluded they were right. Cuban farmers and peasants were the rebels' natural allies and they were to be courted. Not taxing at all for him, albeit he had to pretend a little and smile too much. Well known and respected, he hadn't failed to notice that unbridled admiration shone in the eyes of plain folks when he addressed them. None of his men, he felt sure, elicited a similar response. Therefore, he started testing political, administrative, and negotiating aptitudes.

"Listen, Enrique. Last week the women of the Versalles hamlet sent word they want to talk to me. I don't know about what. I agreed to see them this afternoon at five. But I'm too busy today. Go there and listen to what they have to say. If you think you can solve the problem, do it. If not, report back to me."

Consequently, Reeve found himself facing an assembly of prematurely aged women who were exasperated that Agramonte hadn't come in person. He'd sent a kid instead, a damned beardless kid, for God's sake, who, judging by his lousy accent, wasn't even Cuban. Unbelievable.

No *bohío* in the poverty-stricken village could accommodate all present, and so the meeting was taking place outdoors, under a clear sky and the lambent light of late afternoon, with those in attendance standing. To show courtesy to the ladies, the commander removed his hat.

Informal groups had informal leaders, and this was not an exception. White, in her thirties but looking in her forties, husband serving as infantrymen with General Boza, the leader of these women had borne two sons and three daughters, all currently under the age of fifteen.

"Look, my child," she began. From time immemorial, when Cuban women wanted to rebuke and belittle a person, they started the oral barrage with "my child." "Our men listened to you folks and got pretty well fuddled with this 'independence' idea. And what did they do? They took to the jungle to fight this war. When they left, they said they would be back in a few weeks, would defeat the Galicians before Christmas. Ha, ha, ha. That was five Christmases ago."

"No, four," a concubine said, correcting the spokeswoman.

"Four or five, it's the same. Feels like ten Christmases. Thing is, we began to sweat it out in the field. We take care of and milk the goat, those who have a goat; feed the fowl; plant and weed and harvest beans, onions, pepper, garlic, sweet potato, and cassava. Some of our hombres had horses or burros, but they took the damn beasts to war, so, when there's a little money, we have to trudge all the way to the general store—a league and a half, mind you—to buy rice, salt, sugar, coffee, soap, tallow dips, thread, buttons, and all other things a house and a family need, put it all into a sack, and haul it back home! Tell me, my child, is that fair?"

"No, ma'am," Reeve said.

A surprised silence followed.

"No?" the informal leader said, suspecting a trap.

"Not fair at all, ma'am."

"Well, makes me glad you said that. But you think that's all? Wish it were. 'Cause we've got to keep doing all things we've been doing since God took one of your ribs and made it a woman. We've got to clean, cook, wash, mend clothes, nurse sick children, fetch water from the well . . . pick up eggs from nests . . . feed the dog. . . ."

The leader appeared to be groping for additional chores.

"Sharpen hoes and knives," said one of the sixteen women in attendance.

"True," agreed the leader.

"Bathe the kids," contributed another woman.

"True."

"Feed the pig."

"True."

"Milk the goat."

"I already said that."

There was a two-second pause as brains were racked.

"Only thing missing," said a mulatto woman, "is that once in a blue moon the men take a night off, come home, and even though we are so exhausted that we fall asleep standing, they want to make love till kingdom come."

This was received with applause, laughter, and a chorus of "Yeah" and "That's right" and "True, true, hee, hee, hee."

Reeve blushed, but he believed it best to keep silent.

The mirth subsided and the leader, crossing her arms over her bosom, stared at the commander.

"Now, my child, tell me, what is Agramonte going to do about that?"

"What do you want?" Reeve asked.

"Well," the leader said, "we know that if we ask you to send our men home, you'll say, 'No,' 'cause you've all taken leave of your senses with this 'independence' thing. So, what we pray for every night is for you to win the war and our men to come back home. What we require is for you to help us with a little money, clothes for the kids, and medicine to treat colicky symptoms, measles, agues, and toothaches. We don't ask for food, 'cause we know you are always on the run, ain't got any; if you had, you wouldn't look famished. On top of that, we require our men have a holiday from time to time—say one week—so they can lend us a hand here. We ain't stupid; we know you can't let them all go at once, so you send my man one week, another man next week, another the third week, and so on. There're sixteen of us here. So I'd get to see my man once every sixteen weeks; it's not asking too much. This will make everybody happy. We'll be happy on account of having one whole week to tend only house—"

"Won't sleep much, though," interjected the mulatto woman, smiling this time.

The other women snickered and exchanged amused glances.

"Well, I wouldn't mind a little of that, too, I daresay," the leader.

More snickering followed. Again, Reeve blushed.

"Our men will be happy, too, 'cause they'll get to see their kids and help us out. And it occurs to me Agramonte will be happy, too, 'cause if he's half as good and kind and brave as he's cracked up to be, he's gotta know men need to spend time with their families. You know, I says to myself, Cuba Libre will be a bunch of Cuban families, nothing more. So, what do you figure, stranger?"

Reeve cleared his throat and swallowed.

"Well, ladies, believe me when I say Major Agramonte understands the situation you are in. As I was about to ride here, he said to me, 'Enrique, go see what those brave women of the Versalles hamlet want from us. Explain how sorry I am I can't keep my word to see them today. Be sure to tell them it's because very urgent matters came up. Apologize, and apologize properly, for these women are as hard as the steel of our machetes, so listen carefully to what they have to say and hurry back to me.' Those were his exact words."

A murmur of approval was heard, but the leader remained silent, arms crossed over her bosom.

"We know how things are," Reeve continued. "We know how taxing life is for you. But what you *don't* know is that you are fighting this war with us. You are our rear guard."

"What's rear guard?" the spokeswoman asked.

"The rear guard is . . . the people standing behind us who cure our wounded and take care of our children, and old people, too; they tell us when the enemy is coming and how many there are and if they have cannons or not. That's the rear guard."

The leader nodded. "Go on."

"Without you behind us, the Galicians would've crushed us long ago, because they are more and are better armed than we are. And I want you to know that your men are fighting this war for you, your children, and your elders. You are Cuba. Your men are fighting this war so all Cuban men and women, of any race, can become free, so your children can go to school, so each family owns a piece of land and you can put food on the table every single day of the year."

Several women nodded, with the exception of the leader.

"To achieve all this, we must win this war. Because the Spaniards—I know you call them Galicians, but Galicia is merely a province of Spain; many Spaniards are not Galicians—the Spaniards, I was saying, want to keep enslaving you, not only blacks, but all of you. They want to keep you under their

laws, don't want you to be free; they deport or shoot or gar-
rote those Cubans who want Cuba to be independent. And we
want that to end."

"All right, you've told us where the wind lies," the leader
said. "Now tell us what you're gonna do for us."

"Well, it occurs to me we can do a few things. For instance,
we can buy food from you. You have extra beans you want to
sell; we'll buy them and pay a good price. Cassava, sweet potato, whatever, we are willing to buy them from you. You
slaughter a pig, don't have enough salt to conserve what you
can't eat, we buy it, too. That would put a few coins in your
purse, wouldn't it?"

All women, including the leader, nodded.

"We have a burro that's too old and tired to keep up with
younger animals. So maybe we could give it to you. You take
good care of him, let him rest and graze, and then when one of
you goes to the general store to buy provisions, you ride the
burro, or lead him on, and he would carry the load back for
you. Would you like that?"

"That's a good idea," said a white woman who hadn't spoken earlier. "Darn good" and "Yeah" were voiced by a few.

"I have other ideas, but I must discuss them with the Major
first. So, I'll go back, tell him what you want, make suggestions, and he'll tell me what else we can do for you ladies."

"Fair enough," the spokeswoman said. "But make clear this
idea we have about our men having a holiday to Agramonte,
'cause that's the most important thing. A burro is not a man."

There was laughter behind her, and she turned in anger.
"You know what I mean, for Chrissake!"

Reeve refrained from asking the woman not to take the name
of Jesus Christ in vain.

"So, ladies, what I suggest is, I'll leave now and come back in the morning, around eight. Then we'll meet here and I'll tell you what the Major has decided. Meanwhile, you make a list with the names of all your husbands and give it to me tomorrow, so we know what units they are serving with. Are you in agreement?"

Gazing around, Reeve made sure there were no objections to his proposal, then smiled.

"Very well, see you in the morning, ladies," he said, putting on his hat.

And with this, he did an about-face, ambled to where his two escorts waited, mounted Tiger, and rode back to camp.

"You promised them a burro?" said Agramonte, his eyelids drooping.

"Well, sir, I had to promise them something. And it's true one of my burros is older than Methuselah."

"And the money?"

"I didn't promise them money; I said we would be willing to buy whatever surplus they have. We buy from other folks, so why not from these women?"

"Hmm."

"And, sir, I reckon we should give a little cash to these women. The emergency fund you gave me, a hundred reales, is in four-, two-, and one-real silver coins. I have twenty one-real coins; I counted them. I want your permission to give a one-real coin to each of these ladies. We won't be any poorer with sixteen reales less, and they can buy a little salt and sugar, and maybe dried beef."

Agramonte did not approve the request for one-week holidays and ordered Reeve to give his reasons to the women. But when the Major lay in his hammock that night, he knew he could count on Reeve to deal with people.

On July 23, Agramonte engaged a heavily guarded, huge Spanish supply caravan at Jacinto. The cavalry's role was absolutely decisive because the rebels were so low on ammunition, most infantrymen had to watch from the sidelines. Reeve's extraordinary battlefield performance left his brothers in arms speechless. As was customary, he spearheaded the charge, Battle at his side. He ran through enemy lines slashing and cutting. So much blood spurted from severed arteries and veins that when the colonialists fled, he and Tiger were drenched in it.

The booty seemed substantial. Reeve dismounted, seized Tiger's lead, and started striding in front of the horse. He threaded his way among inert bodies and wounded men who wailed and groaned and cried and asked for help in desperation. Scared by the sound of gunfire, the screams, and perhaps by the odor of terror, the teams of oxen pulling the wagons wandered all over the place, stepping on and running wheels over the dead and the injured. Reeve wiped away blood-spattered sweat from his face. He halted briefly by wounded Cubans to say, "Hold on. Help is coming," but he was indifferent to the suffering of Spaniards. He had been at this for more than a minute when he crossed paths with Battle, who still rode his horse and gripped his machete. His second in command seemed so astonished that Reeve asked, "What?"

"No . . . nothing," muttered Battle.

"Speak up, Captain. Why are you looking at me like that?"

"Are you all right?"

"Of course I'm all right. Not a scratch on me. Why do you ask?"

"You are covered in blood, Enrique."

Reeve inspected his clothes. On his right side, the boot, buckskin legging, pantaloon, and shirt were soaked; his left side was profusely sprinkled with stains. He lifted his eyes to Battle and smirked.

"Guess I took down a few Galicians today."

The hairs at the back of Battle's neck stood on end. "Your face, too," he mumbled.

Again, Reeve wiped rosy sweat away from his face. "Send men to seize the wagons and steer the oxen. The booty is enormous."

Fifteen minutes later, while inspecting the place, Agramonte bumped into Reeve.

"Holy Virgin Mary," mumbled the staring Major.

"What, sir?"

"Are you wounded?"

"No, sir."

"Then you . . . need a bath, Enrique."

"That can wait."

"No, it can't. Ride back to camp; tell the quartermaster I authorize a change of clothes and hat for you. Take a bath; clean your leggings and boots, too. And have a soldier bath Tiger and clean your tack."

"But, sir, the booty—"

"We'll take care of that. You fought gallantly today. Did your share, more than your share, I should say. I'm proud of you. Now, go take a bath."

The booty exceeded all expectations—so much so that part of it was shipped to the government to restock other units. But the hundreds of infantrymen who witnessed the charge from a distance had gaped as Reeve killed or maimed perhaps as many as eight men in less than ten minutes. As he went out the battlefield riding the big charger, showing the satisfied expression of the artisan who has shaped a masterpiece, a young rebel mumbled, "He's possessed."

That day, El Inglesito earned several nicknames that no man had the courage to tell him to his face. Those who didn't know he had survived an execution learned it from those who knew. Blacks, depending on the tribe from which they descended, called him "Nfunbe" (the Spirit of the Dead), "Horey" (the Terrible), and "Taivadu" (the Little Evil One). Lots of white soldiers and noncoms referred to him as "Lucifer" or "Satan." Having kept to himself the depth of his devoutness, not a soul could imagine that he believed the Lord guided his actions.

September 21. On our way to San Antonio, we killed Francisco Jimeno, second sergeant in the Queen's Battalion. His horse, saddle, and a Remington carbine were seized. At Camalote, we attacked a guerrilla unit and took four prisoners, who disclosed the guerrillas were camped at houses in Pennsylvania. We considered whether to engage them in combat, and did. The guerrilla evacuated and we seized five firearms (two precision rifles) and a significant number of machetes, horses, victual, and so forth.

"So you've reached the journal stage?" asked a smiling Battle as he got closer.

It was late afternoon and the squadron had camped for the night. Firewood burned beneath three big pots where sweet potatoes and dried beef boiled. The cooks had been assigned three burros to transport provisions and kitchen utensils. Reeve, sitting in his hammock, lifted his eyes from the red notebook supported on his knees.

"Give me a minute," he said, and proceeded to scribble in the journal. "We will spend the night at La Americana,"

Then he set the pencil inside the notebook, closed it, and stuffed it into the saddlebag resting by his feet.

"Yeah, the Major said I should, and he gave me that journal," he told Battle. "He says as time goes by, one forgets things, and to write accurate reports to the government, we should keep a record. Skirmishes, ambushes, battles, weapons and things we seize, money spent, that kind of thing."

Battle sat on his haunches, facing Reeve. "I know. Figueredo made a practice of dictating reports to his adjunct."

"Well, I want to practice writing in Spanish."

Reeve rested his left foot on his right knee and started struggling with the pieces of rope serving as shoelaces. "This place is named the American Woman; the Spanish guerrillas camped at a cluster of houses named Pennsylvania. You know if an American lives around here?"

"I haven't got a clue. You know this is not my turf."

"I know."

"Want me to find out?"

"No, just wondering."

Battle sat on the ground. "I haven't shit in three days," he said.

"You don't eat much, you don't shit much."

"I know, but I take a crap every day, even if it's only a little turd."

"Oh yeah? Well, I don't keep track. When I have to go, I get behind a bush and shit."

Reeve took the boot off, vigorously scratched his foot for half a minute, then started working on the other boot's rope. Battle grimaced.

"With all due respect, Commander, your foot stinks."

"Really! I'm sure your feet smell of rose water."

"Take off your sock. I want to see," Battle said.

"What's the matter with you?"

"No, really, I want to see if you have fungus."

Reeve dismissed Battle's concern by concentrating on unlacing the other boot. He took it off, dropped it to the ground, and scratched the right foot no less furiously than he had the left one.

"For Chrissake!" Battle said, turning his head away.

"Don't swear, Captain."

"Sorry for that. But listen, Enrique. Fungus gets worse and worse, till you nearly can't walk. Take off your socks and let me see if your feet are reddish and blistering."

"It's dusk; you can't see anything, Battle. They *are* reddish and blistering. There's nothing I can do."

"Well, you could cure your damn feet in three nights; you could do that, you know?"

"How?"

"You know Bonifacio Campos?"

"Black, Second Section, D Platoon."

Battle was taken aback.

"I don't know how you do that," he said after a moment. "Well, Bonifacio learned all sorts of herbal remedies from his mom. He boils several herbs to make an infusion. Before going to sleep, you wash your socks, your feet, then apply this infusion on your feet and let it dry. Go to sleep then. If by the time you get up, your socks are dry, put them on. If not, don't wear socks. Do that for three consecutive nights and your feet won't stink like vultures no more; neither will you have to scratch them like you had scabies."

"What herbs are those?"

"How should I know?"

"Have you applied this infusion to your feet?"

"I have. Bonifacio is happy to give it away."

"All right. Get me some."

"Should I send a soldier?"

"What for?"

"To wash your socks."

Reeve couldn't believe his friend had said that. "Are you out of your mind? You reckon I'm gonna order one of my men to wash my socks? I'll wash my damn socks myself!"

"Whoa, calm down. Sorry. I'll go fetch the infusion."

"Tell some soldier to bring me soap and water."

"All right."

"And Battle?"

"Yeah."

"Find out if Bonifacio has something for constipation."

At noon on November 29, the rebels were surprised by a mixed Spanish column—infantry, cavalry, artillery—at Santa Beatriz. The day was overcast, windy, and unusually chilly, which made it ideal for Reeve. The moment the first shots were fired, they tacked up their horses. The American galloped ahead to confront the enemy. The Spanish infantry, unperturbed, was firing volley after volley at the riders.

Reeve felt a blow in his abdomen and got winded. He dropped the machete, took hold of the pommel, and bent over Tiger's neck. Battle realized what was happening.

"Henry!" he shouted.

Battle spurred his horse until he caught up with Tiger, snatched the reins from Reeve's hand, and, with bullets whizzing by, gradually forced both animals to turn back to Cuban lines. Having gained the protection of the forest, he reined in the horses.

"Henry, what's the matter? Are you hit?"

Reeve grimaced. "I took one, yeah. Help me dismount. Assume command of the squadron."

A quarter of an hour later, the Cubans were retreating. The most seriously injured, Reeve and Captain Tomás Rodríguez, were being carried on improvised stretchers by infantrymen, who were relieved every ten minutes or so to keep the column moving fast. Agramonte rode by their side, urging each fresh foursome of stretcher-bearers to hurry up, watch their step, and be careful.

Bouncing up and down, swinging to and fro, gazing at the sky or at treetops, attentive to the labored breathing of the soldiers carrying him, Reeve apprehended this was the closest call of all and wondered if he'd die any minute now. Before winning the war? Missing the victorious ride into Havana? Lacking the pleasure of seeing the final Spanish battalion board a steamer on its way back to Spain? Without kissing Mom and Dad and his sisters good-bye? You live by the sword, you die by the sword, he thought. "Yea, though I walk through the valley of the shadow of death, I will fear no evil: for thou art with me; thy rod and thy staff they comfort me."

At San Joaquín, Agramonte sent for Antonio Luaces, a rebel M.D. in charge of the Génova field hospital, and asked him to escort the two wounded officers to the hospital and take good care of them. The Major knew the Cuban revolutionary junta in New York had sent Luaces a strange contraption with a rubber mask. The thing produced some substance that rendered patients unconscious and permitted one to operate on them.

It was midnight when Luaces examined Reeve's no-exit wound. Considering that the patient's vital signs were stable, he decided to postpone operating until morning, when bright sunlight would facilitate things. In the small hours, feeling his mouth parched, Reeve asked for water on several occasions. When his request was denied for the fifth time, he tried to get up. Then his arms and legs were tied to the bed. This infuriated him so much that he lost consciousness.

Hours later, when his eyelids opened, he had to force them shut immediately, then reopen them a crack, giving his pupils time to contract. Was he floating on sunlight? He couldn't move his arms or legs. Why? Was he dead? Was this heaven? He turned his head to where the daylight was coming from. It streamed through an open window, but . . . his head was level with the bottom of the frame. To his left, indistinct shadows moved and whispered. Couldn't be heaven. There was no pain in heaven. And who was this bearded and bespectacled man with—what was that? What was he going to—

He tried to struggle when his nose and mouth were covered by—what the hell was that? He took a deep breath and . . . lost consciousness again.

Luckily for his patients, Dr. Luaces had a colleague and friend, Jacinto Solano, who was a graduate of London University, class of 1867. Solano had told Luaces about Pasteur's theory that germs could be the cause of infectious diseases and how Lister had reduced mortality among his patients by sterilizing instruments and using carbolic acid as an antiseptic agent. Rosa la Bayamesa—who, after Najasa, had been reassigned to Génova and who, for reasons unrelated to medical science, had had high standards of cleanliness even before serving as Luaces's head nurse—had always ordered that the strips of cloth utilized as dressings be washed before they were reused. Luaces extracted the bullet using steel surgical instruments boiled in water after each operation.

Taking into account Reeve's age and the possibility that no major organ had been punctured, the physician figured the wounded American had a reasonable chance of survival. He knew two things: that the Liberation Army lost twice more men to malaria, typhoid fever, and unknown conditions than to bullet or saber wounds; and that after he sewed up the incision, all was in the hands of God.

December 16

Captain Battle approached the Najasa Highlands *bohío* where Agramonte slept, had his meals, read and wrote during the rainy season or, for any other reason, when a lull in military operations took place. An adjunct stood guard outside.

"Miguelito, tell the Major I'm back," Battle said.

But as the adjunct was about to announce the visitor, Agramonte raised his voice.

"Send the captain in, Miguelito."

Sitting in a *taburete,* elbows on top of a rustic table, Agramonte lifted his eyes from the page he held the instant Battle entered.

"Well?" the Major asked.

"Luaces says Enrique is recuperating satisfactorily," Battle began. "He walks with difficulty, stooping a little, because he's still hurting, I reckon. Huge scar, Major, believe me. But he asked me to take him back here. When I refused, he pulled rank on me, said he would have me demoted."

Agramonte chuckled and laid the page on top of the others. "Same old Enrique. What did you do?"

"I pretended to be exasperated, stomped off to fetch Luaces, and took him back to Enrique. Then I requested he discharge Commander Reeve today. The doctor wanted to know if I was serious. I said I was asking because Commander Reeve was threatening me with demotion if I didn't take him with me today. Enrique is sickly pale, Major, but believe me, he actually blushed when Luaces stared at him and asked, 'Are you crazy, son?' Enrique stared at the ground and shook his head. 'Well, if you think you can be discharged today, you're crazy as a loon. So, remember this: I'm not discharging you till I pronounce you sound as a bell, weeks from now. Is that clear?' Enrique nodded to this. Luaces continued. 'And let me tell you: Your rank is not worth a fart in a whirlwind to me. You could be President Céspedes in disguise, but I won't discharge you till I'm dead certain you've completely healed over. Is that clear?' Enrique nodded again. 'You steal a horse and run away in the dead of night, be forewarned that I won't take you as a patient should you be wounded again. And I will report you to Major Agramonte, and, you better believe me, *he* will demote *you* and arrest *you* should I ask him to.' Then Luaces turned, flapped his arms, and walked away, muttering, 'After all the effort I go through . . .'"

Agramonte, in stitches, threw his head back. The adjunct outside smiled. He couldn't wait to tell others that Captain Battle had made the Major roar. Battle, too, was smiling broadly. Agramonte dried tears from his cheeks and calmed down.

"Luaces is my kind of physician. Nobody intimidates him. Ah . . ."

During the briefest of pauses, Agramonte snuffled back mucus.

"Enrique was wounded on November twenty-ninth, almost three weeks ago. Did Luaces tell you when he reckons he'll discharge him?"

"No specific date, sir. Before riding back, I talked to Luaces in private. No sooner than mid-January, he said."

Agramonte raised his eyebrows and clucked his tongue. "You are doing a great job, Captain, but I need Enrique back. He's worth a hundred men; he's an inspiration to all."

"I know, sir."

"Well, thanks for the news, Captain. We'll be here for two or three more days, so I want you to choose two men every day. . . . Just a minute, let me think. . . . Raffle off two daily visitors to the hospital, men who'll spend the day with Enrique, amuse him. Oh, and tell them to take lunch with them. Hospital food is only for patients, the doc, and the nurses."

"Yes, sir."

"All right. And thanks for doing this for me."

"A pleasure, sir.

Fragment of a letter addressed to the government of the Republic in Arms by Maj. Gen. Ignacio Agramonte, dated December 17, 1872:

> . . . and the government should not find it odd that this distinguished officer is time and time again nominated for promotion to colonel and brigadier general. I need a second in command in Camagüey and, unfortunately, among the many superior officers under me in this Department, I have not

met one with the indispensable aptitudes to second me that this officer possesses. Bearing in mind all his outstanding qualities, Commander Reeve has gained all my trust and I consider it my duty to highly recommend this young foreigner to the government of the Republic.

FOUR

March 3, 1873

★

Reeve had not been throwing handsprings or standing on his head when he rejoined the column in late January, but from the initial days of the insurgency, Agramonte had instructed that convalescent patients were to be properly nourished, so El Inglesito had recovered and gained a few pounds. For several weeks, however, riding took a lot out of him and in the evenings, although mentally alert and in high spirits, he felt and looked utterly drained.

In the early hours of March 3, Agramonte approached the hammock where Reeve slept like a log and tapped him on the shoulder.

"Uh?"

"Get up, sleepyhead. Let's go see how the shops are doing."

The workshops razed when General Zacarías González attacked the Najasa Highlands had been rebuilt and were fully operational. The workmen and their relatives, as most countrymen, started work well before sunrise.

Escorted by ten riflemen, Agramonte and Reeve rode to the shops. Pale moonlight and the chill in the air combined to make the coatless men shiver occasionally. Far away, several roosters were crowing and, as it still happened to city boy Reeve every once in awhile, he wondered whether they were welcoming a new day, participating in a singing competition, or simply advising rivals their hens were not to be messed with. As was their wont when there was no hurry, horses defecated and farted to the bored indifference of riders. Now and then a pack of dogs trotting ahead of the mounted men stopped and looked back, making sure they were moving in the right direction. Bats flitted about. The pervading scent was a combination of dewy grass, wildflowers, rotten fruits, and animal droppings. In the firmament, millions of celestial bodies twinkled at the blue little planet where, in the beginning of time, cosmic folly settled down.

Reeve stole a look at the Major, who appeared to be absorbed in his thoughts. He had no clue that, once again, Agramonte was mulling over putting him forward for military chief of Camagüey. Soon the Major would be moving to Las Villas to assume command of all rebel forces there. Julio Sanguily, his friend, highly admired second in command, and most logical substitute, needed proper medical attention and rest. Doctor Luaces had warned Agramonte that should Sanguily be kept on active service indefinitely, he would become unable to ride a horse, not even strapped to the saddle; engaging the enemy would be out of the question. Agramonte was making arrangements for Julio to travel to New York and undergo what Luaces guessed would be "a quite complex orthopedic operation" and the consequent rehabilitation program. On the island, in hiding from the authorities, that was impossible.

The Major felt certain that, on strictly military terms, Enrique was a much better leader and soldier than his dear friend or any other officer under him, but he also realized that the government would proceed very cautiously concerning his nomination. Twenty-odd patriotic, rich, and prestigious Camagüeyan families who were extremely proud of their Cuban lineage and in favor of independence had sons, grandsons, or nephews with the Liberation Army. After Jordan's departure, judged reprehensively by many, the reaction of the patriarchs and matriarchs to having their male heirs under the leadership of an American would be weighed. If Reeve were Mexican, Dominican, or Venezuelan, no objections would be voiced, Agramonte thought. It vexed him to think that political deliberations should inevitably take place. Having the most capable man in charge should override all other issues, he firmly believed.

But then again, the Major was on familiar terms with a few scions who had learned about, met, or fought alongside Reeve. These folks, without any coaxing from Agramonte, had expressed great admiration for the young American. Three war wounds and his decision to remain fighting for Cuba Libre when most of his compatriots had laid down arms and gone back to their country were held in high esteem. That the courageous Reeve had never been known to show off was the object of appreciation and praise, as was how he took care of his subordinates, and his having learned to communicate in Spanish, both in spoken and written form. The chips might have written letters to their old blocks about El Inglesito, and maybe the heads of the families wouldn't raise a fuss about his being military chief of Camagüey.

What precious few knew, the Major further reasoned, was that Enrique had a knack for dealing with civilians and earning their trust and respect. Therefore, he deemed it wise to train the American in the logistical side of warfare. Taking him to the workshops was another poorly disguised lesson.

Reeve, who preferred to stay in the background except in battle, listened in silence at each workshop and made mental notes. Agramonte greeted the artisans, inquired after their wives' and kids' health, sipped freshly brewed coffee five times in an hour, asked if they had all they needed to repair guns or make slaked lime, ropes, baskets, saddles, tack, and saddle pads. The Major also wanted to know if they had apprentices, if a record of articles made was kept, and what he could do to facilitate their work. Then he delivered a quick overview of the recent victorious battles, forgetting to mention defeats, and embraced each and every one present before moving on.

At half past eight on a beautiful morning, the twelve men were on their way back to the camp when the distant sound of gunfire reached them. Horses were reined in, heads cocked.

"Where is it coming from?" Agramonte asked.

"I'm not sure," Reeve said after an instant.

"Back to bivouac," Agramonte ordered, and kicked his horse's flanks. Perceiving the echo of sporadic firing, the twelve riders galloped back to camp and found that Captain Battle had the Mounted Hunters' Second Squadron ready for combat. He seemed relieved when his commanding officer reined in Tiger a couple of yards from his charger.

"What's going on, Captain?" Reeve asked.

"Our explorers are exchanging fire with an enemy cavalry regiment and a company or two, I'm not sure, of Guardia Civil infantry. One scout reports two hundred men, the other three hundred. Maybe they are looking for us, I don't know," Battle reported.

"Where are they coming from?"

"Northwest."

Reeve paused and squinted, then turned to Agramonte.

"I suggest charging, Major."

"It's your unit. Act as you deem best, Commander."

A few minutes after ten in the morning, the Cuban bugler sounded beheading. In the ensuing battle, Reeve's combat performance amazed his brothers in arms. Of the twenty-eight dead Spaniards abandoned on the battlefield, some men swore Reeve had slashed ten and shot another ten, a glaring exaggeration. But El Inglesito killed six or seven men and wounded as many. Five rebels died and thirteen sustained severe injuries. The Cubans took two prisoners, twenty-six horses, twenty-seven carbines, as well as sabers, revolvers, and ammunition.

After midday, once the wounded rebels had been evacuated and the dead were strapped to riderless horses, according to Agramonte's request, Battle ordered the men to fall into formation. Drunk on victory, their adrenaline levels still high, their sweaty rags bloodstained, most were smiling widely; Reeve's fairly new trousers and shirt were a mess. Riding Tiger, he stood to the right of Agramonte; Battle, also on horseback, was to the Major's left. The bugler sounded silence and the men piped down. Some horses kept snorting, kicking the ground, and bowing their heads. A flock of buzzards flying overhead eagerly waited for the departure of bipeds and quadrupeds to start feasting off dead Spaniards.

"Mambises," roared Agramonte. Some rebels snorted, others chuckled, and a few doubled up.

Mambí was a derogatory term applied by the Spanish military to Cuban and Dominican rebels. The Major waited for the laughter to subside.

"I am honored to have fought alongside you," he bellowed at the top of his lungs. "You fought like lions. I am proud of you. Cuba is proud of you. If you ask me to mention those who showed extraordinary courage, I would say all. All of you! And especially those soldiers who fell in the faithful discharge of their duties. We will give them a Christian burial this afternoon. Not one of you fled the battlefield; not one of you surrendered or was captured by the enemy. But a certain fighter outdid all others. And I ask you, who is that fighter?"

Right away the men started shouting "El Inglesito, El Inglesito." Agramonte turned in his saddle and, smiling contentedly, watched Reeve blush and incline his head. Wondering what the hell was going on, most horses dropped their ears.

When the cheering abated, Agramonte continued. "Given the fact you saw what I saw, by the powers invested on me by the government of the Republic in Arms, I hereby promote Commander Reeve to lieutenant colonel, active immediately."

More cheering followed.

"And tonight," Agramonte continued, "I shall write a letter to the president of the Republic in Arms proposing that Lieutenant Colonel Reeve be promoted to the rank of full colonel."

Looking at Tiger's ears, Reeve shook his head in confusion and embarrassment as the men cheered once again.

"¡Que viva El Inglesito!" a soldier hollered.

"¡Que viva!" the whole squadron shouted, save for the man being acclaimed.

"¡Que viva Cuba Libre!" Agramonte yelled.

"¡Que viva!" And this time Reeve joined the bawling horsemen.

At sundown, the brand-new lieutenant colonel was reluctantly taking a bath. Regular bathing was unheard of, but from time to time he enjoyed riding to a nearby brook, creek, or river and jumping in. Should the stream be too shallow, he would take a tin basin to pour water over his naked body, soap himself if lye soap was available, rinse off, then energetically run his hands all over his torso and legs, shaking off droplets. As he let the sun and the breeze dry him before donning his soiled clothes, he flew back in time and became the snotty Brooklyn kid he had been ages ago, possessing the same carelessness and identical state of innocence. He felt weaker and sweated much more for the next ten or twelve hours, but for a day or two he enjoyed feeling fresh and clean.

But Reeve bathed reluctantly after battle, when he had to shed his bloodstained clothes to wash away the stench of other men's dried blood. His armpits, tolerably smelly most of the time, reeked disgustingly following combat. El Inglesito wanted to believe he disliked those baths because he was forced to clean up at bivouac, amid bushes to hide his nudity from others, standing on the oilskin Ryan had given him as a present so as not to muddy his feet.

When Agramonte promoted Reeve to commander, the Major ordered that some rebel unfit to engage in combat was to be appointed his orderly. Reeve disliked having a servant, but it came to him that doing without one would be contrary to custom and might upset other rebel officers. Antonio, a freed slave whose right index and middle fingers had been severed while feeding sugarcane stalks into a mill, was assigned to care for Reeve. More often than not, streams and wells were not within walking distance, so Antonio had to ride to the nearest source, fill a bucket, and then go back holding the container and steering the horse. He made two trips. Reeve managed to wash off with one bucket; his soiled garments were dropped into the other for Antonio to wash and hang them to dry.

What made Reeve dislike those baths was that as he watched the pinkish water run down his abdomen, thighs, and calves, his mental screen started projecting the terrified expressions of the men he had killed or maimed that day. Reeve couldn't discern if this happened because the powers of darkness wanted to show him their appreciation or if God Almighty was telling him he had placed himself beyond the bounds of human compassion. He thought of the forty-something lieutenant who had stared at him in disbelief when Reeve's blade cut into his neck and a powerful two-yard-high jet of blood shot into the air; the young fair-headed soldier who felt, yet couldn't believe, that two slugs were boring into his heart, lungs, and spine; the soldier sporting an incredibly large mustache with curly ends who gasped in terror the instant the blade cut into his ear and kept going into his long sideburn, skin, upper jaw, tongue, larynx, and the top of his spine.

That sundown, Reeve retched three times before vomiting the rice and boiled sweet potato he had eaten earlier.

On May 7, as the rebels repelled a Spanish charge at Cocal del Olimpo and achieved a resounding victory, Tiger was wounded. Reeve had learned the importance that rider and horse know each other well, so he was concerned and tinged with sadness, as though one of his new recruits had been hurt. He asked the squadron's marshal, a horse lover, if he knew someone in the surrounding area who could take good care of Tiger during his convalescence. The marshal said his brother-in-law lived two leagues away and would be honored to care for Reeve's horse.

Reeve's first Cuban fiesta took place on May 10, at the Jimaguayú field camp. Officers born in Camagüey held a banquet in honor of the officers of Las Villas, one of the ideas that Agramonte conceived to ward off unwanted regionalism and build bridges. The cooks worked two full days to feed more than five hundred men, for the Major made it very clear that all rebels, regardless of rank, would eat the savory dishes on the menu.

On the first day, helped by a few gluttons who volunteered, the cooks peeled and dropped into cauldrons, pots, pans, and pails three hundred pounds of cassava, *malanga,* sweet potato, plantains, pumpkins, and *ñame*; later they covered them with water. Hundreds of crushed cloves of garlic and finely chopped onions and green peppers were dropped into earthenware containing the juice of several dozen bitter oranges. A rich fellow living nearby judged it prudent to donate the sack of sugar and half sack of salt that Captain Battle was willing to pay for. Two herb connoisseurs marched into the woods to gather coriander, mint, parsley, marjoram, and basil. A young ox and ten pigs were slaughtered and left hanging overnight.

The next morning, around four, fires were lighted. At ten, two carpenters finished putting together the rustic tables and benches for ranking officers. Most soldiers were chitchatting about this and that; others were playing practical jokes; a few sharpened their blades and cleaned their firearms. Surrounding a rebel strumming a guitar, a bunch of white Cubans were singing at the top of their lungs. Dissimilar groups of freed slaves grouped around four of them who, tapping endlessly on a wooden box, a four-legged stool, and two washbasins, intoned sad-sounding chants in tribal dialects. Agramonte instructed his quartermaster to provide two bottles of *aguardiente de caña,* hard liquor made from sugarcane molasses, to each platoon. The goal was accomplished: The men appreciated the moderate elbow bending and a mere five got pretty well fuddled.

After four years of eating simple, unseasoned, and hurriedly cooked dishes, Reeve had forgotten the fragrances and scents that came from spiced food. By noon, the pervading smells of roasted pork and beef, of a stew that Cubans called *ajiaco de monte,* of black beans, and of *cusubé*—a dessert made from cassava starch—made officers, noncoms, and soldiers salivate profusely. Those who would be waiting on the officers' tables gorged beforehand; later, as they carried platters to the tables, their satisfied expressions and bulging bellies spoke volumes. Around one, Agramonte, his staff officers, and the guests from Las Villas sat on the benches. Agramonte's salutary words took less than a minute; then they toasted with fermented sugarcane juice, *zambumbia*, and attacked the first course immediately.

"Don't eat too much *ajiaco*," Battle counseled Reeve after a minute, "or you'll be full when the main course arrives."

"It's delicious."

"I know."

"What's this?" Reeve asked, lifting a whitish piece with the spoon.

"Looks like *ñame* to me."

"Name?"

"No, not name, *ñame*. The emphasis falls on the *a*. Forget it. I've yet to meet an Anglo-Saxon who can correctly pronounce a word with an ñ."

"Umm. So tasty."

"No, it's not. You find it tasty because it boiled for several hours in a stew that had beef, pork, onion, corn, and other things. You boil a *ñame* in plain water and it's insipid."

"And what's in that plate?"

"*Fufú*."

"What's *fufú*?"

"Mashed green plantains with salt, garlic, onions, and small pieces of pork crackling."

"Sounds tempting. Mighty peculiar name, though."

"Well, my dad says English slavers used to feed the cheapest grub available—boiled plantains and *malanga*—to slaves.

When they threw the food into the ship's hold, they shouted, 'Food, food.' So, for African slaves, boiled plantains were *fufú*. Eventually, Cubans adopted the name."

"For land's sake!"

Battle cocked his head for an instant, then said, "What a socially acceptable alternative to taking the Lord's name in vain."

"Don't call me to account for my language, Captain," Reeve said wryly as he served up *fufú* on his plate.

To Battle's mind came the thought of the ingenuous kid who four years earlier had volunteered to get him a glowing ember to light a cigar. The kid had turned into one of the Grim Reaper's favorite warriors, Battle thought.

When the black beans and the rice were served, Battle gave an approving nod.

"Not bad," he said.

"Not bad? These are the best black beans I've ever had!" Reeve exclaimed.

"You haven't tasted my mom's black beans."

The beef and pork were served. Reeve and Battle didn't touch the beef, but they gorged on pork.

"Delicious," said Reeve after polishing off a rib, then wiping his fingers on his pantaloon.

"No, it's not," countered Battle, still halfway through his rib.

"What's the matter with you? Lost your sense of taste or what?" Reeve said as he stuck his fork into the brimful of ribs on the flat piece of wood serving as tray.

"If instead of hanging the animal," Battle said with the patient tone of good teachers, "they had left it level all night long and spread *mojo* over its rib cage every few hours, these ribs would be truly delicious."

"What's *mojo*?"

"A mixture of bitter orange juice, garlic, oregano, cumin, black pepper, and salt."

"You sound like an honest-to-goodness cook."

"Our cook took Sundays off, and now and then I enjoyed cooking something. On my mother's or my wife's birthday, too. I like to cook. But these guys probably lacked pepper and cumin."

Later, Battle went into ecstasies about *cusubé*, the dessert.

"You know what? Too sweet for my taste," Reeve said.

"Of course. Cubans have a sweet tooth because we eat sugar from the time we are in the cradle; it's what makes the rich rich. And it's cheap, so the poor eat a lot."

Coffee and *aguardiente* followed.

"You can have mine," Reeve said, extending his gourd of liquor to his second in command.

"Thanks. You never touch the stuff, right?"

"Nope."

"On account of your faith?"

"Well, the Lord said, 'Do not drink wine nor strong drink,' but religion aside, I tried whiskey on board the *Perrit*, and *aguardiente* one day when I was soaking wet and cold after a downpour. I didn't like it, not in the least. Makes me cough; my throat burns. I can't figure why so many men drink spirits. In New York, ragpickers spend it all on liquor."

"Well, I suppose picking rags you don't make enough money to get drunk."

"Wrong. Ragpickers make pretty good money, as much as eighty cents a day. It's hard work, you know. They have to be done by six in the morning, when street sweepers start working. But eighty cents buys a lot of bad whiskey."

"I didn't know that."

The rich meal brought about heavy somnolence to men living hand-to-mouth, and several hundred took a siesta. Sentries had to fight off sleep. At half past four, Agramonte sent word that those who wanted to have supper would have to make do with leftovers—no more cooking today, just coffee at sundown. Three hours later, as the wonderful aroma of fresh coffee was invading the camp, a Cuban informer brought the news that a seven-hundred-strong Spanish force—infantry, artillery, and cavalry—under the command of a lieutenant colonel had camped a league away, at the Cachaza farm.

Agramonte convened a meeting with all officers, delivered the news, ordered them to have their men ready, and addressed Reeve last.

"Enrique, send scouts and tell them to get back here at three."

Betting that the enemy had acted on reliable information about where they were and would start hunting for them soon after sunrise, Agramonte ordered his 400 infantrymen and 130 cavalrymen to head north at a quarter past four the next morning. By six, the rebels had taken positions in a forest to the south of the savanna the Spaniards would have to cross to hunt for them. The savanna's tall guinea grass forced lookouts to climb up trees.

Waiting for the enemy on horseback, Agramonte became pensive. He had been summoned to a meeting that would take place in Las Tunas in two weeks. A source close to the president had told him he would be designated general in chief of the Liberation Army. He had been asked not to risk his life unnecessarily. He turned in the saddle and spoke aloud to those near him.

"I won't charge today, friends. You stay here with the chief of the cavalry."

Then he addressed Reeve in his normal tone. "Assume command. Trounce them, Enrique. I'll inspect the troops, then ride to El Guayabo. Meet me there after the battle."

The Spanish lieutenant colonel turned deeply suspicious when he realized his men would have to go through a savanna flanked by dense forest; he took all precautions. His foot soldiers, concealed by the tall grass, advanced unimpeded; his cavalrymen, though, were visible, and the Cubans opened fire. After a few volleys, the rebel cavalry charged twice and contained the enemy.

For some reason, Agramonte had second thoughts. Maybe he wanted to give instructions to Reeve, or perhaps he reckoned that leaving the battlefield would give a bad impression to the ranks, but whatever the reason, he tried to cross the savanna from east to west and stumbled on Spanish infantrymen. He caught a bullet in his head and died instantly. Two of his four-man security detail fell trying to recover his body; the others fled.

Having lost the element of surprise, aware that he was not knowledgeable concerning infantry tactics, and believing that Agramonte waited at El Guayabo, Reeve ordered the Cubans to back off. Fifteen minutes after the bugler sounded retreat, a Cuban captain on a galloping horse caught up with Reeve.

"Inglesito, the Major was shot. A man from his security detail says he's dead," the man announced as his horse, displeased at being reined in so brusquely, kicked the ground and bent his neck several times.

Reeve yanked both reins, knit his brow, and froze. It couldn't be. The riders around him also reined in their horses and stared at the messenger in complete disbelief. Then all eyes moved to Reeve, who was looking around, wondering what to say, what to do, wishing someone would take the matter in his own hands. It dawned on him that he had become number one, at least for a few hours. He forced himself to react.

"Captain Battle."

"Yes, sir."

"Take a squad, ride back to the savanna, and look for the Major."

"Yes, sir," said Battle, and turning his horse, he shouted. "First squad, second section, A platoon. Follow me!"

"Captain Sánchez," Reeve said.

"Yes, sir," said Serafín Sánchez.

"Tell all other officers the news. We'll wait here for Captain Battle. Set remote sentries."

Fearing another ambush, the Spanish column started retreating to a nearby sugar mill and came across Agramonte's body. Two days later, following identification, the corpse was incinerated, the ashes scattered to the wind.

Taciturn and feeling really blue as news traveled back and forth, and even though vengefulness consumed him, Reeve abstained from launching offensive actions for two reasons: As a foreigner, he believed he shouldn't take initiatives; and as a mere lieutenant colonel, he knew he should wait for Agramonte's replacement.

The loss imbued him with a deep sense of sadness, on a par with losing a beloved older brother. After Jordan, he had looked up to Agramonte. But he felt certain that in all his life he had not met a man like the Major. One of the dark thoughts recurrently crossing his mind was that the war was lost. Riproaring fellows came once in a coon's age. Nobody could take his place. Julio Sanguily was an invalid. No highfalutin sugar aristocrat would do. Nobody would go across lots as

Agramonte had or unite blacks and whites as he had; nobody else was as persuasive. Reeve knew he outclassed the Major at one thing only: He was a much better killing machine.

Had the time to hang his fiddle arrived? Should he return to Gotham? Or should he keep fighting for Cuba Libre and achieve the goal the Cuban major general had died for? His only firm decision was to wait and see how things turned out.

For Reeve, though, the most serious repercussion of Agramonte's death consisted of his doubting religious dogma. If "the Lord God omnipotent reigneth," if "the Lord searcheth all hearts, and understandeth all the imaginations of the thoughts," then how could He permit such a man to die before liberating his country and abolishing slavery? The Major had been a believer, a patriot, had taken a virgin of his own people to wife and had been faithful to her, didn't drink spirits or smoke, and not once had he taken the name of the Lord in vain, Reeve mused. Yes, Agramonte had killed men, but a war was going on, and that same reason had prevented him from resting on the seventh day. The Bible said the children of Israel fought wars in their land against the enemies oppressing them. Didn't they kill their oppressors? Did they always rest on the Sabbath, even if the enemy charged on that day? It was the same here. Was it possible that God was not omnipotent? That He wouldn't read every single man's thoughts? That He didn't always protect his children?

Five days after the tragedy, Reeve camped at El Majagual, a lush green pasture not too far from the Spanish camp of Vista Hermosa, to wait for Julio Sanguily. To protect saddles from the drizzle, they were removed from the horses; orderlies and soldiers took to the forest and cut branches and twigs and gathered dry palm fronds to build and thatch ramadas. The night was uneventful. Early the next morning, a sentry who had been more concerned with keeping dry than with performing his duty discovered that the enemy was fewer than five hundred varas away, closing in fast. He ran to the camp as fast as he could.

"*Arriba, caballero, que los gallegos están ahí mismo, pegaitos,*" he hollered.

Time was so short, most cavalrymen rode bareback. Antonio, however, managed to saddle and bridle Reeve's latest horse. With blood racing through his vessels, Reeve mounted and drew his blade.

"Men, let's avenge the Major," he said, and, forgetting all he knew about horses, angrily spurred the stallion's flanks.

In that battle and the next, which took place a few days later at Hacienda Yucatán, Reeve and his men killed 16 enemy officers and 122 noncoms and soldiers. Close to three hundred Spaniards were wounded. The Spanish high command concluded that Agramonte's death would not end hostilities in Camagüey.

July 6

Reeve squeezed the flanks of his horse and approached the row of horsemen he was facing. Capt. Federico Diago rode alongside him. Behind them, Reeve's cavalry squadron was lined up. Both men reined back their stallions when the strangers were a mere fifteen feet away.

"Good morning, gentlemen, and welcome" were Reeve's opening words. "May I inquire which of you is Major General Máximo Gómez?" he asked, looking at the brown eyes of a thin middle-aged man whose military bearing made Reeve suspect this was his new superior officer. The protruding cheekbones of the undernourished man stood in stark contrast to his impressive mustache.

"I am Gómez," the man said. "May I learn your name and rank, sir?"

"I am Lieutenant Colonel Henry Reeve, sir."

"Very pleased to meet you, Lieutenant Colonel. Your fame has preceded you."

"Thank you, sir; likewise. Aligned behind me is the Second Cavalry Squadron, Camagüey Army Corps. This gentleman is Captain Federico Diago, the Corps adjunct. I would be honored if you allow me to introduce my officers and the rest of the squadron."

Thirty-six-year-old Maj. Gen. Máximo Gómez looked ten years older. Born in Santo Domingo, he had joined the Spanish army when Haitians invaded his homeland and reached the rank of master sergeant. Transferred to Cuba in 1865, Gómez resigned his commission a year later and settled down with his family in Oriente. He made a lot of friends among Cubans who favored self-determination, joined the rebels in October 1868—six days after they rose up in arms—and was appointed major general. Reportedly, he was the most knowledgeable person concerning military tactics and had taught his brothers in arms many things, including the cavalry charge with machetes. But certain strategic discrepancies had surfaced. Two contradictory versions had circulated: Some said he wanted to burn sugar plantations; others said he didn't. Nobody knew for sure why, a year earlier, President Céspedes had removed Gómez from his post as commander of all rebel formations in the Eastern Department. But when the president had to appoint a substitute for Agramonte, he felt certain that Gómez was the best man for the job.

In the afternoon, Reeve presented Gómez with a five-year-old sixteen-hand Spanish-Norman stallion and said that all its tack

had been handmade at the shops Agramonte had ordered rebuilt. The general reciprocated with a .44-caliber Colt model
1860 revolver, fifty paper-wrapped cartridges, and the same
number of percussion caps.

After supper, both men went into the *bohío* hastily assembled for Gómez, took off their hats, hung them atop the rear
posts of the *taburetes* they sat in, and, illuminated by a tallow
candle, discussed the military situation in Camagüey for nearly
two hours. But the discussion turned personal in the final five
minutes.

"We have something in common, Reeve," said Gómez, his
mustache concealing the hint of a sad smile on his thin lips.
"Both of us are foreigners."

"We are, yes."

"And we lead Cubans. You over a hundred, me over a thousand."

"Indeed, sir."

"I'll take you into my confidence, Reeve," Gómez said,
averting his eyes, clasping his left knee with both hands, and
then returning his gaze to Reeve. "It's been almost five years,
and still I'm not used to it. I believe that . . . concerning certain
issues . . . I should keep my opinions to myself. Especially on
politics. I steer clear of taking sides. But I have other concerns,
like this tendency to exaggeration a number of officers and
many soldiers have, like pulling practical jokes constantly and
throwing tantrums over things . . . inconsequential. They either fall short or overshoot. Many's the time I've felt like repri-
manding them, but not being Cuban, I abstain. I feel I may be
missing a trait inherent to the nature of this people that justi-
fies certain behaviors. Have you felt something like that?"

Reeve raised his eyebrows and smiled. "Well, sir, to be honest with you, yes, I have. In my case perhaps even more so, on

account of the fact that maybe your country is more like Cuba than Flatlands. To me, it's another world: people, climate, plants, animals, everything is different. I've had to learn your mother tongue, too. And I share your view that I should keep my mouth shut concerning politics. I know there are differences of opinion, but it's not my funeral."

Gómez nodded twice and smiled; this time, his mustache failed to conceal the unhappiness of his smile. "I expect things will get tougher for me now. I will occupy the place of Agramonte, a Cuban hero much admired by his subordinates."

"I daresay that admiration doesn't begin to describe what men felt for Agramonte, General. And it wasn't only soldiers; plain folks revered him, too."

"Exactly. So I suppose you realize that whoever occupies his place will be constantly compared to him, and I want to do things the regular way. Agramonte had a pretty good opinion of you; currently the government is studying a letter of his proposing your promotion to colonel. I reckon that your bravery is admired, and other officers think you are mature beyond your years. War does that to men. You know where the wind lies in this neck of the woods, and since we are both foreigners, I would be grateful if you would advise me on how to deal with officers and civilians. Sometimes I may disregard your advice, but I will always consider carefully what you say before making a decision. Would you be willing to help me on that, Lieutenant Colonel?"

"Honest I would, sir. It's what the Major would've wanted me to do."

"Thank you. Is there anything else you want to discuss?"

"No, sir."

"Then good night. And thanks for the stallion. Impressive animal."

"You're welcome, sir. The gun you gave me is excellent. Sleep well," he added, turning and taking three steps to the opening that served as an entrance to the *bohío*. He stopped and turned again.

"Welcome to Camagüey, Major General."

Reeve was promoted to colonel on July 27. Two weeks later, Major General Gómez formed two columns: one composed of three hundred cavalrymen under General Julio Sanguily; the other, with eight hundred infantrymen and one hundred horses, was led by Col. José González. One hundred cavalrymen from Sanguily's column, led by Reeve, were directly under Gómez.

After slaughtering a column of Spanish infantry on August 12—the Cubans counted thirty-five dead enemies—Gómez ordered Reeve to ride to Najasa with his horsemen, and to allow the Spaniards to see them.

"Show ourselves, sir?"

"Yes, Colonel."

"And may I inquire why, Major General?"

Reeve detected that, on this occasion, Gómez's smile was not in the least sad. Was it . . . mischievous?

"You may, Colonel. But this is not to be shared with any other officer. A Cuban trait I find displeasing is how few men are capable of keeping a secret. The moment you ask one of them to hold his tongue, the intimate confidant he'll tell it to springs up in his mind. Cubans are brave, generous, affectionate, . . . and gossipy. Not all, but most.

"Life has taught me a lesson. Secrets win wars and save lives. The enemy should never learn our intentions. Even better, we should try to deceive them, make them think they know what we'll do, so they drop their guard, maybe divert forces from where we will strike, in order to reinforce the towns or places where we won't go. I am getting ready to attack Nuevitas, so I want the enemy to figure all Cuban forces are retreating to the south. Particularly, I want them to see a full cavalry squadron moving south."

Reeve reflected on this for a moment.

"I see your point, sir. But does this mean we won't participate in the attack on Nuevitas?"

Stroking his mustache, Gómez said, "Exactly. But en route to Najasa, you are free to provoke and engage the enemy when you deem it proper."

Reeve and his men moved out from Gómez's camp at the crack of dawn. Although he missed the freedom and constant alertness that scouting required, and the responsibility of leading the vanguard, he was getting accustomed to riding at the center of the squadron, as commanding officers had been ordered to, surrounded by subordinates, all especially wary after the Major's loss. Even though instinctively he kept looking for signs of an ambush his scouts might had overlooked, for over an hour nobody said a word and he was lost in thought.

Most of his musing had to do with the leadership qualities of Jordan, Agramonte, and Gómez. Jordan, the West Point graduate and veteran of several wars, knew all there was to know about strategy and tactics, but he had been unfamiliar with the terrain and the Cuban national spirit. Agramonte, the courageous idealist, the indefatigable patriot, had had what Jordan lacked and had been able to arouse his men like no one else. He had marched and countermarched to confound the enemy, had grasped the importance of logistical self-reliance and having medical facilities to care for the sick and the wounded. But before he took up arms, the Major's understanding of war had been purely academic. That Agramonte had been able to achieve so much was a tribute to his innate military genius.

Reeve was mature enough to realize that it takes a long time to impartially assess the strengths and weaknesses of a man, and he had met Gómez less than six weeks earlier. Adding to his impressions what he had learned from others, Reeve theorized that the Dominican appeared to be a cross between the Major and Jordan, but with an astuteness that Reeve had not discovered in the other two men. Gómez had been trained by the Spaniards, but as far as Reeve had been able to glean, the basic training Spanish soldiers and noncoms got did not include tactical or strategic concepts. Despite this, the man had risen fast in the rebel hierarchy because, having seen combat in Santo Domingo, he had the experience that almost all top Cuban leaders lacked, and could provide the sound advice they badly needed. Perhaps, like Agramonte, he had a natural talent for waging war. On the whole, from a military standpoint, perhaps Gómez was half as good as Jordan, but twice as good as Agramonte.

If not as idealistic as the Major, Gómez had to have a strong tendency to idealism to side with the oppressed, take up arms against the metropolis, and even live with a young Cuban who, for being his wife and bearing his children, was sought by the Spaniards. Several reasons precluded his being adored as Agramonte had been: He was an alien and lacked the Major's eloquence, looks, and passion. But concerning his adaptability to Cuba and the Cubans, he outclassed Jordan. Coming from an island nation colonized by the Spaniards, he probably had been brought up saying the prayers, playing the games, and singing the songs Cuban kids said, played, and sang. Possibly he had read the same books, learned identical rules of etiquette and dress code. But most important of all, he knew how the Spanish soldier *thought*.

And this scheme to send his squadron four leagues south to Najasa while preparing to attack a big town eight leagues due north was so . . . *clever.* Reeve checked his memory and concluded that in all his born days he hadn't met a foxier guy. The Major, Ryan, even Jordan, had attracted the Spaniards into ambushes by relatively simple means: tricking them into believing that a small band of rebels had run into a Spanish column and fled, and by countermarching. But Reeve was not aware they had ever done this sort of distraction, or that they had attacked a major settlement. Although displeased by having been excluded from the main operation, Reeve found himself looking forward to the outcome and decided he would do as much as he could to deceive the enemy.

And he did. He captured an enemy convoy near Maraguán, provoked the Spaniards at several places, approached the city of Puerto Príncipe, exchanged fire with a fort, and cut the telegraph line between Puerto Príncipe and Santa Cruz del Sur. Meanwhile, Gómez destroyed the defenses of Nuevitas, dispersed its garrison, and captured an important booty. Then he rode back to Najasa and reunited with Reeve.

Gómez demanded high standards from his men, but he kept to himself those who lived up to his expectations and those who did not, those he considered brightest or bravest or less prone to indiscretion. Careful not to show favoritism toward any one, he held private conversations with all senior officers, including the unremarkable or too talkative, since this served as a front for the truly important conversations, those where he disclosed the next operation he was hatching in his mind. Therefore, none imagined that anything especially significant was going on when on September 19, after supper, he sent for Reeve.

"At your service, Major General," Reeve said on entering the *bohío,* saluting, and taking off his hat. As with Jordan four years earlier, rank gave Gómez the privilege of illuminating his hut with a tin candleholder suspended from the ceiling.

"Pull up a *taburete*," Gómez said, lifting his eyes from the letter he was penning to his wife. He shook the nib twice and a droplet of ink fell on the topsoil floor; then he blew on the paper to hasten the drying of the ink. As he sat, Reeve took in the writing table. It hadn't been there three days earlier, and it was smaller than Jordan's.

"Your squadron is eleven men short, right?" asked Gómez as he rested the wooden stylus alongside the pewter inkwell.

"Nine men short, sir."

"Only nine?"

"Yes, sir."

"I was told you arrested two perverts early this morning."

"Oh, you included— Yes, sir, I'm eleven men short."

Gómez nodded and looked at the unfinished letter. "And what do you intend to do with the two *maricones*?"

"They will be court-martialed tomorrow morning and most likely sentenced to death. If that's the case, I'll have them hanged."

Gómez rested his left elbow atop the table and gazing pensively at a point above Reeve's head, stroked his mustache.

"Hang them, Colonel?"

"Yes, sir."

"Are you familiar with the Act of Military Organization?"

Reeve blinked twice. "The what?"

Gómez successfully suppressed a smile. "It was enacted four years ago. Article Seventy-four stipulates that military crimes and sentences would be defined by an act. Are you acquainted with this act?"

"No, sir."

"Well, neither am I. Perhaps the government has had to

deal with more pressing matters. Military crimes and sentences have not been defined. Of course, I assume the responsibility of trying, sentencing, and executing traitors and deserters. But sodomy is depravity, not a punishable military crime. You can't hang these men, Colonel."

Reeve cocked his head and stole a glance at the toe cap of Gómez's boots before lifting his eyes to the general.

"Then what am I supposed to do with these two degenerates?"

"Discharge them dishonorably."

"And they go back home and live in sin while true men fight?"

"I don't know. Maybe they'll kill themselves. It's what a white officer chose to do when he was caught in the act with a slave near Bayamo. Shot himself. The man had a wife and two children."

"A married pretty boy?"

"Yep. I suggest you conduct a trial and, if they are found guilty of sodomy, sentence them to dishonorable discharge. Then have the squadron fall in, read the sentence aloud, and let them go. Now, let's move on to more important matters, shall we?"

"As you order, Major General. But perhaps—"

"Dishonorable discharge. End of discussion. Tomorrow I will assign eleven riders to your squadron. Now, let me show you."

The general got to his feet, with a few steps reached the gloomiest corner of the hut, extracted a folded single sheet of paper from a battered leather briefcase with a shoulder strap, and returned to the table. He moved the inkwell and the stylus to the edge, unfolded and spread out the folio over the unfinished letter. The ten-by-sixteen-inch paper showed a crudely drawn diagram of a coastal town and a compass rose.

"This is a map of Santa Cruz del Sur," Gómez said, and paused.

Nodding slowly while contemplating the diagram, Reeve recalled that Ramona had said the most delicious fish came from this town. Gómez sat down.

"All fortified posts, arm depots, main streets, and buildings are marked," the major general went on. "I have a written report with police and army units, number of men, and the names of ranking officers. I know how many sentinels guard headquarters, arm depots, and advance posts. There are three watches; each guard stands two hours of duty and has four off. The officer conducting the rounds is escorted by a sergeant and two soldiers. Countersigns are changed weekly."

The general fell silent. Reeve lifted his eyes to him.

"We have a spy in Santa Cruz del Sur," he said, smiling.

"We have a patriot in Santa Cruz del Sur," Gómez replied, correcting him.

"Right. And you are contemplating attacking."

"I am."

"How many Spaniards?"

"Under three hundred. I'm getting reinforcements from Las Villas. I could send into combat five hundred infantrymen and two hundred cavalrymen."

Reeve, the former bookkeeper did the mental arithmetic.

"Wow. Almost three to one in our favor. I'm not used to that," he said after a moment.

"Neither am I. Tell me what you think. We would begin at dawn, your cavalry squadron charging along this street as the infantry, deployed here, here, and here would . . ."

For the next six minutes, moving his finger over the diagram, Gómez delineated his plan of attack. Looking at the map, Reeve listened. When the general finished, Reeve lifted his eyes from the folio.

"With due respect, sir, I would suggest that rather than sending my full squadron charging along here, I take this gateway to the town with thirty riders. That would make it easier for Lieutenant Colonel Montejo and his infantry platoons to cross the main street. The rest of my squadron would charge here. . . ."

The exchange lasted a quarter of an hour. Sometimes, Gómez nodded and remained silent; on other occasions, he shook his head and gave his reasons for disagreeing.

"We'll need three teams of mules" was Reeve's final remark.

"Excuse me?"

"We ain't leaving behind three artillery pieces and shells, right?"

"The kind of warfare we wage, artillery excessively limits mobility," countered Gómez. "I don't know about other generals, but I've never shelled an enemy position before attacking. So I'm in favor of rendering useless the pieces we seize."

"Very well."

"Any other observation, Colonel?"

For a moment, Reeve wondered if he should ask, then decided to. "What sort of diversion are you contemplating, sir?"

Gómez gave a chuckle. "None at all. After Nuevitas, the Spaniards will figure we are moving south because we want them to believe we'll attack Santa Cruz, when in fact we will be headed west, to Guáimaro, or east, to Jobabo."

Reeve stared at his superior, thinking to himself, The old dog is full of new tricks. "I see. Well, I have nothing else to say."

"Have your men clean their firearms and sharpen their machetes; then let them bum around. We'll probably leave here in a couple days. Now, I want to finish this letter to my wife. Good evening, Colonel," Gómez said as he picked up the folio and folded it.

Reeve nodded, stood at attention, and saluted. "Rest well, sir."

Without getting up, Gómez halfheartedly returned the salute. "You, too," he said.

Brandishing the machete with his right, holding the reins with his left, and bending over his horse's neck, Reeve started off the attack on Santa Cruz del Sur by leading a full-gallop charge at the town's main entrance on the overcast morning of September 28, a Sunday.

As was to be expected, the Spaniards turned their attention to the cavalrymen. A minute later, Col. Gregorio Benítez and a hundred infantrymen advanced from the west with the mission of occupying the Spanish headquarters and the pier. From the east, Lieutenant Colonel Montejo commanded three infantry platoons that closed off the dirt road to Playa Bonita. Three hundred rebels stood in reserve.

Reeve and his thirty riders went past the first line of defense and Colonel Benítez occupied the headquarters. Even though the sound of gunfire unambiguously signified what was going on, church bells started tolling madly to warn townsfolk. Ten Spaniards barricaded themselves at a pillbox and put up a determined resistance. Reeve and his men launched an attack on a fortified position that had a small cannon; their thrust was so daring that most defenders fled. El Inglesito approached the artillery piece, tapped on it with the point of his blade, and said the customary "Conquered." A fraction of a second later, a Spanish soldier who had stood his ground fired his carbine point-blank at Reeve. The bullet entered through his right upper thigh, smashed the head of the femur, and ruined the sacro-iliac.

Sharp pain exploded into burning agony. For a moment, Reeve was blinded. He squeezed his eyes shut and yanked the reins right. A blur gradually dissolved when he blinked again and again. After a moment, he focused. Twenty feet away, Battle emptied his revolver on the Spaniard, who fell to the ground with three chest wounds.

"Henry, Henry, you are bleeding!" the frightened captain shouted.

"It's nothing. Charge after the cockchafers. Charge, god-damn it, charge!"

Sheer determination made him spur his horse and give chase. But at a gallop or a trot, he was constantly thrown off balance as the jagged edges of fractured bones bit into muscles and nerves. The pain was unbearable. Fifteen minutes after getting shot, the hatless Reeve was being carried away on a stretcher.

Again, he was seeing treetops and fragments of an overcast sky. Once the bullet cooled down to body temperature, the pain dulled into a bearable ache. Reeve checked his vague notions of anatomy. A certain major organ was above the hip, to the right; he wasn't sure if it was the liver or the spleen. But his wound was below the hip, so presumably nothing vital had been punctured. Just the thigh, he guessed. Two weeks, maybe three, he was reckoning, when the carrier who held the back left side of the stretcher lost his balance and tumbled over. Reeve's right leg hit the ground and he almost fell from the stretcher; a fresh wave of excruciating pain engulfed him.

"Oh God," he wailed.

Antonio, riding alongside the wounded colonel, reviled the stretcher-bearer. Reeve wanted to tell his orderly to let it be, but he couldn't articulate a word. The trek resumed at a slower pace. Lightning flashed, thunder pealed, and soon after fat raindrops were falling. After half an hour, Reeve was soaking wet, yet clearheaded. The blood that kept flowing from his wound, thinned by the downpour, dripped to the ground and left a trail that the rain dissolved soon after. Remembering how thirsty he had been the last time, he kept licking his lips and swallowing rainwater. He would be taken to a mad doctor, like the good Luaces, who wouldn't let him take a sip before putting that nasty mask on him and rendering him unconscious, so he figured he'd better fill up now.

He wondered where they were taking him. In Santa Cruz, after staring at his bloodied pantaloon, asking how he felt, and complimenting him, Major General Gómez had taken Battle and Antonio aside and given instructions he couldn't overhear. But Reeve knew the most probable destination was the twelve-bed field hospital at San Diego del Chorrillo. The old field hospital was dismantled and moved there on account of the fact that the Spaniards were planning a raid on Génova. The silver lining was that Dr. Luaces and Rosa la Bayamesa were stationed at the new medical facility, and he felt sure they wouldn't let any one else care for him. Feeling a little dizzy, Reeve closed his eyes.

Antonio kept stealing glances at the colonel, and when Reeve shut his eyes, the orderly thought he had died. Relief came after a second; dead men didn't stick their tongues out and run them over their lips. Reeve was the whitest white he had ever seen, but now he was as white as a mariposa petal, the softly scented snow-white flower thriving alongside rivers and lagoons. Like most Afro-Cubans, Antonio didn't know that losing blood caused paleness, and he imagined that Ikú was claiming the son of Ogún. Was this his fault? Had Ikú hidden in Reeve's canteen or a jug that he, Antonio, had inadvertently left uncapped? The orderly started mumbling an invocation to Oyá, the just, wise, and bellicose *orisha* of the strong winds, the tempests, and the dead that dwelled at graveyards. Ikú had to obey all her wishes.

Around nine o'clock, Reeve was admitted to the field hospital. Like all others, it had walls of dry *yaguas* from royal palms and was thatched with dry *pencas* from the same tree. He opened his eyes to the worried expression of Dr. Luaces and Rosa's dazzling smile. He smiled, too, and closed his eyes, knowing he was in the best of hands.

The insurgents occupied the town for two hours. They seized 271 rifles, 80,000 bullets of diverse calibers, 130 pounds of gunpowder, shrapnel, sabers, swords, three hundred uniforms, pharmaceuticals, and significant amounts of money and jewelry. The cannon that Reeve had conquered was rendered useless. The rebel casualty toll, however, was surprisingly high: seventeen dead and fifty wounded.

The report that Maj. Gen. Máximo Gómez sent to the government included this paragraph:

> In all justice, I must say that on the morning of September 28, the Cuban forces covered themselves in glory. All behaved admirably, without exception. But Col. Henry Reeve deserves special mention for charging into the muzzle of cannon . . .

Luaces examined Reeve and got ready to remove the bullet. After washing his hands, he applied chloroform to the mask, held it over the patient's mouth and nose, and withdrew it when unconsciousness was achieved. With Rosa holding two tallow dips near the wound, Luaces guessed, rather than observed, the condition of the head of the femur and the pelvis and sighed deeply. Should El Inglesito survive, the war was over for him; he would be leaning on a cane, if not on crutches, for the rest of his life. Rosa sutured the wound.

Having eased Reeve's pain with morphine—sent by Cuban exiles in New York—over the next two days, on the third, judging that his patient was clearheaded enough to understand what he had to say, Luaces thought it necessary to have a short exchange with Reeve.

"Look at me," the doctor said. "Can you hear me?"

Reeve nodded feebly.

"Blink once if you understand what I'm saying."

Reeve blinked.

"Blink once for yes and twice for no. Do you want to die?"

Two blinks.

"Do you want to be a paralytic the rest of your life?"

Two blinks.

"I thought so. Now, listen to me. Are you listening?"

A blink.

"If you want to live, and if you want to stand on your own two feet again, you can't move from the waist down for the next three weeks. You pee in bed; you shit in bed; you drink water and eat your meals lying down. Don't disobey me, Reeve. I know you; if all goes well, in a couple of weeks you'll feel much better and will start pestering Rosa, saying you want to sit in bed or even stand up. Everybody in this place will be under orders to report to me if you start asking someone to get you out of bed. If that happens, I'll strap your hands and feet to the bed. Do you understand what I'm saying?"

A blink and the shadow of a smile.

"All right."

Luaces made no distinction between officers and soldiers, but he knew that Reeve was special. Mildly guilt-ridden, he devoted more time to El Inglesito than to his other patients. He fought inflammation and suppuration by changing dressings soaked in a 5 percent solution of carbolic acid every four hours. There was osteomyelitis, a common surgical infection causing fever and inflammation of the bones. The patient mumbled incoherently in English when asleep. When fully conscious, he couldn't ignore the moans and screams of the other patients; he also witnessed a leg amputation. Reeve was deeply embarrassed every time Rosa changed the cloth she placed beneath his penis to absorb urine, and especially when she removed his excrement and wiped clean his anus after defecation.

"This pee cold. You pee hours ago, but no call Rosa. You pee, you shit, you call Rosa. I'm not here, you send for me. I sleep, you send for me. My *bohío* is next to this. You wan me complain to Dr. Luaces?"

"No, Rosa, please. I'll call you next time."

"You promise?"

"I promise."

"This afternoon, I shave you. You have little funny mustache. Becoming old man, eh? Ji, ji, ji."

As he recovered, hours of reminiscence filled the day: the sweet smile of his mother as she laced her bonnet under her chin before going to the market; his father in a collarless dress shirt and suspenders, reading the Bible in his armchair, a permanent frown on his forehead; his bawling sisters getting home after school and demanding cookies.

Summer was the gayest of times in New York, albeit on

very hot evenings many stayed outdoors until almost midnight; the destitute slept on roofs and in the streets, or went to
the docks. Yet, heat waves were bearable, whereas the bliz-
zards and snowstorms made the destitute miserable. He had
seen homeless urchins gathering at steam grates on the side-
walks. But ice skating in Central Park was wonderful! He
hadn't sleighed, though; his family couldn't afford horses and
a sleigh.

Remembering Central Park made him chuckle. Yeah, the
lakes and footpaths and bushes and woods had seemed fantastic, despite the fact his father had told him it was all artificial;
all those hundreds of acres had been swampy land where thousands of squatters dwelled, Reeve senior had maintained. Only
now, after four years camping outdoors in the tropical wilder-
ness, did he realize the artificiality of Central Park. But, oh
well, there had been the concerts and the socializing. It wasn't
bad. And it should be completed by now, he thought.

He acknowledged missing a few things—playing baseball,
watching a horse-drawn fire engine rushing to a fire, the
Brooklyn Navy Yard and the Brooklyn Theater, the huge Manhattan buildings and residences. He hadn't been in a Cuban
city, but Battle had said none compared with New York.

Several events he had attended were etched in his mind, like
the huge triumphal procession when the Civil War ended. Just
sixteen days later, he had stared in disbelief at President Lincoln's coffin as it was drawn up Broadway to the Hudson River
Railway Depot. Where had they interred Lincoln? He couldn't
remember. Perhaps in Springfield, Illinois, the same place where
rifles were made.

And, of course, he frequently recounted his final months in
New York. The long conversations with Federico and Ricardo,
the passionate young Cubans whose ardor had won him for

the cause. How where they? Where? He had no clue. The meetings at Delmonico's, the bearded and mustachioed men in bowlers and top hats, wearing coats, vests and trousers, heatedly discussing in Spanish in smoke-filled rooms how to win their country's freedom. Standing on a corner, awestruck, he must have looked pretty stupid and immature. No wonder Jordan had been reluctant to accept him as messenger boy. Well, he had proven he could do a thing or two besides delivering messages. He remembered how guilty he had felt the final days at home, watching his parents and sisters, feeling he would give them a reason to be worried sick, especially his mother. But his father would've tied him down in bed had he revealed his plans.

Like most medical workers who served in military hospitals during wartime, Luaces found the resilience of the human body awesome. Reeve's gradual recovery reaffirmed his opinion. On the morning of October 18, twenty days after the battle of Santa Cruz del Sur, Luaces approached Reeve's bed.

"How are you today?"

"Ready to be discharged."

Luaces gave a chuckle. "I'm going to help you sit up. I will slip my arm under your shoulders and lift you slowly. You feel a little dizzy, don't worry; it's usual after three weeks in bed. If it hurts, tell me to stop. All right?"

"All right."

It hurt so little that Reeve didn't complain. For the next six days, he was lifted and sat up in bed for five or six minutes each time to have breakfast, lunch, and supper.

"Today you'll stand up," announced Luaces twenty-seven days after Reeve was wounded.

"Wonderful. Let's do it."

"Put all your weight on your left leg. Then, little by little, shift it to your right leg. Not all, just some weight. Do you understand, Reeve?"

"Oh c'mon, Doc, I'm not stupid."

Reeve felt fine below the knee. But the right side of his body, from waist to knee, felt stiff as a board and it hurt somewhat.

"How do you feel?"

"Never better. How soon can I rejoin my squadron?"

Three weeks after that day, Luaces, Rosa, and others who watched Reeve painfully hobbling around the field hospital, a rustic cane in his right, believed that never would El Inglesito lead men into combat again.

FIVE

November 25, 1873

Emilio Battle, Antonio, and a security detail composed of six of Reeve's riders arrived at the hospital midmorning, fifty-eight days after the raid on Santa Cruz del Sur. The visitors were taken aback by the gaunt, deathly pale, and disabled man who greeted them, yet all tried their best to conceal their surprise. Even so, Reeve noticed that they embraced him and patted him gently, as though dreading that a hug and a slap on the back might send him into a relapse.

To comply fully with Agramonte's previous order concerning hospital food, the visitors brought three chickens, five pounds of rice, a few tomatoes, onions, garlic, and salt. After the patients and the staff had lunch, the hospital cook loaned his pots and pans to Antonio, and by five o'clock something resembling chicken fricassee and rice was served. All ate like famished wolves. By sundown, Antonio and four cavalrymen tied their hammocks to trees, lay down, lighted up, and started jabbering. Two riders assumed sentry duty until ten. Dr. Luaces took his patient and Battle to his hut; they sat on *taburetes* around a small table where a tallow dip in a candleholder stood. The physician produced a box of Lucifer matches and lighted the candle. The smell of sulfur made noses wrinkle.

"All right, Battle. Bring me up-to-date," Reeve said.

Battle, promoted to commander five weeks earlier, made a ten-minute summary of military actions he had participated in, none of any significance.

"But we are in a big political fix," Battle said, addressing his main concern.

"What do you mean?"

"About a month ago, the Chamber removed President Céspedes from his post."

Reeve frowned and turned to Luaces. "Did you know this?"

Luaces nodded. "I found out three weeks ago."

"Why didn't you tell me?"

"I thought best to spare you the worry."

"Jesus, Doc, I appreciate all you've done for me, but—forget it. So, Battle, who is president now?"

"Salvador Cisneros. People are evenly divided, though. Some support Cisneros, others Céspedes. I, for one, believe that Céspedes should be president. He organized the rebellion. If it weren't for him, we wouldn't be where we are now: Better than ever, militarily speaking. Calixto García controls almost all the Eastern Department. Vicente García has the Spaniards confined to Puerto Padre and Tunas, and a few weeks ago he took an enemy camp by surprise and seized two hundred thousand bullets. Can you imagine? Wars have been won with fewer bullets. General Gómez has achieved . . . Well, you know that. The insurgents from Las Villas have gained experience and are ready to return to their turf. And all of a sudden, this political bomb explodes. . . ."

There were a few moments of silence. Battle extracted a cigar, bit its end, got to his feet, lighted it on the tallow dip's flame, and sat again.

"I don't think politics can affect the war," Reeve said, a smile playing on his lips. "Let politicians argue while we fight."

Battle's expression suggested he didn't share that view.

"Any other news?" Reeve asked next.

Battle threw a swift glance at Luaces, who barely shook his head, but not fast enough.

"Oh for God's sake, Luaces," Reeve said. "Don't treat me like a five-year-old. What is it, Battle?"

Again the commander shot a look at the doctor. He got a resigned nod.

"William Ryan, the Canadian?"

"What happened to him?"

"He was executed three weeks ago."

Reeve stared at Battle for a few seconds.

"Wasn't he in New York?"

Battle shook his head. "He was in Jamaica, with Varona and President Céspedes's brother, getting a two-hundred-man expedition ready. They sailed on a steamer, the *Virginius*. A Spanish battle cruiser intercepted them in international waters. They dumped the weapons and ammunition overboard, but they were towed to Santiago de Cuba. Both rebels and crewmen were court-martialed immediately. Every single man on board the *Virginius* was sentenced to death. Ryan was . . . one of the first executed by firing squad."

Reeve hung his head. In his mind's eye, he pictured the Torontonian riding his black stallion, pulling his leg, leading his squadron's charge, presenting him with his oilskin before leaving for New York.

"Luckily, an English frigate came into port," Battle continued. "The captain found out what was going on and told the Spaniards he would shell their bloody fortress unless they stopped the executions. So they stopped. But fifty-some men had already been shot."

"Butchers."

"Yeah."

Reeve stared fixedly at the flame for a few moments before breaking the silence. "We've lost two pillars: Agramonte and Ryan. Politicos should pay heed. While they argue, heroes die."

"It's war, Reeve," said Luaces.

"I didn't know that. I thought we were playing soldiers. Playing dead is hard, though."

Luaces lowered his eyes to the ground.

"Now, Battle, is there any other bad news you've been asked to keep from me?"

"No, Henry."

"Honest?"

"I give you my word."

"Then I guess I'll turn in. When are you leaving?"

"At dawn."

"After breakfast," said Luaces.

"We don't want to trouble you."

"Just coffee and crackers."

"Very well. We'll have breakfast with you."

"See you at breakfast, then," Reeve said. Wearing a serious expression, he got up and hobbled out. Battle sighed deeply.

"Doc, give it to me straight. How is he?"

Luaces lifted a hand to signal a pause, stood, approached a crack in the wall of *yaguas,* and spied on Reeve as he reached the hut where convalescents lodged; after seeing him go inside, he returned to his seat.

"He'd have stayed here until midnight, shooting the breeze, if you hadn't told him the news on Ryan. That hit him hard," the doctor said.

"Well, he asked and you nodded."

"I know."

"You figure—not now, I know, not now, but in a month or two—you figure he'll be able to . . . resume command of the squadron?"

Luaces shook his head. "No. I don't think he'll be able to ride a horse, much less command a cavalry squadron. The bullet must have damaged the head of the femur and the pelvis. His leg seems severely disabled. To put his left foot into the stirrup, he would have to support all his weight on his bad leg. Suppose he can. He won't be able to swing his right leg over the saddle. But even if he found a way to do it, riding may prove impossible for him."

"How so?"

"You know something about the human body?"

"Not much."

"Oh, well. I'll try to not sound too . . . medical. As horses walk, canter, trot, or gallop, as they swerve right or left, as they buck, horsemen keep their balance because their muscles and joints react instinctively. Henry's feet, calves, and thighs would be moving constantly. The head of his right femur and its socket are damaged, so he may well be in pain every time he rides. How much pain? I don't know. Henry being Henry, he may endure whatever pain he experiences, but maybe the pain will be unendurable."

"I figure he won't be able to charge, either," Battle said, as though talking to himself. "I mean, you have to bend forward, swing the machete, turn right and left in the saddle. You reckon he could do that?"

"No chance, I'm afraid."

"Has he asked when you'll discharge him?"

"Every week or so. I've told him not before March. But he doesn't give up. He keeps moving around the camp, goes every morning to the clearing where we keep four crow baits and two burros and tends after them. I warned him that if he tries to saddle and ride a horse, I'll report him to General Gómez. That'll keep him quiet for a while. Besides, he's too weak."

A reflective silence followed. Battle puffed on his cigar. The hut was filled with the potent aroma. Then he spoke again.

"You know what, Doc? We've lost in his prime the most courageous soldier I've ever met."

"I know."

"What a waste."

"I know."

"I guess I'll turn in now, Doc. See you in the morning."

"Sleep well, Battle."

Supine in bed, his head supported on interlaced fingers, Reeve was wondering if he had become a soulless beast of war. Ryan had been a friend; they had shared language and, to a certain extent, cultural values, too. He had served under him, had taken a liking to Ryan, and the man had reciprocated. Yet, Reeve's sadness was mild. When Agramonte was killed, he hadn't cried, either. He measured their deaths in military terms only: loss of leadership, of tactical brilliance, of audacity. He failed to see them as men with parents, wives, and children who would mourn them; men with dreams, expectations, and beliefs. He hadn't been so unfeeling before coming to Cuba. When he learned that President Lincoln had been assassinated, and when sixteen-year-old Richard fell from an elevated track and died, tears had welled up in his eyes. Yet, although Agramonte had meant more to him than a president he hadn't seen and a neighbor he had gone to school with, his sadness had been bearable, his regret mild. It was even more bearable and milder concerning Ryan.

The best he could do to honor their memory was to keep fighting for Cuba Libre, he concluded, and to that end he had to complete his recovery. He would exercise his leg daily, master his pain, eat like a horse to recover his strength, and if riding proved difficult, well, he could do what Julio Sanguily did, have himself strapped to the saddle. Now, what was that contraption Sanguily had devised? Eventually, Reeve slumbered.

However, the next morning, after seeing his visitors off, El Inglesito fell completely and uncontrollably in love and all his noble ideals about Cuban independence were temporarily deferred.

For Henry Reeve, she had the most beautiful liquid brown eyes in the entire world, and the sweetest, yet saddest look of all. He found stunningly attractive the thick reddish brown hair cascading down to her waist. The colonel also found adorable her full lips and the rosy angelic skin of her wide unlined forehead and high cheeks. Her neck was gracefully thin and slightly blue-veined, as were her hands. Her name was Anunciación, which in English meant "announcement". It was the Spanish term for the day when the Archangel Gabriel announced to Mary that she was carrying God's son in her womb.

Any other man would have gladly agreed that the nineteen-year-old virgin was a good-looking young woman, albeit she stood a mere five one, weighed a hundred pounds, and was noticeably shy and rather unassuming. But to the mesmerized Reeve, she was the loveliest, most perfect human being born

since God made Eve. His heart raced and his legs felt all wob-
bly every time he saw her. He spent sleepless nights imagining
tender scenes where he told her how much he loved her and
wanted to marry her and she timidly admitted that she adored
him, too. But all his firm resolutions to approach Anunciación
and introduce himself the next time he ran into her vanished
the instant she entered his field of vision, especially if she was
coming his way.

Reeve assumed he had been able to conceal from all the
roaring emotional fire consuming him, but even the less per-
ceptive souls in the hospital realized that the top-ranking patient had fallen head over heels for the daughter of a patient.
Luaces, like most physicians, a keen observer of humankind,
found baffling that love would transform a totally fearless
warrior into an openmouthed idiot incapable of mustering the
courage to approach the object of his affection and make his
feelings known. He knew a few abject cowards who didn't
think twice before making advances toward any woman they
fancied. He started wondering about how love affected different types of men. He gave it up, reckoning he had much more
important things to do.

Anunciación Filomena de la Concepción Heredia Menocal
had been born on March 25, 1854, in a small hamlet named
Jobabo. Her mother had died giving birth, and she'd been
raised by an older sister. On the morning that Reeve's visitors
departed, her father, a lieutenant in the rebel army suffering
from typhoid fever, was admitted to the hospital. She arrived
with him and stayed at his side from morning to midnight, then
lay down in a hammock alongside Rosa's at the *bohío* especially
built for the field hospital's sole woman. After two days of this,
not wanting her to catch the disease, Luaces asked Anunciación
to step outside for a moment. The doctor complained that his

staff was overworked; help was urgently required and would be most appreciated. Would Lieutenant Heredia's daughter be willing to lend a hand? She readily agreed.

The young woman cherished having a reason to leave the gloomy *bohío* where her father and three other delirious patients were kept. She would rather boil hospital linen, update the inventory of pharmaceuticals, help the cook, or perform any other chore than spend eighteen-hour days watching how her father, unconscious most of the time, wasted away, but she felt guilty about it. Moving around the camp, she experienced a strange combination of relief and remorse. Absorbed in her thoughts, she failed to notice the fair-headed, slightly built, lame young patient who watched her from dawn to dusk.

On November 30, Lieutenant Heredia died. Reeve was among the convalescents who expressed their condolences to Anunciación, but she was so devastated that all she could do was shake hands and mutter "Thank you" to each mourner. But at the internment that afternoon, the accented Spanish of the man saying a prayer intrigued her.

"Depart, dear brother Federico Heredia, out of this world in the name of the Father, who created thee, in the name . . ."

For the first time ever, Anunciación shot a glance at Reeve. El Inglesito always closed his eyes to pray, but on this occasion he was staring at the woman he loved as he intoned in Spanish what he had learned in English. When her gaze fell on him, he had to muster all his courage to mumble the rest of the prayer.

". . . of the Son . . . who, who redeemed thee, and . . . in the name of the . . . Spirit, who redeemed thee . . . whole. Amen."

Dr. Luaces and Rosa la Bayamesa exchanged a glance and wiped smiles from their faces.

"Do something. Keep her here," Rosa said that evening to Luaces.

"What can I do, Rosa?"

"I no know. Tell her she insinpendable."

"Indispensable?"

"What you say I am."

"You are indispensable, Rosa. She is not. I won't kick her out, but if she wants to leave, I can't keep her against her will."

"You say her she indinpen . . . whatever, and ask not leave. I take care of rest."

"Rosa, I know what you are trying to do."

"So?"

Luaces paused and looked off thoughtfully as he searched for reasons. "Maybe she's in love with someone else. Or maybe she is not attracted to cripples; in case you don't know, Henry will limp for the rest of his life. Besides, she'll be in mourning for a year or two. No decent woman would marry while in mourning. If Henry can't engage in battle anymore, perhaps he will return to his country, to his family and friends. But even if he stays here, that girl can't—"

"Sh, docto. You put oxcart ahead oxen. You fix leg. I fix heartache. Do something. Keep her here."

Luaces always avoided making Rosa angry, so he asked Anunciación if she would stay at the hospital for a few weeks, until he found another person willing to lend a hand. He added that she had become indispensable. The young woman said she was so grateful to Dr. Luaces and Rosa for having cared for her father that she would remain at the hospital to help in whatever way she could for as long as she was needed. What's more, she had no place to go. Her home had burned to the ground and she suspected the Spaniards had torched it.

Four days later, after lunch, Rosa began her offensive.

"In morning, Inglesito saddle horse," the black woman said, pretending to be enraged.

"Who is Inglesito?"

"He can't ride. He know. But his head? Hard as rock."

"Who is Inglesito?"

"He alive, thank God and Docto Luace. Now he want ride and go back war. He crazy. Too soon he go back."

"Rosa, who is Inglesito?"

"You no know?"

"No."

"He prayed at you daddy burial."

"Oh, yes. I remember him. Is he from England?"

Rosa had grasped years earlier that, concerning love, white people dragged two chains: religion and convention. African cults glorified sex, whereas Christians considered it a sin. Whites deeply in love announced their engagement and then convention dictated they had to wait a year or two before getting married and having sex. If one of the woman's parents died, the mourning period could reach five years, and no Christian woman would marry while in mourning. Concerning sex, she found whites ill-advised. But these two were white, so she spun her web slowly and waited six days before making the introduction.

It happened on December 10. That day, Capt. Federico Diago, the Camagüey Corps adjunct, and a five-man security detail rode to the hospital to inform Reeve that the Chamber of Representatives had promoted him to brigadier general.

Mesmerized by love, nothing was further from Reeve's mind than a promotion. The news baffled him.

"Me, a brigadier general?"

"Yes, sir, you," Diago confirmed.

"But, but . . . why?"

Diago cleared his throat. "Well, sir, I'm not aware of the factors the Chamber weighed, but I reckon they took into account all you've done for Cuba Libre and . . . that you were wounded at Santa Cruz."

"I didn't want to be wounded! Cowards are wounded, too, and nobody promotes them."

"Well, sir, you ask me, wound or no wound, no man I know deserves the promotion over you."

Reeve ran his hand through his hair and shook his head, pretending to be in dismay and nonplussed, but in fact, he was very pleased. Anunciación would be proud of him, he thought.

"What's all the fuss about?" Anunciación asked Rosa that evening.

"Men happy 'cause Inglesito promoted."

"Oh. What's he now? Lieutenant?"

"Brigadie general."

"Is that more important than lieutenant?"

"Oh, girl. Genral is . . . more than lutenan, more than captan, more than commander, more than colnel. Genral is big chief."

"Oh my. He's so young."

"He hero, girl. He very big hero. He most brave man of all. But he sweet, he kind. Maybe you thank him for prayer, and congrotel him, yes?"

Half an hour later, a proud Rosa approached Dr. Luaces's smoke-filled *bohío*, which was full to bursting with a dozen men who, after supper, went there to boisterously celebrate the promotion.

"Inglesito," Rosa shouted from the doorway, wrinkling her nose at the smell of burning cigars.

Silence descended; all turned and stared at her. "Yes, Rosa," Reeve said.

"Come here. Plis."

Reeve exited. The night was cool and starred. He took a deep breath of clean air. "What's the matter, Rosa?"

"Congrotelation."

"Thank you, Rosa. But you are a general, too, the general of all Cuban nurses. To the last day of my life I'll remember how you—"

"Shut up. Friend of mine want congrotel you, too. Come with me."

To everyone's delight and to Henry Reeve's sheer bliss, by Christmas Eve Anunciación had fallen in love with the new brigadier general. Every single day, after supper, they spent until midnight sitting together in Rosa's presence. She was the only other woman at the hospital and the girl was an orphan, so Rosa assumed the role of chaperone. She knew this was totally wrong, but she had to respect white people's ways, even if white people didn't respect black people's ways.

They chatted, sighed, stared, and when Rosa nodded off in her *taburete*, they held hands for brief moments and whispered the terms of endearment lovers have been murmuring since time immemorial.

Reeve learned that Anunciación had been home-schooled by her sister. She had read nine books, including *Don Quijote*, *La vida es sueño*, and translations of *The Count of Monte Cristo*, *The Hunchback of Notre Dame*, and *Pride and Prejudice*. In Spanish magazines she had learned about the United States in general, and Washington and New York in particular. She knew that snow fell from the sky in those cities, that people skated on frozen lakes and ponds, and that slavery had been abolished after a long and bloody war between the Northern and Southern states.

Her father had been a moderately prosperous cattle rancher. In 1870, he had freed his ten slaves and joined the Liberation Army. She'd kept living at her father's with her sister, brother-in-law, two nephews, a niece, and a cook. Eventually, the Spanish Army had confiscated the herd, and six months earlier a mysterious fire had burned their house to the ground. The rest of the family had moved to Puerto Príncipe, but one of her father's friends had helped her to locate him. She'd ridden to his camp and told him the news. She had begged the lieutenant to let her stay there washing, cooking, and helping out in all she could. He had reluctantly agreed and she had spent nearly five months there, until her dad fell ill.

Their first serious conversation took place at night on New Year's Eve, as they waited for Luaces's Breguet to say it was twelve. There was a chill in the air and their clean yet ragged clothes weren't warm, so they had draped clean sheets around their shoulders. Rosa, sitting two yards away, had warned Anunciación the sheets were to be boiled again in the morning.

"What are we going to do, Henry?"

"What do you mean?"

"I am in mourning. You are still convalescent. We have no money, no land. We can't get married. What are we going to do?"

In a fraction of a second, it dawned on Reeve that he had not reflected on any of this. Even worse, since meeting Anunciación, he had not given a thought to returning to the squadron, to finding out if he could ride again, and, if that proved impossible, to mulling over his future.

"I don't know," he said. "But we'll think of something. We'll defeat the Spaniards soon and then we'll get married."

Rosa smiled.

"Oh, Henry, I love you so much."

"And I love you immensely, Anunciación. I have never loved any one, not my parents and sisters, even less my friends, as I love you. I started loving you the first time I saw you."

"You are so sweet."

"You bring out the best in me."

Rosa rolled her eyes.

"But how are you going to make a living once we win the war?"

After an instant, he said, "I have no idea."

"Henry, after the war, will you stay in Cuba or go back to Flatlands?"

"I haven't thought about that. Hmm. Your rival is Cuba. I began to fall in love with Cuba before I met you. But now that the most beautiful woman in the world is a Cuban who loves me and, on top of that, I love Camagüey, we may go visit my family once a year, but we will live here."

Good reason to feel smug, Rosa thought.

Anunciación clapped in delight, then knit her brow. "Maybe you could get a job as bookkeeper or teller at a bank."

"Maybe."

"I could be a dressmaker. I cut and made dresses for my sister and my niece."

"You won't have to. I'll support you."

"But I want to help you."

"You will help me by cooking my favorite meals, keeping house, and waiting for me to get home and kissing me."

"Oh Henry."

"We've never kissed."

"I am in mourning, Henry. You know I have to show consideration for my father's memory."

Rosa felt so sorry for both of them that she shook her head compassionately.

"I know."

"We will kiss endlessly when the war is over and we get married."

Anunciación was as ignorant about sex as Reeve had been before meeting Ramona. The day her sister calmed her fears and explained that menstruation was not a disease, she added that people only slept together to have children and that love and fornication were two different things.

"Kiss only?" Reeve asked.

"Of course, my love. We can't have children until we can provide for them."

Rosa grunted.

Reeve was confounded. Had he fathered a child with Ramona?

"Of course," he said.

"Henry?" Anunciación said after a five-second pause.

"Yes, my love."

"Do you have to go back to your squadron?"

"I'm afraid so."

Rosa knit her brow. Afraid?

"Oh, Henry, if something happens to you, I'll die."

"Nothing will happen to me, my darling. Well, I may be wounded. But if that happens, Rosa and Dr. Luaces will be there for me. Won't you, Rosa?"

No response.

"Rosa?"

"Uh?" she replied, pretending she had been dozing.

"I was telling Anunciación—"

"One minute to twelve!" shouted Luaces from his hut.

1874

From the next morning on, Reeve started reflecting on his outlook. He wanted to spend every minute alongside Anunciación, but common sense and experience told him that couldn't be. Marriage wouldn't convert them into Siamese twins, like the Chinese brothers Barnum had brought to New York and who became the talk of the town. His father went out early in the morning, returned at lunchtime, left again, and reunited with his mother in the evening. Should the war and Anunciación's mourning end simultaneously, thus permitting them to get married, he would still have to make a living. They would spend evenings together, though, sleep in the same bed and make love.

But the war wouldn't end anytime soon, he felt sure. Going back to the squadron meant renouncing the woman he loved. Did he want that? No, he didn't. Could he return to active duty? He didn't know, so he decided to find out. He fulfilled his New Year's resolution to stop using the cane. And a few minutes before midnight on January 5, once Anunciación and Rosa went to bed, and seeing candlelight escape through the cracks of Luaces's *bohío*, he decided to have a talk with the physician.

"Doctor, you still up?" he asked from the doorway.

"No, I'm sound asleep. I sleep sitting up and with a candle burning," Luaces said, lifting his head from the letter he was penning. The surgeon was sitting behind a small writing table. What a coincidence, he thought.

Smiling, Reeve went in. "Sorry to interrupt; I know it's late. Listen, Doc. I have to find out if I can ride again. My leg is not what it used to be, but the pain's gone, so I want your permission to ask someone to help me tack a horse and get on it."

Luaces sighed. He had been replying to a letter from Gen. Máximo Gómez, in which the Dominican had asked about Reeve's condition. The doctor capped the bottle of ink and rested the stylus alongside the paper.

"Well, to tell you the truth," Luaces said, "I'm not surprised at all. I know you discarded the cane, which is good, and that you spend the better part of most mornings with the horses, so I figured you'd eventually try to ride one."

"Is that a yes?"

"Provided you agree to certain conditions."

"Which are?"

"First, a man holds the horse steady as you mount. Second, left foot in the stirrup, you grab the pommel, pull yourself up. Then you rest your right foot on a *taburete* another man holds. Next, gently and very carefully, try to swing your leg over the saddle. It may hurt. You may not be able to mount the first time you try. Don't force it. Stop. Try again the next day."

"Anything else?"

"Just walk the horse, no cantering or trotting."

"All right. Would you demand that an adult take the lead and walk in front of the horse? Like when a four-year-old rides a pony?"

Luaces chuckled, shook his head, then grew serious. "Listen, Henry, I know you. If it hurts, you'll grind your teeth and say you feel fine. Don't do that. If it hurts now, it may hurt less in a month or two, or nothing at all in six months. If it hurts, it means the bone and the joint are not yet ready, that they need more rest. Don't force them."

"I won't."

"Then you have my permission."

It did hurt, but not as much as Reeve had feared. He realized that Luaces's advice was sound: He could only mount and dismount if someone held a *taburete* to rest his right leg on before lifting it and swinging it over the saddle. He should ride smaller horses so as not to overburden Antonio with too tall a stand. What worried him most was that he had to keep his left hand gripping the pommel. His body constantly slid a little to the sides as the horse cantered or trotted. But when he pressed his right foot down in the stirrup to regain equilibrium, a sharp pain ran up that side of his hip and groin. The only way to restore balance was by pulling at the pommel with his left. He would fall off the animal if he failed to do that. But being right-handed, he would still be able to swing the machete and shoot firearms.

Was the Lord letting him know he had done all he could for Cuba Libre and it was high time to get married and live a normal life? Or was he looking for an excuse to remain at the side of the woman he loved? Had the wound made him a coward? Had love made him a coward? Maybe he could insert the leather strings riveted to the saddle's left rear housing under his belt and tie a knot. That should prevent him from sliding rightward and free his left hand. And if it didn't, then he would find out about the leather contraption utilized by Julio Sanguily to strap himself to the saddle. If nothing worked, he would ask to be honorably discharged with a clear conscience.

Tying himself to the strings helped, but it didn't solve the problem. Because of his riding, walking without the cane was more painful. After twenty or so steps, it hurt, really hurt. He tried to conceal this from all, but Dr. Luaces *knew* what was going on and Rosa had the experience to *guess* what Reeve was living through. Neither was fooled by the patient's smiles and reassurances. On January 23, Reeve had another serious conversation with Luaces.

"Doc, I need to find out about that leather thing General Sanguily uses to strap himself to the horse."

"Why?"

Trying to make it sound funny, Reeve explained the sliding problem. Luaces listened with a solemn face.

"I can draw you the thing," Luaces said after his patient finished. "It's a harness. We can send a letter to the Najasa leather workshop, asking them to make one for you. They know; they made Sanguily's."

"Great! Let's do it."

Luaces nodded in agreement as he wondered whether he should say what he had been mulling over for weeks. He decided to take the plunge.

"Listen, Henry. You outrank me, so from a military standpoint, I have to—"

"Oh c'mon, Doc, this has nothing—"

"No, let me finish. I'm a junior officer. I'm not supposed to argue with you. But I'm also a doctor. You can't fool me. I know it hurts; walking, riding, it hurts. I haven't spied on you when you take to the bushes to take a crap, but I've seen you carry your oilskin and a jugful of water. I know why. You have to shit lying down 'cause you can't squat, and after you are through, you wash the oilskin."

Reeve reddened and lowered his eyes to the ground.

"Your willpower is admirable, as is your devotion to the cause of Cuba Libre. You've fought gallantly for four years, you've been wounded four times, and you've proven conspicuous valor. But you can no longer sustain the rigors of camp life. As a doctor, I have to warn you: You keep pushing yourself to the limit, your leg and hip will get worse and worse and the day will come when you will be confined to a wheelchair for life. The time has arrived for you to take it easy. You are twenty-two years old, Henry. You are in love with a fine young woman who loves you dearly. You can go back to your country and live in peace. You could work for Cuba Libre in New York, with the Cuban exiles. But you can stay in Cuba if you wish. I'm sure the government of the Republic in Arms will consider it a privilege to employ your services as . . . as . . . an adviser or . . . I don't know, something. As a doctor, as a friend, and as a Cuban, I ask you to give up this crazy idea of going back to the squadron. With all due respect, you shouldn't, Brigadier General."

Without a word, Reeve turned around and hobbled away.

Three days later, early in the morning, Gen. Máximo Gómez and his security detail of two dozen men visited the field hospital. Accompanied by Luaces, Gómez spent around twenty minutes in a question-and-answer session with the six fully conscious patients, stared for a few moments at the three who were unconscious or sleeping, visited the kitchen and the pharmacy. He paced the graveyard, where thirty-one rebels were interred, and on his way back greeted Anunciación, who was boiling linen in a huge pail near the kitchen. He had a quarter-hour chat with Rosa la Bayamesa before spending a full hour talking in private with Dr. Luaces. The paramount tête-à-tête, the real reason for his visit to San Diego del Chorrillo, was the ultimate thing Gómez did.

"How are you feeling, Enrique?" he asked, smiling and gazing into Reeve's eyes. They were at Luaces's *bohío* by themselves, sitting, hats hung atop the rear posts of the *taburetes*, facing each other.

"I'm sure Dr. Luaces gave you his opinion on that."

"He certainly did. But you know medics. You let them rule, all one can do is party and have fun," he said, attempting a light touch. "They would proscribe trains 'cause they derail, horse-drawn carriages 'cause they turn over, horses 'cause folks fall and break bones. They would order all knives and machetes melted to prevent people from cutting themselves. They hardly ever weigh the consequences. You tell them that without machetes there are no cane cutters, no sugar, they just shrug. It's why I want you to tell me how you feel."

Reeve smiled. "I'm feeling well."

"Well, General?"

Reeve took a deep breath, averted his eyes, sighed.

"No, in fact, I'm not well. But I hope soon I'll be able to ride. Yesterday, I ordered a . . . thing from the leather workshop at Najasa, sort of a harness, similar to the one used by General Sanguily, so I can strap myself to the saddle. When I get it, I figure I'll be able to return to my squadron."

Gómez stared at Reeve for a moment or two. Reeve stared back.

"Listen, Enrique. Cuba needs you and I need you. We are at an especially defining moment. Nonetheless, if you reckon that you are no longer fit to serve, rest assured that not one rebel will doubt your courage. There are hundreds of men who haven't met you and yet respect you on account of hearing about El Inglesito and the things you've pulled off. Your war record ranks among the most distinguished, and all of us will respect your decision. I'm certain the government of the Republic will find ways to express its gratitude for your years of service."

Again, Reeve breathed deeply.

"Thank you, General," he said. "In a month or so, I will know if I can or cannot rejoin my squadron. If I'm certain that I'll become an impediment to my men, limit their maneuverability and fighting ability, I'll resign my rank. If that is not the case, I'll keep serving Cuba."

"Very well. But don't force your leg. Maybe you need two months, or three. Take all the time you need. There is no hurry."

"I will. Now, sir, tell me about my squadron. How are my men doing?"

Five minutes later, the conversation was over. As Reeve limped alongside Gómez to the clearing where the detail waited, he recognized the sound he had been unconsciously missing since Diago's visit: the faint jangling of spurs when a rider walked. Those insurgents who knew El Inglesito spotted him and came forward. One by one, they shook hands, wished him a fast recovery. The others, who had heard about but never met the fabled warrior, eyeballed him from a respectful distance. After a minute, Gómez nodded to the chief of his security detail.

"Mount!" the man hollered.

All hurried to their horses. A soldier rode away ahead of the others to let the posted sentinels know they were leaving. Gómez's orderly brought his horse.

"I see you keep him," Reeve said.

"It's a fine animal."

"Glad you like it."

Gómez extended his right hand. Reeve took it.

"Hope you rejoin soon."

"I hope so, too."

"Take your time."

"I will, sir."

Gómez turned around, reached for the pommel, and heaved himself up. His orderly was the last to mount. The older general saluted the younger one. Reeve saluted back. Then Gómez giddyapped his horse. Reeve kept his eyes on the party until tears clouded his vision.

Henry Reeve's plans were in a state of flux for the next three weeks. In the mornings, he did all he could to adapt to the harness a man had died for. The only reason Luaces had sent a man to Najasa was to bring the harness to Reeve. The Afro-Cuban had been two leagues away when a band of *guerrilleros,* Cubans who fought for Spain, spotted him and gave chase. The freed slave knew the region well, so he spurred his horse and managed to escape, but he took a bullet in the back and died an hour after he surrendered the harness to Reeve. "Here you are, General," he had said with a feeble smile.

This gave Reeve one more reason to learn to ride with the damn thing around his waist, swing the machete, and even gallop a little. To regain his strength, he asked for second helpings. To rest his leg, he started using the cane again when moving around the hospital grounds. But at nighttime, when he watched the smiling Anunciación approaching, his heart melted and his resolve dwindled. By the time he went to bed, he was utterly confused, so he prayed: Oh Lord, please guide me. What should I do? I love her so much. But I came to this island to fight this war. Please show me the way.

But the Lord never spoke to him.

"Many men use canes because it's fashionable. Is that why you are using the cane again, Enrique?" Anunciación asked one evening.

"I just want to . . . you know, not force the leg when I move around."

"Well, if it makes you feel better, that's good."

After a moment, she said, "You haven't told me what you and General Gómez talked about."

"Military things. Nothing you'd understand."

A fresh pause ensued.

"Did he . . . I mean . . . does he want you to . . . go back?"

"Well, yes. He wants me to rejoin my squadron and said my boys ask him every time they see him if I'm getting better and when he figures I'll rejoin. But he said I should take all the time I need, make a full recovery before going back."

"I don't want you to go back."

"I don't know if I'll go back."

"But you harness yourself and ride every morning. I've seen you trotting and swinging the machete. It seems you are practicing 'cause you want to go back."

Rosa gave a firm nod.

"What I'm trying to find out, my love, is if I can still do the things a cavalryman does. That I won't be a burden to my squadron should I rejoin."

"So, if you decide you won't be a burden, will you leave?"

"I'm afraid so, darling. Rosa and Luaces will look after you, and I will visit whenever I can."

Rosa gave another firm nod.

"Henry, you talk as if you would be going to Puerto Príncipe on a business trip! You would be going to war, darling. I love you. If something . . . terrible happens, I can't live without you. I don't want you to go to war, because I don't want you to run any more risks and because you're the most important person in my life."

"And *you* are the most important person in my life, Anunciación. I love you like . . . I haven't loved anyone in my whole life. I love and miss my family, but what I feel for them is nothing compared to what I feel for you. But please, my love. Try to understand. The Major? Agramonte? Have you heard about him?"

Anunciación nodded and wiped a tear from her cheek. "My father admired him very much."

"Well, he had a wife whom he loved very much, too. They had a son. But he concluded that he would betray his homeland if he stayed at home while other men—"

"But Cuba is not your homeland, Henry."

"It's as if it were, darling."

Anunciación sobbed, got to her feet, and ran away.

"Anunciación! Anunciación!" Reeve called after her as he struggled to get up, but she kept going and rushed into Rosa's *bohío*, where she lived.

Rosa sighed and stood.

"Rosa, what can I do?"

The black woman slowly turned to face the white man she ranked third in order of preference. Number one was Agramonte; number two, Dr. Luaces.

"Do what you think better," she said staring intently. "You think you can't go back squadron, stay here. You think you can go back, do that. You go back, she never unnerstand; never. All women want men they love at their side. All. Even the Major's wife. Don't worry; good women resign themselves after time abandoned. Anunciación good woman. So-so women find other man. Good woman realize her man has values, put hide on the line, has *cojones*. That comfort her."

The next evening, Rosa interceded and they made up. But from then on, as both tried to avoid the paramount subject on their minds, conversations turned forced and awkward when they were not cooing to each other and swearing their love would last forever. They would stare at and comment on the star-studded heavens, the moon, discuss the shapes of clouds drifting over it, the call of night birds and bats, the weather, the most recently admitted patient, the meals. Reeve abstained from mentioning military subjects or the news he had learned from Luaces or new patients.

By virtue of the phenomenal healing power inherent to the human body, El Inglesito gradually got better. Walking and riding, he experienced less pain in his right leg. The left one, after months of inactivity, slowly but surely was getting stronger. The combination of rest, standard nourishment at regular hours, and exercise made his wiry pectorals, biceps, and triceps regain their full strength and endurance. He got accustomed to the harness and drew conclusions. Smaller horses were easier to mount and dismount; more to the point, their flanks were narrower and his thighs were not as spread apart as with bigger animals, like Tiger. The less spread, the less pain. So he would have to find a rather lean, medium-size horse. That wouldn't be a problem, he felt sure; soldiers' horses were not as tall and wide as generals' horses.

On February 1, after lunch, Dr. Luaces asked Reeve to his *bohío*.

"The reason I'll ask this is not personal curiosity, all right?"

"All right."

"Have you decided what are you going to do?"

"You mean concerning . . ."

"Rejoining your squadron."

Reeve bit and then released his upper lip. "I am not one hundred percent sure," he began, "but I'm feeling much better. I have no pain. I'm—"

"Hey, it's me, Luaces, your doctor," the physician said, jabbing his forefinger at his chest.

Reeve looked confused. "Yeah, so?"

"Don't lie to me."

"Lie?"

"About feeling no pain."

"Oh, well, I feel a little pain."

"A little pain?"

"Well, when I ride, it gets worse, but it's endurable."

"How many hours are you riding now?"

"A couple."

Luaces stared at Reeve and nodded before marching to the small table where he kept several bottles, picking a green one, and turning to face his patient.

"Come here."

With three steps, Reeve reached him. Luaces uncapped the bottle.

"This is salicylic acid. Extend your hand, palm up."

The intrigued Reeve did as he was told. Luaces tipped the bottle and about a gram of colorless crystalline needles fell in the hollow of his hand.

"Touch the tip of your tongue to it."

Tentatively, Reeve complied, sucked his tongue, and made a face.

"So bitter."

"That's right. Listen," said Luaces as with thumb and fore-finger he recovered the acid remaining in Reeve's palm and returned it to the bottle. "If you rejoin, you'll spend ten to twelve hours on horseback. Then this 'endurable' pain you experience will be worse. This will help you; it's a painkiller that's good for the bones and the joints. Take half of what I just put in your hand, dilute it in water, and drink it when you need it. But mind you, this is hard on your stomach, so take it only when the pain is intense."

Luaces capped the bottle and extended it to Reeve.

"All this for me?"

"You'll need it. I have more. Got a fresh shipment this morning. I also suggest you start riding three hours next week, four hours the following, so your leg will get used to the punishment."

"'Punishment'?"

"General, why don't you go take a nap?"

Battle's second visit took place on February 16 and both men had a long conversation. The commander updated Reeve on all significant developments and then learned the brigadier general was getting ready to rejoin the squadron.

"Really? When?"

"Soon. Tell General Gómez I want you, Antonio, and six men to ride here on the morning of February 27, a Friday. Bring a horse that's lean and short. Have him wormed and free him of ticks, lice, and botflies."

"You mean a crow bait?"

"The best crow bait you can find. And a light saddle."

"Why the dickens, Henry?"

Reeve explained, then added, "I have my Colt and twenty-one cartridges with me. Bring me my carbine."

"And clothes."

Looking mildly surprised, Reeve lowered his eyes to his clean rags before smiling at Battle. "I reckon I ain't dressed fittingly for a brigadier general."

"You sure ain't."

The evening of February 26, an emotional hurricane lashed two souls, maybe three, as Rosa's eyes misted over a few times.

"My love, tomorrow, Battle, Antonio, and six men will come to the hospital."

"To pay you a visit?"

"Not exactly."

Anunciación had a premonition. She turned a little in her *taburete* and stared at Reeve.

"Why are they coming, then?"

"They are coming . . . to get me."

She swallowed twice; a tear trickled down her nose.

"Are you telling me you are leaving of your own free will, Henry?"

"Yes, I am."

She grabbed his hands. "Henry, please don't go."

"Darling, I have to rejoin the—"

Anunciación slid from the seat and got down on her knees. "Henry, I beg you, for the love of God, please, stay with me."

Rosa dropped all pretense of indifference and stared.

Reeve choked and sobbed. "Please, my love, stand up, please."

"I won't stand up before you swear you won't leave."

"Stand up, please. I can't kneel," he said, rising.

Rosa got to her feet and in two paces reached Anunciación.

"Girl, raise, please, girl," she said, grabbing Anunciación's forearms and forcing her to stand.

"Take me with you," Anunciación bawled.

Once Rosa had forced Anunciación to sit, Reeve tried to explain why she couldn't go with him, but the young woman was so frustrated and panicky, her mind could not process his reasoning.

"You won't take me with you?"

"I can't take you with me, darling. It's impossible."

"It's not impossible. I lived in my father's camp."

"That was different."

"No, it's not."

"Yes, it is. We are constantly on the move. The only places where women can stay are the Najasa workshops or one of the infirmaries or field hospitals."

"If you don't stay here and you refuse to take me with you, your love is not what I thought it was."

"You are my reason to live."

"No, war is your reason to live."

Stunned, Reeve leaned back in his seat. Was she right? With trembling hands and a heaving chest, Anunciación kept her flaming eyes on her fiancé.

"This war is important," Reeve said, racking his brain for a proper refutation, " 'cause Cuban independence is important. I want you to be free. I want all Cubans to be free."

"You know what I want, Henry?"

"I know. You want to be with me."

"In second place. First of all, I want you to *live*! I want you to live even if Cuba remains under Spain. I lost my father in this war. I lost my home. I fear I will lose you. Damn the war, damn independence!"

Rosa clucked her tongue in disapproval.

Reeve shook his head in dismay. "Listen, honey. We met thanks to this war. I have . . . risen through the ranks and now I lead over a hundred men who respect me, a few even admire me. Do you want those men to think that a Spanish bullet made me a coward?"

Her head lowered, Anunciación was crying silently. Her hunched shoulders shuddered.

"What kind of example would I be setting? That when one is shot one hangs up his fiddle and goes home?"

She raised her head. "Isn't love a reason?"

Reeve considered it. "Yes, it's a reason. But most of my men left behind wives and children. Battle? My second in command? He adores his wife and daughters. But he hasn't seen them since he joined the Liberation Army. He confided to me that he thinks of them every single night. Can I tell Battle that I won't rejoin my unit 'cause I found the love of my life?"

The discussion went on and on for two hours. Anunciación cried her eyes out, Reeve's tears flowed more than once, and Rosa, the hardened woman who had looked death in the face on countless occasions, was moved to tears twice. The heart-to-heart talk dragged on and on. It would have gone on until sunup had not Anunciación suddenly gotten to her feet and run away.

Reeve felt simultaneously relieved and sad. He shot a sidelong glance at Rosa.

"What do you think, Rosa?"

She gave a deep sigh. "Love, war—bad mix."

"I can't say to my men that I am deserting them 'cause I'm in love."

"But you can say can't ride no more."

"But I can ride, Rosa."

"You can say can't ride. Can say too much pain ride horse, walk. Nobody know how much pain you suffer."

Reeve nodded. "Yeah, that's true. Tell me, Rosa. What do you figure the Major would've done in my place?"

Feeling he had her there, Rosa smiled for the first time that night. "You know what he do," she said.

"Tell me what you figure he would've done."

"Two legs amputated, two arms amputated, Major would go back just to shout 'Viva Cuba Libre' to Spaniards."

"That's the kind of man I want to be, Rosa."

*   *   *

The next morning, a heavyhearted Reeve was about to mount his horse, when Rosa approached him. She held a folded paper.

"Come to say good-bye and give you this," she said.

Reeve took the paper and slid it into the pocket of his new long-sleeved shirt.

"She's not coming?"

"No. She says that says what she says. She awake all night."

"Tell her I will love her until the last day of my life."

"She know. She, too."

Reeve shook hands with Luaces before hugging and kissing Rosa. "I love you, too, Rosa," he said with watering eyes.

"Go now, man."

Reeve turned. A made-to-order three-foot-tall stool was placed alongside the lean thirteen-hand seven-year-old stallion with a blaze on his head, the mount that Battle had chosen. Pascual and Nicolás, who had scouted with Reeve for more than two years, stood by: one held the reins, the other Reeve's harness. Once El Inglesito had both feet into the stirrups, Nicolás handed the harness to Antonio. Following Reeve's instructions, the orderly helped the general strap himself to the saddle. The rest of the men mounted. Then Pascual drew the reins over the horse's head and Reeve took them. Antonio picked up the stool and fastened it to the back of his saddle before mounting his horse.

"On your order, Brigadier General," Battle said.

Reeve turned and glanced at the *bohío* where Anunciación and Rosa lived. No one stood at the door. Next he locked gazes with Luaces.

"Thanks for all, Doc."

"You're welcome, General."

He moved his eyes to Rosa la Bayamesa.

"See you soon, Rosa."

"God bless you."

"Men, ride!" Reeve ordered.

That night, before going to sleep, he read:

I love you with all my heart, mind, and each and every bone and muscle in my body. I love you since I was born and until I die. I love you because of how you are; I love you despite how you are. I love you because loving you is the greatest of pleasures and the most heartbreaking of sufferings. As I love you, I become part of you; I disappear in you. As I love you, I grow old and retract to childhood at the same time. I love you because my only reason to live is to love you.

From the next day on, life took a new meaning for Reeve. His dearly loved, distant fiancée displaced Cuba Libre as his be-all and end-all. He started paying attention and enjoying things that had left him unmoved in the past: the concerto performed by a dozen species of warbling birds at sunup, the soft babbling of a stream when riding riverside, the respectful concern of his subordinates, the loving gaze of the skeletal canine bitch that followed him everywhere. Those and other gifts from nature stirred emotions that he shared with Anunciación. Watching him smile without apparent reason, Antonio, Pascual, and Nicolás, who lost sight of Reeve only when he hobbled into the undergrowth to defecate, exchanged intrigued looks, then lifted their eyebrows and pulled down the corners of their mouths in incomprehension. They couldn't imagine he was conversing with her. *Aren't those birdsongs beautiful, dear? Day and night that stream murmurs that I love you. See, they are my friends; they take good care of me, don't fret. Wouldn't you like to have puppies from her?*

She intensified his urge for achieving final victory, which made him even more audacious. His orderly and escorts discussed the situation. Antonio felt sure that Oyá, the *orisha* of the strong winds, had taken Reeve under her protection and nothing would happen to him. Pascual and Nicolás reckoned that Oyá wouldn't mind should they lend a hand. For two and a half more years, they would flank Reeve at charges and bludgeon with their machetes all Spaniards behind their general's back, and at his sides, too. Reeve couldn't fail to notice, but he didn't resent it. He knew he needed it on two counts: his physical limitation and his desire to marry Anunciación and grow old at her side.

Henry Reeve returned to the battlefield with a serious internal conflict between his greatly enhanced survival instinct and his extraordinary courage.

At a bivouac midway between San Cayetano and Ciego de Najasa, beneath a canopy of teak, cedar, mahogany, fruit trees, and numerous royal palms, Maj. Gen. Máximo Gómez finished updating El Inglesito on the overall military situation. Both men sat in hammocks as their orderlies and adjuncts performed their duties, keeping out of earshot and shooing away noncoms and soldiers wanting to take a peek at Reeve. The flames of his legend had been fanned by onlookers who had watched from a distance as Pascual and Nicolás helped their young brigadier general unfasten his harness and dismount. El Inglesito was back, they told anyone who lent an ear. He couldn't walk; escorts had to carry him in their arms; he had to strap himself to the saddle; he was looking good; the countless women he had fucked claimed he had grapefruit-size *cojones* and a thick ten-inch-long prick. A year ago, he had single-handedly beheaded nineteen Spaniards (three hours later, the number of severed heads counted by an unnamed eyewitness was fifty-five); both he and his horse finished drenched in enemy blood. Beware *gallegos*. El Inglesito was back.

Reeve had learned from his superior that he would lead Gómez's Independent Cavalry Squadron; the Camagüey Army—cavalry and infantry—was under Julio Sanguily. Gómez had reliable, albeit not yet official, information, that the government and the Chamber of Representatives, frustrated that peace reigned west of Camagüey, had decided to take the war as far away as Havana. In a few weeks, Brig. Gen. Antonio Maceo and his men, from the Eastern Department, and the infantry from Las Villas, under Brig. Gen. González Guerra, would join Gómez to organize and carry out the invasion. The Dominican general was not at all pleased by the rumor that the full Chamber and all members of government would join him; they would hinder the soldiers' progression, he argued.

"Now that you are back, I want you to hear it from me," Gómez said to Reeve as they were concluding the exchange.

"What, sir?"

"Someday someone will tell you I was opposed to your getting promoted to brigadier general."

For a moment, wondering, the frowning Reeve stared at the older man. "Well, I guess you had a reason. To be promoted solely on the ground that I was wounded—"

Gómez shook his head energetically and raised his hand. "No, no, wait, let me explain. You deserve the promotion; I wasn't opposed to it. What I opposed was the procedure. As your commanding officer, I should have proposed your promotion. The Chamber has the authority to approve or deny promotions to colonel and general, but not before a general submits them in writing, and I hadn't. They didn't even have the courtesy of consulting me. So, I wrote a letter expressing my disagreement with the procedure, not with the promotion. But as versions change over time and there's so much dissension among politicos, I'm sure someone will tell you that I opposed your promotion."

Reeve nodded twice and pursed his lips. "I see."

"I wanted to wait until you got well."

"Of course."

"How do you feel?"

Reeve smiled. "I can't say I'm as good as new, sir. But all things considered, I'm fine."

"How many hours did it take you to get here?"

"Three and a half."

"Did it . . . hurt?"

"No, General. I had been practicing, riding as long as four or five hours a day around the hospital. Dr. Luaces used to say I reminded him of a kid in a merry-go-round."

Gómez forced a smile. "Good. But I want you to take things easy for a while. Do not charge until you feel combat-ready."

Reeve pondered how to better word his objection. "Sir, I lead men."

"So do I. Have you seen me charge?"

"Yes, I have."

Gómez grunted in annoyance. "Well, maybe once or twice. When victory was uncertain, morale low. But a commanding officer is not supposed to risk his life unnecessarily. Your courage has been amply proven. You can order a charge and remain behind. Nobody will accuse you of cowardice."

"I know that. It's just that—"

"General Reeve, I'm giving you a direct order. I forbid you to lead cavalry charges until I say so. Is that clear?"

A pause ensued. Agramonte came to Reeve's mind. The Major would've tried to reason him into staying behind. "It's clear, sir," he said.

Gómez lowered his eyes to the ground and clucked his tongue. "For God's sake, Inglesito, don't force me to pull rank on you. Go rest now."

For the next few days, sheer willpower made Reeve do without salicylic acid, but one night he couldn't sleep and took more than a gram dissolved in water. Soon after, his pain started decreasing. A quarter of an hour later, it was bearable; before an hour, he was sleeping soundly. The next morning, his stomachache was so severe he refused the gourd of coffee his orderly brought. Lunch around eleven in the morning—sweet potatoes and dried beef—extinguished the fire in his belly. Similar episodes made Reeve realize he should always take the medicine after meals.

One evening, Antonio unintentionally discovered that the son of Ogún had to lie down to defecate. The next day, the orderly took Battle into his confidence. When Battle's eyes moistened, Antonio felt sure the commander would help him out. The illiterate orderly suggested that Battle measure the length and width of the seat of a *taburete* and made a drawing. Perhaps he could also ask the Najasa workshops to build a removable wooden seat *and* a removable hollow wooden frame, both having identical dimensions.

If they were made, Antonio explained, before Reeve went to the bushes to defecate, he would take the rustic chair to wherever Reeve wanted, remove the seat, put on the frame, and leave. Once the general finished, he would recover the *taburete,* clean it if necessary, and affix the solid seat. The added advantage was that at all other times Reeve could sit comfortably. Antonio had been assigned a mule to transport Reeve's personal possessions: a change of clothes, the stool he utilized to mount and dismount, his diary and official papers, and a few odds and ends. The animal could carry the *taburete,* too.

Three weeks after telling Battle, Antonio presented the peculiar chair to Reeve and described its purpose. Reeve had stared for a long moment at his orderly before hugging him tightly—one of the many reasons El Inglesito felt brotherly love for Antonio.

On another evening, as he was tying Reeve's hammock to the trunks of two young teaks, Antonio made a suggestion.

"Genral, you give permission I prepare bed in ground?"

"What do you mean?"

"I cut grass, collect dead leaves, put hammock over them. You lie down on left side, try sleep one night. You give permission?"

Four and a half years outdoors had persuaded Reeve that Afro-Cubans knew much more about life in the open than other people. He might as well give it a try, he thought.

"All right, Antonio. Do it."

Once Reeve was lying down on his good side, Antonio offered a fresh suggestion.

"Genral, bend legs."

"What?"

"Like this."

Gently, Antonio maneuvered Reeve's legs until both knees were drawn in toward his chest. At four, he awoke flat on his back, his bladder about to burst. But he hurt less than when he slept in the hammock.

While sipping his coffee, he said, "Antonio, from now on I'll sleep on the ground. Thanks."

"You welcome, Genral."

"How did you know?"

"My father, back ache, always slept like that."

On March 12, the members of the government and reinforcements under Antonio Maceo and González Guerra arrived. Gómez reviewed the troops. Later, as introductions were made and the officers socialized, Reeve shook hands with Antonio Maceo.

"General Maceo, meet General Reeve," Gómez, the proud owner of two top-class gamecocks, announced.

Maceo's eyes narrowed a little and the hint of a smile pulled at the corners of his mouth. "Glad to meet you," he said.

"It's my pleasure, sir."

"I've been told you are American."

"That's right."

"Why do people call you El Inglesito?"

"I have no idea."

"Do you reckon Cuba should be annexed to the United States?"

"I do not."

"That makes me even gladder to have met you. At your service."

"Likewise."

Gómez and Maceo moved on. Maceo's chief of staff faced Reeve and they shook hands. Afterward, from a distance, Reeve studied the newly arrived. Light-skinned black, late twenties, nearly six feet tall, powerful build, wide face, jet black eyes, full beard, trimmed mustache with twisted tips. He had the lithe movements of a large mountain lion. And lion he was, according to rumor. Antonio, his father and brothers, all freemen, had joined the insurgents days after the uprising started, in October 1868. Soon thereafter, Gómez had named Antonio his adjunct, but before long the Dominican grasped that the man's uncommon valor and quick mind were worthy of superior endeavors. Maceo had meteorically risen through the ranks because of his innate sense of military tactics, leadership qualities, discipline, and raw courage.

Over the next two days, the generals discussed strategy and scheduled the invasion. As it was his custom, Reeve kept a respectful silence and gave his views only when asked.

He was already lying on the ground on the evening of March 14 when, out of nowhere, Antonio Maceo materialized and sat on his haunches alongside Reeve, who tried to scramble to his feet. Maceo placed his hand on the disabled man's shoulder.

"Please, don't." This was uttered in a gentle tone, a request. But out of courtesy, Reeve sat on his left buttock, supported himself on his left hand.

"What can I do for you, General?"

"Well . . ." Maceo let his gaze roam. "I want to know if you feel . . . in the mood to meet someone tonight."

"Who would that be?"

"On my way here, the last night, we camped near a hamlet a couple of hours away. I met two beautiful sisters there, half-breed, true patriots. I spent the night with Carmen. Incredible woman. Next morning, as I was leaving, her sister, Pura, asked me if I knew El Inglesito. I said I didn't but that I would meet him soon. Then she said she had heard so many fantastic stories about El Inglesito, she was dying to meet him. So, I wonder if you would want to ride with me there tonight and meet Pura."

Reeve smiled and shook his head in wonderment. The randy whoremonger. "No, General, thanks. I am in love with a Cuban girl. We are engaged. I will marry her when the war is over."

"I'm sure Pura won't ask you to marry her."

"Yeah, I know. But I won't cheat on my fiancée."

"Sleep well, then," Maceo said as he stood and sauntered away, wondering if all Americans were so upright.

Grinning widely, Reeve's orderly approached him.

"He same name I," he said.

"I know. You like him?"

"He honor to my race."

"Forget race, Antonio. He's a brave man; you're a brave man, too. Let's go to sleep."

"What he want with you, Genral?"

"Antoniooo . . ."

"Good night, genral."

At dawn, a Cuban sentry let through a collaborator who reported that five leagues away, at Jagüey de San Pedro, a huge enemy column seemed to be hunting for rebels. Gómez asked Reeve to send explorers out. A few minutes later, the Dominican frowned as he watched Antonio Maceo returning to the field camp. He waved his ex-adjunct over.

"Where were you?" Gómez asked.

Maceo shot a swift glance at Reeve, who shook his head.

"I went to take a crap, sir."

"On horseback?"

"I was looking for a clean spot. All the underbrush around here is covered with stinking turds. How long have you been camping here?"

"All of a sudden, you start acting like a señorita," Gómez fumed. "Get your men ready. It seems an enemy column is heading this way. I'll go see if the government will authorize me to engage with them."

"Excuse me, Major General," Maceo said in disbelief. "Are you asking the government's permission to engage?"

"The government is here, Maceo. When they are fifty leagues away, I make the decisions and assume the responsibility. But civilian authority overrides that of the military. I have to ask them. Never forget that."

The government told Gómez he should act as he considered best, thus clearing the way for the most important military operation ever waged on Cuban soil, the battle of Las Guásimas. Gómez deployed fifteen hundred men around his chosen battlefield, a huge savanna between a hill and a four-line cattle fence, hours in advance. Then he sent Cuban riders to tempt the enemy into giving chase and bring them to the selected terrain.

"You think the Spaniards are stupid, Battle?" Reeve asked his friend, who was to his right, as usual.

Three squadrons had been positioned at the fringe of the wood, covering the small elevation. Gómez put them all under Reeve, expressly indicating Reeve's squadron was to be kept in reserve. The two other units were under Col. Gabriel González and Col. José Surí, who knew and idolized El Inglesito.

"I don't think so. Why do you ask?"

"You think they are stupid, Gabriel?"

"No, sir."

"What do you think, José?"

Surí took off his hat and scratched his head. "Well, sir, some Spaniards are stupid. But some Cubans are stupid, too. Why do you ask?"

"Because they keep making the same mistake, battle after battle, year after year."

"Yeah, I know," Gabriel said. "We send a group of riders, they show themselves, the Spanish cavalry gives chase, and they ride right into our ambush."

"Exactly," Reeve concurred. "Why?"

The silence lasted almost a minute. Halfway into the pause, horses pulled their ears back, wondering what made these talkative two-legged creatures, so lazy that they always rode on their backs, keep quiet for so long.

"Maybe the officers we ambush are sent back to Spain before they get a chance to fraternize with their substitutes, pass on their experience," ventured Gabriel.

"Could be," said Reeve.

"I don't think so," Surí said. "It's a problem of pride. Spaniards are too proud. They refuse to admit that a bunch of improvised soldiers are kicking their asses over and over again. The notion that we outwit them is inadmissible, so they figure we were lucky and next time they'll wipe us out."

Battle, always the scholar, opined, "Maybe it's half and half, lousy communication and too much pride."

Reeve shot him a sidelong glance. "Maybe. But I guess they'll eventually learn the lesson. Then we'll have to figure out something."

"But I hope we get to trounce them today. Oh, please, Holy Mother of God, please, let us rout the bastards," said Gabriel González.

The short invocation made Reeve ponder whether God's Mother ever took sides, as lots of Spaniards were probably requesting the opposite of her.

Over two hundred enemy riders fell into the trap and the Cuban infantry fusilladed them. Then Reeve sent two squadrons to finish the job. The day concluded with great carnage.

Having lost part of their cavalry, the Spaniards excavated trenches at the center of the savanna, forming a huge square, hoping to fend off the attack.

"The man must be crazy as a loon," El Inglesito said to Battle, who had tied his hammock near Reeve's, spread on the ground; both were hoping to snooze two or three hours. "He should have sounded retreat and gotten the hell out. Instead, he locks himself in."

"Perhaps out of pride," Battle ventured. "You know, not to be accused of having fled with his tail between his legs."

"Perhaps, but he's going to pay for it."

At intervals throughout the night, the Spanish brigadier general sneaked out four dispatch riders carrying notes that requested reinforcements be sent. The rebels captured two, but two got away. Even so, it was not until March 19 that two thousand men led by Brigadier General Bascones reached Las Guásimas under hostile fire. That evening, Bascones persuaded Armiñán that their position was indefensible. The next morning, the victorious but exhausted and red-eyed rebel officers watched the enemy retreat.

In merely five days, the Spanish army's casualty toll reached 1,037 men. Twenty-nine rebels had died; 130 were wounded. Strategically, however, that victory set back the Liberation Army, because nearly all the munitions held in reserve to conquer the western part of the island had been spent. The invasion had to be deferred.

During April and early May, not wanting to prolong the postponement indefinitely, the rebels restocked, eluded important military engagements, and just harassed the enemy. Hostilities all but ceased when the rainy season began and the Spanish troops barracked.

Distant flashes of lightning and the rumble of thunder were so frequent that humans and animals got accustomed to them; they froze only when lightning struck nearby. Humidity made Reeve miserable. Even though he wore Ryan's oilskin constantly and kept dry while sleeping in a ramada erected by Antonio, Pascual, and Nicolás, his old wounds hurt, especially his upper thigh and hip. He took so much salicylic acid that he suffered from indigestion, nausea, and vomiting. When his mood became as dark as the clouds that hid the sky along the four points of the compass, he went over Anunciación's letter in his mind, which he had read so many times that he knew it word for word. He was hurting all over the day Máximo Gómez sent for him.

"I have a very important mission for you," the Dominican said.

"At your service, sir."

"The biggest responsibility you've ever had."

"I'll try my best."

"I know you will. So, I'm asking you to ride under escort to San Diego del Chorrillo and take a one-week pass. When you come back, I will explain the mission to you."

"But, but General, I—"

"Dismissed."

"With all due—"

"I said, dismissed."

Reeve always obeyed orders quickly, but this time his haste amazed all. Their reunion at noontime the next day was a sight for sore eyes. Anunciación was hanging bed linen on the clothesline when Reeve and his seven escorts arrived. She stared, unsure, holding her breath, her pulse racing faster, until a black rebel jumped to the ground, unfastened a stool from the hindquarters of a mule, and approached a white man still on his saddle. She dropped everything and broke into a sprint.

Custom dictated they should abstain from embracing or hugging, but she threw herself in his arms and rained kisses on his face and lips. Reeve's hat fell to the ground, and, struggling to keep his balance, he embraced her tightly. Antonio stood back-to-back with Reeve pretending to care for the general's horse; in fact, he was hoping to provide support if El Inglesito lost his balance. Suddenly, she drew apart from Reeve and gripped his arms.

"Are you wounded?"

"No, my love."

Again she embraced him, renewing her kissing spree.

The rumble of hooves as the party came into the clearing had made staff and convalescent patients emerge from *bohíos*. Men were chuckling; a few clapped. With outstretched arms and smiling widely, Rosa hurried to the couple and brought them even closer with her hug. Luaces stepped out of his hut and approached Reeve's party.

"Well, well, look who's here," he said.

Anunciación kept her arms around Reeve as tears started streaming down her cheeks.

"Now, now, girl. He salute others now, yes?" Rosa whispered in her ear.

Anunciación nodded and stepped back, wiping away tears. Reeve kissed Rosa and shook hands all around. After the exchange of greetings, Luaces mentioned that three of his riders were recovering in the hospital, and Reeve, flanked by his fiancée and Rosa, followed the physician to where they lay. As Agramonte's loyal disciple, he conversed with all conscious patients, made them feel important and esteemed.

The insurgents were almost certain the enemy hadn't learned about the field hospital, but Reeve's escorts began carrying out Battle's precise instructions. Antonio's sole responsibility was to care for Reeve. Nicolás and Pascual led two trios that would perform outpost duty day and night. Should Spanish troops get closer than a thousand varas, they were supposed to evacuate the general to a safe place, even by force and against his will if necessary.

Goaded by Rosa, Luaces told Anunciación to take the rest of the day off. The couple spent the afternoon sitting and cooing to each other at the clearing, not to flout convention. In the evening, it started drizzling and they moved to Luaces's *bohío*, the most appropriate spot to be indoors, as nobody could suspect they would even kiss in the presence of the doctor. But around nine, Rosa asked Luaces to check on a delirious patient.

"Rosa, he's better than he was this morning," Luaces affirmed after examining the man.

"You think so?"

"You know he is, Rosa. What's the matter? I'm warning you, don't hornswoggle me."

In frustration, the black woman stamped on the packed-earth floor. Why white people were so dumb concerning love? "General and girl in your hut. Give them little while alone," she said.

Thus, for the first time ever, the sweethearts were able to kiss passionately and incoherently murmur words of endearment. Half an hour after obliging Rosa, Luaces headed for his hut. He started harrumphing and coughing loudly fifty varas away from the doorway.

After Anunciación retired at midnight, Luaces asked Reeve to bunk at his *bohío*. The doctor listened intently as his patient and friend mentioned that he slept more comfortably lying on the ground on his left side, both knees drawn toward his chest, and Reeve gave all the credit to Antonio. Then Luaces confessed his perplexity concerning the understanding of the human body and the remedies for sicknesses that black people had accumulated from time immemorial. He mentioned a few of the amazing things he had learned from Rosa. Reeve nodded as Luaces expressed his amazement that covering a wound with mold hastened healing. The American mentioned that salicylic acid alleviated his pain but ruined his stomach. Luaces gave him precise instructions on how much to take after meals and then refilled Reeve's bottle. They kept talking until after two, when the emotionally drained general fell sound asleep.

The week was unforgettable for the lovers. Reeve had the physical benefit of a much-needed rest and the spiritual fulfillment of spending time with the woman he loved. But suddenly it was their final night together, chaperoned, as always, by Rosa. Time had simply flown. It felt as if a mantle of melancholy had fallen from the heavenly vault dotted with a trillion pinpoints of light.

"Life is so short, Henry."

"I know."

"Since you went away, I've been thinking. People get sick and die unexpectedly at any age—they drown, get struck by lightning, fall and break their necks. My mother died giving birth to me. Hurricanes and earthquakes kill more. Some are hanged or garroted. Thousands starve or freeze to death. And all that makes me wonder, if so many die before reaching old age, if happiness is so elusive, why do men fight so much? Couldn't you resolve your differences in courts of law? Are wars inevitable?"

Rosa grunted.

Reeve remained silent, head bowed.

"Do you know the number of men who have died here from gunshot or machete wounds since I started counting? Twenty-two. That most likely means twenty-two widows and maybe fifty, sixty, or seventy orphans. And that's just here. I'm not counting those who die from disease, like my father, because nobody can be certain they wouldn't have fallen ill and died if Cuba were at peace. The number of those who die in battle and get buried in the middle of nowhere is anybody's guess. Why do you wage war, Henry?"

Reeve lifted his head and took a deep breath.

"Nothing I say would change your mind, my love. I beg you, let's not argue over such complicated . . . things. I don't want this night to end like our last together back in February. Let's dream the war will end soon and we'll get married and be happy and have many children."

"Yes, let's dream."

Resignation never breeds happiness, though, and all of Reeve's efforts to lift her spirits failed. As part of her preparation for the inevitable, she had promised herself she wouldn't behave as desperately as she had a few months earlier, so she managed to fight back tears and put on a brave face when Rosa, in deep slumber, almost fell from her *taburete*.

"Uh," the black nurse mumbled.

"Let's go to bed, Rosa," Anunciación said while standing up and gently caressing the woman's shoulder. Reeve got to his feet, too. Rosa stood and yawned prodigiously.

"Is it late?" she asked a moment later.

"Very late, Rosa, time to go to sleep," said Anunciación. "Good night, Henry. I'll see you off in the morning. Will you leave after breakfast?"

"Yes, my love."

"Until then. Let's go, Rosa."

The next morning, she approached Reeve's group with a sad yet loving and beautiful smile on her face. Unconcerned by the presence of others, she embraced the man she loved, kissed his cheeks.

"Take good care of yourself, Henry. I don't know what I will do if I lose you."

"I'll be careful. And I shall visit you again as soon as I can. I may not be able to spend a whole week, but a day or two may be possible. At least six or seven hours."

"I'll always be waiting for you."

Reeve did his stirrup-stool routine and mounted. Antonio helped him strap himself to the saddle. Seeing this brought tears to the eyes of both women. Nicolás handed Reeve the reins. Reeve blew a kiss to Anunciación and waved to Rosa, Luaces, and the patients watching.

"Men, ride!"

He lacked the courage to look back.

SIX

★

Reeve reached the camp near Ciego de Najasa a little after ten, and Battle immediately reported that a day earlier one of his subordinates, Aquilino Acosta, a white lieutenant in his late twenties, had allegedly raped a fourteen-year-old girl. The previous evening, the teenager's father had ridden his wretched crow bait to the camp, asked around until he found Acosta, and then challenged him to a machete duel at the top of his voice. Others intervened and the fight was prevented. Perplexed, Battle took the poor peasant aside to determine the cause of his anger. Right away, he placed the accused under arrest and notified General Gómez. The trial was to take place in the afternoon and Reeve, as the squadron's superior officer, had to be the judge. He asked Battle to fetch Capt. Serafín Sánchez, and without further ado, the three of them and a six-man security detail rode to the family's *bohío*, half a league away.

The father had missed work, the mother was cooking lunch, and the girl was in bed. The parents affirmed that a week earlier

Acosta and two scouts, while reconnoitering, had stopped at their humble home, met the head of the household, and exchanged pleasantries with him. The lieutenant had returned on three occasions, in the evenings and on his own, to chat and sip a gourd of coffee. The unsuspecting adults had befriended him. Acosta learned that the father spent the day working at a nearby farm; the teenager, her mother, and a four-year-old son were on their own from dawn to dusk. It was why Acosta's last visit had taken place the previous morning, the parents assumed. When the mother excused herself to go to a well two-hundred varas from her home to fetch a bucket of water, the lieutenant said he would be glad to do it for her if her daughter would ride pillion on his horse to show him where the well was. Half an hour later, the adolescent came back home alone, in tears, hauling the empty bucket, her face scratched, her arms bruised, blood trickling down her thighs.

Reeve questioned the victim last; Battle and Sánchez only watched and listened. A very late bloomer, she looked three or four years younger than fourteen because she was under five feet tall, had a flat chest and narrow hips. She answered the general's questions while looking at the packed-earth floor in red-cheeked embarrassment. "Did the man who, ahem, treated you badly, ask you to . . . do something to him?" Reeve asked as softly as he could. The girl nodded. "Did you refuse?" She nodded again. "What did he do then?" The girl remained silent, staring at the packed-earth floor. "Did he leave?" She shook her head vigorously. "Did he threaten to harm you?" The youngster gave three firm nods. "Did he force you to do things you didn't want to do?" "Yes," she replied in a whisper. "Did he beat you?" "Yes." "Make you lie down on the ground?" "Yes." "Before leaving, did he warn you against telling your parents?" She nodded. "Did he say what he would do to you if you told your parents?"

"Yes."

"What did he say he'd do?"

"He'd wring my neck and break it, like Mamá kills chickens."

Reeve thanked her and asked her father to ride back to camp with them.

The trial began at three o'clock sharp. Battle served as prosecutor, Capt. Serafín Sánchez was the defending counsel. No tables were available; the three officers, the accuser, and the defendant sat on *taburetes*. Attendance was compulsory and the squadron formed a circle around them. Reading from a paper, Reeve announced that Lt. Aquilino Acosta was charged with raping an underage girl and that the trial would try to determine whether he was guilty or innocent. Then he asked the girl's father to stand up and tell all those present what the defendant had done.

"That man," he said, pointing a finger at Acosta, "forced my child yesterday morning. She is in pain, dishonored, no longer a virgin."

Nobody expected the peasant's allegation to be so brief; for a moment, stunned silence reigned over the clearing.

"Thank you," Reeve said eventually. "You may sit down." Then, turning to the accused, he asked, "Do you plead guilty or not guilty?"

"Not guilty, General. The girl was burning with desire. She begged me to make love to her."

"That's a lie!" hollered the father, jumping to his feet.

"Keep quiet, Don Jacinto. Please sit down. Prosecutor, do your job," Reeve said.

On his feet and raising his voice so all could hear him clearly, Battle made known that the judge, the defending counsel, and he had interrogated the accuser, his wife, and the victim earlier that day. Next, within ten minutes, he recounted how and when the accused had met the family and won their trust. Acosta had willfully and purposefully abandoned his platoon the day before, with the intent to commit the rape, Battle went on. He had deceived the girl's mother, sexually assaulted a minor, and threatened to kill her should she tell her parents what he had done. Having heard the testimony of the girl and her parents, and having seen the scratches and marks the victim had on her face and arms, Battle said he had no doubt whatsoever that Lieutenant Acosta had committed the crime he was being tried for.

Battle mentioned next that any sort of wrongdoing brought shame and disgrace on the entire Liberation Army. The Cuban people wouldn't believe in, trust, or provide for the Liberation Army if its soldiers, noncoms, or officers raped, pillaged, stole, murdered, or committed any other crime against the peaceful civilians they were striving to liberate from the Spanish yoke. It was why he asked the defendant to be found guilty and condemned to capital punishment.

"Your turn, Captain Sánchez," Reeve said as Battle sat down.

Serafín Sánchez stood and said the possibility that the girl had deceived them couldn't be discarded. Maybe she had aroused Lieutenant Acosta.

"You lying son of a whore!" the victim's father shouted, standing up.

Reeve ordered him removed from the court-martial.

Once this was done, the defending counsel argued that even if it could be proved the girl had been unwilling to fornicate—which had not been proved, as the defendant's version contradicted the accuser's and there had been no witnesses—the judge should take into account the lieutenant's military record. Aquilino Acosta had joined the Liberation Army as a plain soldier two years ago, had been wounded once, had been promoted to corporal, to sergeant, and then to second lieutenant. Since January of this year, he'd been a platoon leader. Should the Liberation Army lose a distinguished combatant? Wouldn't it be better to demote him to soldier and give him the opportunity to win back the trust and respect of his brothers in arms?

"The defense rests, General," Sánchez concluded.

"Very well. I will now pronounce sentence," Reeve said. "I find you, Lieutenant Aquilino Acosta, guilty of rape and sentence you to the death penalty. The defense counsel knows he can lodge an appeal with Major General Gómez. If he confirms the sentence, you shall be hanged tomorrow at sunup. May God have mercy on your soul. This trial is over."

There were rumblings of both approval and disapproval throughout the squadron.

Acosta rose, his eyes flaming, and in a hateful tone fulminated Reeve: "You rotten, good-for-nothing Yankee invalid—"

"Shut up!" shouted Serafín Sánchez, jumping to his feet. Acosta didn't even glance at him, just kept staring at Reeve.

"You have the insolence to sentence me to death? You? After spending an entire week fucking your private whore?"

Reeve, his face draining of color, scrambled to his feet.

"Shut your mouth, imbecile," Sánchez said.

"You shut up, you lousy defender," Acosta replied, "He sentences me to death for fucking a bitch? What about him? He rides his whore much more than his horse. I hadn't fucked in a year."

The two men who had removed the girl's father from the clearing dragged Acosta, kicking and insulting all members of the court-martial, to the supply cart where he had been bound since his arrest.

Reeve was livid, trembling with anger.

"Commander Battle!" he yelled.

"Yes, General."

"Order the squadron into formation."

"What for?"

"Never mind what for, Commander. Order the squadron into formation. Standing at attention, not on horseback. That's an order."

"Henry, please, think. Don't act hastily."

The hardness of Reeve's look made his second in command do an about-face and start shouting the names of platoon leaders. A few minutes later, the squadron was formed.

"Squadron," began Reeve, then paused. "You've just heard Lieutenant Acosta. He accused me of fornicating with a whore for an entire week. That's a damn lie. I have a fiancée; that's true. She works at the hospital where I spent last week; that's also true. But my fiancée is a decent young woman in mourning for her father, who was a lieutenant in our army. We're not married; we've not yet consummated our love, nor will we consummate it before we get married. I give you my word of honor. I went to the hospital obeying a direct order from Major General Gómez; I did not ask for a leave of absence.

"I was not aware that you knew about my fiancée. It didn't cross my mind you could think I went away to fornicate. But I should have realized that most of you have not spent time with your wives in a long while, and you may judge it unfair that your commanding officer leaves camp and has the opportunity to visit the woman he loves. I apologize for not having taken that into consideration. I want all of you to know that I shall write a letter to my fiancée telling her what happened here. That letter will advise her that I won't visit again until all of you have spent at least a day with your wives and kids. At my side stands Commander Battle. The last time Commander Battle saw his wife and daughters was almost six years ago.

Commander Battle is the man you should look up to. Right now I will write a letter to Major General Gómez saying that if I am no longer capable of leading you into combat, Commander Battle should be appointed chief of the squadron."

"*¡Viva Battle!*" a soldier yelled.

"*¡Que viva!*" almost all chorused in unison.

"Dismissed," Reeve shouted.

At eight o'clock in the evening, Reeve, Battle, and Sánchez went into the camp's only *bohío*, General Gómez's abode. It was furnished with a writing table, a tin candleholder, a cot, and a trunk for the safekeeping of documents. With three *taburetes* added to the general's, the place was crammed.

"Good evening, gentlemen."

"Good evening, sir."

"Please take seats."

Hats were removed. Battle and Sánchez waited for Reeve to take the weight off his bad leg, then sat down.

"I have here"—Gómez lowered his eyes to one of several manuscripts on his table—"Captain Sánchez's appeal. Before making a decision, I want to ask a few questions. General Reeve, are you absolutely certain that this officer raped the girl?"

"Yes, sir, I am."

"Commander Battle?"

"I am dead certain, General."

"Captain Sánchez?"

"I'm certain there was fornication. It looks as though he raped her, but it hasn't been proved. I think Acosta's life should be spared."

Gómez cleared his throat and nodded. "And in your opinion, what should his sentence be?"

"Well, sir, were we not waging war," Sánchez went on, "he should be sentenced to years in prison—I don't know how many, as I'm not a lawyer. But since we are at war and have no jails that I know of, I respectfully suggest sentencing Acosta to fifteen years of hard labor, demoting him to private, and having him tend horses, scrub pot and pans, fetch water, and perform all other menial tasks for the duration. After victory, he could be granted a pardon if his conduct has been beyond reproach, or sent to prison for the remaining years."

Gómez gave a nod. "Your thoughts on that, General Reeve."

"I disagree with Captain Sánchez, sir. Civilians within a ten-league radius, maybe more, would learn about such a lenient sentence and lose confidence in us. We don't have jailers to watch over Acosta; the man would run away at the first opportunity. Besides, other subordinates could conclude that raping young country girls is not that great a crime. We may face similar cases in the future and, according to precedent, we would be forced to sentence offenders to years in prison. Are we willing to become a traveling prison?"

The question remained unanswered.

"Commander Battle."

"I share General Reeve's opinion, Major General."

Gómez took a deep breath, stroked his mustache, and lowered his eyes to the paper before his eyes. Then he picked up a stylus, inserted the nib in the inkwell, wrote on the appeal, and signed underneath. Once he carefully positioned the stylus alongside the inkwell, Gómez locked gazes with Sánchez.

"I denied your clemency appeal, Captain Sánchez," he said, moving his eyes to Battle. "Commander, make the necessary preparations to hang the prisoner at dawn. You may both leave now. I want a word in private with General Reeve."

Battle and Sánchez got to their feet, saluted, and left. Gómez moved his eyes from the door frame to Reeve.

"I was told what happened after you sentenced Acosta."

Reeve breathed deeply, lowered his eyes to the ground, and kept silent.

"You did well."

"Thank you, sir."

"Did you bring the letter recommending Battle to lead the squadron?"

"Yes, sir."

Reeve extracted a folded page from the left side pocket of his shirt and extended it to Gómez, who unfolded it and read it.

"You wrote this just in time," Gómez said a minute later as he placed the paper on the table, "because I have a new assignment for you."

"At your service, Major General."

"We won't win this war if we don't break the backbone of the Spanish power in Cuba, which is the hundreds of sugarcane plantations and sugar mills in Las Villas, Matanzas, and La Habana. Most of the slave labor is there, too. Nearly all the money Spain needs to wage this war comes from the west. It's why we will march westward. We kill enemy soldiers, they bring more from Spain a month later. We torch a sugar plantation, it takes a year for the stems to regrow; we raze a mill, they don't rebuild it in one year. We can't destroy mills with bullets and machetes; we will have to raze them, burn them, free the slaves, recruit them for the army. To the west of Camagüey, our main mission won't be winning battles, but torching mills and sugarcane plantations.

"Nobody knows when we will get on our way. It depends on two factors: the dry season and how soon we will be fully restocked. Maybe in July or August, maybe later if the hurricane season is too active. But I'm making plans for reassigning officers and I want to know if you feel well enough to assume command of all our forces in Camagüey when we leave."

Reeve frowned in surprise. "Sir, you mean I would be staying here? Wouldn't go west with you?"

Gómez had foreseen Reeve's reaction. Confirmation brought a smile to his lips. "Agramonte's adjunct made a copy of all letters he wrote to the government. I have them all there." The Dominican moved his eyes to the trunk. "I will read from one of them, dated the seventeenth of December, 1872."

Gómez lifted the candleholder and drew a piece of paper from under it. He angled it for better illumination, squinted, and started reading. "'I need a second in command in Camagüey and, unfortunately, among the many superior officers under me, I have not one with the indispensable aptitudes to second me that this officer possesses.'"

Gómez paused, eyeing Reeve knowingly.

Returning to the page, he continued. "'Bearing in mind all his outstanding qualities, Commander Reeve has gained all my trust and I consider it my duty to highly recommend this young foreigner to the government of the Republic in Arms.'"

Reeve fought a lump in his throat.

"A year and a half have gone by," Gómez said, resting the paper on the table. "You are older, more experienced. People admire your courage. You are well known and respected in Camagüey. You are the best man to assume command over all our forces in the territory."

"What about General Sanguily?"

"General Sanguily will travel abroad to be treated for his ailment."

Reeve kept to himself that he had been hearing that for some time now and yet Sanguily remained in Camagüey. He stared at the ground and racked his brains for a good reason to make Gómez reconsider. "I am a foreigner, General."

"So am I."

"But I am American. And you know to what country the annexationists hope to annex Cuba."

"Precisely. Your not being in favor of annexation speaks in your favor."

"Sir, your strategy of torching plantations and mills will move the war west. You will take with you the bravest men, the best weapons, the best horses and mules. The Spaniards won't stand with their arms folded. They will transfer battalions from east to west. Battles will be waged there, as well."

"Should we all go west and surrender this territory to the enemy?" asked Gómez.

"Of course not, sir. But it would be a privilege to ride west with you. Maybe another general would—"

"Listen, Inglesito." Gómez had had a trying day and was tuckered out. "If for health reasons you think you are not up to the commission, I will designate someone else. But you wouldn't be begging me to ride west with the army should you feel incapacitated. So, be frank with me. Are you not feeling well enough to accept this commission?"

"I am feeling fine, sir."

"Good for you. And good for me. You will assume command of the Liberation Army in Camagüey when the invasion of western Cuba begins. Not a word to any one until then. In preparation for that, next week I will raise a regiment of cavalry, the Agramonte Regiment, composed of ten companies and nine hundred officers and men. You will be its chief. Your squadron, under Commander Battle, will be a company. Any objection?"

"None whatsoever, sir."

"Good. Let's move on. As a brigadier general, you must be protected, have a security detail, four men under one officer—"

"Sir, I don't—"

"Reeve, don't argue with me. All generals, without exception, must have a security detail. I suppose you want those two blacks who always ride alongside you to be part of it, but I want Lieutenant Gabino Quesada to be in charge. Would you object to him?"

"No, sir. Quesada is a fine officer. The Major promoted him two weeks before he died."

"All right. Choose two other men you trust."

"I want my orderly to be part of my escort."

"Your orderly is your orderly and he will ride with you, but he is not part of your escort."

"Well, as long as he rides with me . . ."

"He will. You will appoint an adjunct, too. A literate man who takes dictation and acts as your archivist. Well, you know. I'm done. Anything else you want to tell me?"

"No, sir."

"Then, dismissed."

Before midnight, Reeve was kept awake by the implications of the mission he would have to carry out as soon as the pick of the Liberation Army and the government headed west. In addition to the military side, he would have to deal with political and logistical problems, and he wasn't ready for those, especially the politics of war.

In the small hours, thinking about the execution made him sleepless. Battle would arrange everything, but he had to be present. Who would pull the *taburete* from under Acosta? It would be the squadron's first execution; all would see a new face of death. Sánchez had a point. Under other circumstances, Acosta wouldn't deserve capital punishment. Reeve took comfort from remembering the undernourished girl, her scratches and bruises, her crying mother, her incensed father. He felt confident that probably all other Cuban civilians in the surrounding area would agree that justice had been done.

Battle came for him a little after five the next morning.

"Henry, the sun will rise soon."

"I'm coming. Did you ask the father if he wanted to be present?"

"Yes, he's here. He arrived half an hour ago."

Gómez, Maceo, and their officers were already there when the prisoner, weeping and begging for mercy, hands tied behind his back, was dragged beneath the branch of a huge cedar tree. Acosta kept whining and pleading, saying he would never rape a woman again. He was lifted to a *taburete,* the noose slipped over his head; Pascual yanked the seat. Acosta kicked for nearly a minute and, to the total amazement of those who had never seen a hanging, had an erection and ejaculated. Believing it the work of Satan, many made the sign of the cross. After all signs of life had ceased, Battle regarded the dial of his pocket watch for two minutes. Then he ordered the corpse to be brought down and interred.

White-faced and wide-eyed, the victim's father jumped onto his crow bait and rode away.

Maceo approached Reeve.

"Well done. But you should've stripped him of his rank before hanging him."

July 4

The president of the republic and his staff, several members of the Chamber of Representatives, and Gómez, Maceo, and Reeve were bivouacking three leagues south of Puerto Príncipe when the news arrived that an enemy column was at Merced

Nuñez, a league and a half away. Gómez ordered Reeve to intercept it. Ten minutes later, El Inglesito and two companies from the Agramonte Cavalry Brigade trotted off. Gómez, Maceo, and their adjuncts and escorts joined them.

The mission about three hundred Spaniards—cavalry and infantry—had already carried out had consisted of ensuring the safe arrival at its destination of a long line of wagons loaded with provisions; they were going back to base now, the vehicles empty. The rebels didn't know that and deemed this a golden opportunity to restock.

Having learned from his father that setting a good example was worth a thousand sermons, feeling better, and with the expression "good-for-nothing Yankee invalid" still ringing in his ears, Reeve decided to disobey Gómez's order not to engage in combat. He asked the bugle to play beheading, spurred his crow bait, and, clutching the pommel with his left hand, his revolver in his right, spearheaded twice the number of hollering centaurs he had ever led. A good number of Spaniards barricaded themselves behind the heavy vehicles; the rest ran to the nearby forest, all opened fire. Once the rebels reached the wagons, hand-to-hand combat followed. Maceo, who had remained behind watching, couldn't keep in check his fighting spirit and joined the fracas.

Having spent all his rounds, Reeve holstered his revolver and drew his machete. Chopping the shoulder of the closest adversary, to his left, presented no problem. But swinging at the second man, to his right, threw him so off balance, he almost fell from the saddle. He took hold of the pommel and managed to pull himself up after great effort and what seemed like an eternity.

"Goddamn it," he muttered under his breath.

He watched as Antonio Maceo, three or four yards to his

right, with a powerful swing of his machete, beheaded a Spanish sergeant who had just fired at Reeve. I can't do that, he thought. And as the realization crossed his mind, something numbed his left shoulder. He stopped wondering about the cause of the insensibility when he noticed that a young overweight Spaniard was closing the breech of his Berdan and getting ready to shoot Maceo, who was looking elsewhere. Reeve spurred his crow bait. The Spaniard cocked the hammer. Maceo turned, caught a fleeting glimpse of his rival, and did the only thing possible: duck behind his horse's head. The enemy soldier lifted the stock to his shoulder, pulled the rear trigger, took aim. But before he pulled the front trigger, Reeve's blow almost severed his arm.

Maceo straightened up, smiled, and winked at El Inglesito, then grew dead serious and shot a glance at someone behind Reeve.

"He's wounded. Take him back," Maceo shouted to Antonio and Nicolás, who were both closing in on Reeve. Maceo whirled around, looking for his next Spaniard.

"Wounded?" Reeve muttered. He felt no pain whatsoever.

"Genral! Go back! You bleeding!" Antonio yelled before pulling the reins of his horse right and swinging his machete. It clanged on the bayonet affixed to an enemy rifle. The rifleman dropped his weapon and fled.

"I ain't wounded," Reeve said angrily.

But weeks before Reeve was assigned a security detail, Antonio, Nicolás, and Pascual had foreseen that any day El Inglesito would go back to his old ways, and they had extensively discussed how to react should Reeve get wounded. They had reflected on two scenarios: the general on the ground or on horseback. And since Reeve was mounted and angrily claiming he was all right despite the blood soaking his shirt, Nicolás

and Antonio forced their crow baits to flank the sides of
Reeve's. Nicolás pulled the general's carbine from its saddle
holster and hurled it to Pascual, who caught it in midair and
started firing to cover the retreat. Antonio yanked the reins
from Reeve's left hand. Lieutenant Quesada, the recently appointed chief of the detail, sensed that he had lost the initiative. He recovered fast, though, and started firing his revolver
to facilitate taking Reeve to a safe place.

"What the hell!" shouted the wounded man. "Are you all
crazy? I'll have you court-martialed, the three of you."

Reeve watched the rest of the battle at a safe distance, mol-
lified by the realization that he *was* wounded. Antonio cleaned
his deltoid, which had been grazed by the bullet fired by the soldier Maceo beheaded, and a scratch on his left hand. It was his
first wound after starting to take salicylic acid, and the blood
wasn't clotting properly, but nobody could identify the cause.
By pressing a cloth over the shoulder wound, Antonio managed
to stop the bleeding. Then he placed a spotless linen handker-
chief over Reeve's shoulder and bandaged his hand. Quesada
proved he was a shrewd man. Rather than criticizing Pascual
and Nicolás for ignoring him, he complimented both men and
discussed how they should all act in different scenarios.

Eventually, the Spaniards retreated, leaving thirty-four
corpses on the battlefield. It was then that the insurgents found
out that the wagons were empty. The booty consisted of forty-
two mules, thirty-one rifles, and around two hundred bullets.
Eleven rebels died and nineteen were wounded. Back at the
bivouac, a trained male nurse cleaned and bandaged both of
Reeve's wounds.

"Come here, the three of you," the general said, beckoning
his rescuers over that evening after ordering Quesada to go to
the kitchen and eat his chow. He was lying on the ground, flat

on his back, his knees raised. They approached him and stood side by side, eyes downcast.

"I appreciate what you did today. But you shouldn't have. I could've kept fighting. It was just a scratch. Why did you do it?"

There was no response.

"I want an answer."

No response.

"Antonio, why did you do it?"

Still looking at the ground, Antonio shuffled his feet.

"Now, don't get me wrathy, soldiers. Look at me. Antonio, Nicolás, Pascual. Look at me."

The three men lifted their eyes to Reeve's.

"I can't stay behind every time we charge. All creation will think I'm a coward. So I will charge again and again. If I'm seriously wounded, of course it would be all right for you to take me to a safe place. But if it's a scratch, like today, don't pull me out. You'll put me in a fine puck if you do."

Their gazes returned to the ground.

"Look at me."

Compliance seemed to be the best way to brave the storm.

"You are my brothers. I know you wanted to save me and protect me. But you've got to promise right off the reel you won't do that again, or I'll have to—"

"Sorry to interrupt," a dead-serious Maceo said, coming out from behind a cluster of trees. "I came to inquire how you are feeling, General. But I couldn't help but overhear."

"I'm fine, thank you."

"Don't get up, don't get up."

"Thanks."

"Listen, Inglesito, these men are not to blame. The blood-stain on your shirt was spreading. I had no way of knowing how serious the wound was. I ordered them to pull you out, and they must obey an officer. You want to complain, complain to me."

Reeve moved his eyes from Maceo to his subordinates. "Men, I want to have a word in private with Brigadier General Maceo."

Feeling certain they were in the clear now, all three soldiers disappeared into the woods, but they paused within hearing range.

"All right," said Reeve. "First, I don't give orders to your subordinates, so don't you give orders to mine. Second, they would've done it anyway. This was no spur-of-the-moment thing. They were right behind me, covering my back. I know these folks; you don't. They had discussed what to do if I was wounded. Oh, well. What's the use? By the way, thanks for killing the bastard."

"Well, we're even. Your sockdolager almost severed the arm of that fat *gallego*."

"Yeah."

Maceo took his hat off and scratched his head. "You amalgamate."

"Of course I do. Why wouldn't I?"

"It's not that. . . . I mean, you act different."

"How?"

"Well, some white officers treat black orderlies as . . . if they were still slaves. 'Do this.' 'Do that.' 'Clean my boots.' 'Sharpen my razor.' Others are . . . condescending with blacks. Know what I mean?"

"I reckon so."

"They treat black men like children, call them boys."

"Yeah, I've heard them."

"Like they don't give a damn if they hurt their feelings."

A short reflective silence ensued.

"I suppose," Reeve said, "people don't change overnight. Many Cuban white officers owned slaves. Abolishing slavery is one thing, race prejudice another."

"You may have a point. But tell me, did I hear right? Did you tell those men they are your brothers?"

"Well, maybe I shouldn't have said that, but it's true. Brothers wouldn't look after me any better than those three men. Let's keep that between us, General. You witnessed today the liberties they take with me. If they had their way, I'd ride pillion on Antonio's horse, flanked by Pascual and Nicolás."

Maceo threw his head back and released a throaty laugh.

"It's true; it's true," Reeve said, smiling.

"Don't worry. I won't tell. You know the wagons were empty?"

"I know."

"I wonder why the sons of whores didn't pull foot earlier. What were they defending?"

Reeve weighed the question. "Their honor?"

It seemed Maceo hadn't contemplated that possibility. "You think so?"

"Maybe. They fled when they realized we had them."

"Well, maybe. Get well soon. Good night, Reeve."

"Good night, Maceo."

The mulatto general turned and dashed along too fast for Antonio, Nicolás, and Pascual to disperse and jump into their hammocks. Maceo motioned them over.

"Don't let me catch you overhearing again," he whispered, pretending to be angry.

Their offended expressions made clear such accusation was totally unfounded.

"You better be more careful when covering his back. He's no fool."

This time, they nodded.

"He's a real macho and a . . . nice man."

"We know," Antonio whispered.

"I know you know. So stop acting like you are his mommy."
They frowned.

"Mommy?" Pascual asked, intrigued.

Maceo was at a loss. "Or his big brothers. Dismissed, soldiers."

Soon after, for unspecified reasons, Antonio Maceo and his men were reassigned to Santiago de Cuba. The rainiest August in living memory arrived and military operations ground to a halt. Occasionally, at noon, there was a break in the cloud cover and sunlight streamed through. Then troopers set to drying shoes and clothes; atop trees, buzzards spread their wings. But before long, massive dark clouds streamed in and another downpour started.

Reeve pined for Anunciación, who was a mere four-hour ride away, but going to see her was out of the question. In the longest letter he had ever penned, he had explained the rape case to her, the trial, and Acosta's accusations. He hoped she would understand that he couldn't go back on his word.

Humidity made him hurt all over, so he overdosed on salicylic acid, adding tummy ache, burping, and nosebleeds to his misery. During the long hot days, sweating profusely under the oilskin, he exchanged ideas and recollections with the regiment's senior officers, listened to reports of drenched scouts, scribbled in his diary, wrote letters to his sweetheart, and sipped an herbal infusion made by Antonio (chamomile, mint, old-woman herb, and the root of pine herb), which made him feel better. Four reasons kept him awake at night: physical pain, a repressed sexual urge, nightmares where fat raindrops turned into blood, and the realization that no future was more uncertain than the future of war.

Overseeing the schooling of Antonio, Nicolás, and Pascual was his favorite distraction. Reeve became aware of the full extent of illiteracy in his old squadron the day he chose his adjunct. After Battle had ordered the unit into formation, Reeve had addressed them, saying he would choose an adjunct from among literate noncoms and soldiers. He asked those who could read and write to raise their hands. Out of sixty-one men present, only four were literate. From his copy of *Don Quijote,* he dictated an excerpt to all four. Modesto, a thirty-five-year-old white teacher who had joined the squadron two months earlier, was the best hands down, so he took the man aside.

"Modesto, would you be willing to be my adjunct?"

"I would be honored."

"Good. Did you notice how many illiterate soldiers the squadron has?"

"I did."

"Would you be willing, when there's next to nothing to do, to teach those who want to learn?"

The teacher took off his hat, scratched his head, and lifted his eyebrows in doubt. "Well, we don't have a blackboard, or slates. We don't have chalks. We don't—"

"Modesto, I know what we don't have. Let's see what we have. We have the ground and we have twigs. Writing on the ground with a twig, you can teach them the vowels. Then progress to *ma, mamá*; *pa, papá,* and so forth and so on. Would you be willing to do that?"

"I am willing, Inglesito. But we will—"

"General. 'I am willing, General.'"

"Sorry, sir. No disrespect. We soldiers call you El Inglesito."

"I know. But now you are my adjunct, so from now on you address me as 'General.' It's called military courtesy. You know, saluting, presenting arms, that kind of crap. I couldn't care less, but other officers may reprimand you if they hear you calling me Inglesito." Reeve winked in complicity.

"I understand, General."

"All right. So, your first assignment as my adjunct is to make a list of all soldiers in the squadron who want to learn to read and write; bring it to me tomorrow before sundown. Begin classes as I said—the ground and sticks. At a later time, I'll try to get you paper and pencils. Now, go see Antonio and tell him I want you to sleep where he and the men from my security detail sleep. Now, dismissed, soldier."

Classes began two days later and Modesto discovered that willing adults could learn the vowels and the few consonants he drew on the topsoil. When Reeve assumed the regiment's command, he asked Modesto whom he regarded as most capable among the other three soldiers who could read and write. Modesto said José Caimares was their man, and Battle appointed him substitute teacher. In the regiment, Modesto had only three pupils: Antonio, Pascual, and Nicolás, but Reeve ordered all company chiefs to teach the illiterate. One of Modesto's duties was to act as headmaster to other teachers.

The first two weeks of September were sunny, and Reeve rode with one of his units, the Camagüey Cavalry Company. He wanted to apply the yardstick to its chief, Col. Gabriel González, a Mexican volunteer. It turned out that the man was a good leader: brave, shrewd, with a keen nose for ambushes, and firm yet affectionate with subordinates. On the fourteenth, they learned that seventy Spanish cavalrymen were near Punta de Diamante, a fort not far from Puerto Príncipe. González led the charge, and most colonialists fled to the stronghold. However, sixteen Spaniards—fourteen soldiers and two officers—barricaded themselves in a wooden house to cover the retreat of their comrades in arms. Surrounded and isolated, they proved immensely courageous. The last rifleman bled to death moments after firing the final shot.

". . . fourteen, fifteen, sixteen *cojonudos*" was the admiring comment González made as he finished counting corpses. He and Reeve were inside the house, watching rebel soldiers pick up rifles, revolvers, and bullets. A few hands still clutching firearms had to be pried open.

"Those two killed themselves," Reeve observed, pointing at nearby bodies. "A shot on the temple, revolvers near their hands. Men like these, you've got to respect. It's a shame they sided with a lost cause."

"Yeah. Luckily *cojonudos* like you, the Major, and General Gómez sided with Cuba Libre."

Reeve blushed, mumbled unintelligibly, turned, and hobbled to his crow bait.

On September 20, Gómez and Reeve, under torrential rain, spent the night at Peralejo. Again all military operations had to be canceled for a few days.

Few feats of arms took place in October and November, all inconsequential. Reeve grew impatient and tried to conquer Fuerte Cascorro on November 30. Surrounded by a deep ditch, it had a front door accessible by a drawbridge and a back door where a portable bridge—four oak planks nailed together—was drawn out in the morning and pulled in at sundown. Not to repeat the mistakes made during the failed assault on the Pinto optical tower, Reeve, in the middle of the night, hid forty men in an empty house near the fort and another twenty-five in a pillbox in the vicinity of the enemy stronghold. His plan was that at sunup, as soon as the drawbridge was lowered and the portable one slid out, the men in the pillbox would force the main door and those in the empty house would assault the rear entrance. He also had one homemade wood-and-iron cannon. After the optical-tower fiasco, the Major had argued that a single artillery piece would have changed the outcome.

The drawbridge was lowered and the front entrance was successfully stormed. But the portable bridge was not drawn out and the main force couldn't gain access through the back. Numerically superior, the Spaniards resisted and counterattacked. Reeve ordered his artillerymen to open fire. The initial shot hit the fort, but when the second was fired, the cannon blew up and killed its two gunners. Rebels inside the fort had to retreat. General Reeve suffered his first humiliating defeat.

The next occurred on December 28, when he tried to trounce the garrison at Fuerte Montejo. Informers had reported that at the end of the day most Spanish soldiers enjoyed a leisurely stroll in the vicinity. Reeve intended for the cavalry to mow down as many as possible and then for the infantry to raid the fort. It didn't turn out that way. The sauntering Spaniards, alarmed by something—a weird noise probably—darted back to the fort. All efforts to force open the main door failed and three rebels were killed and eleven wounded before the bugler sounded retreat.

1875

The New Year found Reeve deeply frustrated. Having to control a full regiment was much more difficult than leading a squadron; the failed experiences of Fuerte Cascorro and Fuerte Montejo made him think he was not up to the task. He missed the companionship and sound advice of Battle, who had spent precious little time at his side since assuming command of his previous unit. Physically, Reeve lived in pain. His sentiments concerning religion, second nature to him in the past, had waned. It seemed the Lord wasn't lifting up the meek, nor casting the wicked to the ground; in fact, the opposite seemed to be happening. He increasingly wondered how his father, mother and sisters were doing and would have gladly relinquished his generalship to spend a few hours with Anunciación.

Since early December, General Gómez had been getting ready to march west. His tactical plans included diversionary maneuvers that El Inglesito was to execute. On January 1, Reeve's regiment rode near the railroad track joining Nuevitas and Puerto Príncipe; two days later, he moved nearer the headwaters of the Jobabo River.

The fortified line traversing the island from Júcaro to Morón made the diversion essential. The brainchild of the Spanish general Blas Villate, Count Valmaseda, the Trocha had been built to preclude the possibility of the rebellion spilling westward. Twelve leagues long—roughly forty-two miles—it had sixty forts and pillboxes surrounded by obstacles and stockades. During daytime, communication was through signals, but the forts at Júcaro, Ciego de Ávila and Morón were linked by telegraph. Should wires be cut or out of service for any reason—and at night, sentinels on duty could shout the alarm—the fort farthest from where something happened would learn about it within a couple of minutes. Ten thousand soldiers manned the line of fortifications. A narrow-gauge railroad made possible the speedy transportation of men, ordnance, and artillery from one point to another.

The line's first echelon, to the east, consisted of cavalry outposts where two thousand riders watched over roads and trails.

The second was the fortifications proper. The third echelon, to the west, had four widely spaced forts equipped with telegraphs, where patrolling units camped. Riders liaised with the second echelon when the telegraph was not working.

On paper, the Trocha was impregnable. In real life, on January 6, under fire, Gen. Máximo Gómez and 1,164 rebels crossed it. Gómez was superficially wounded on his neck. A bullet fired from Fort Fourteen missed his carotid artery by a hairsbreadth.

The Dominican had left two sealed letters in the hands of Representative Francisco Sánchez. One, addressed to the president of the Republic in Arms, informed the government that he would march westward during the first week of January. The other, addressed to Brig. Gen. Henry Reeve, appointed him acting commander of the Liberation Army in Camagüey. He would lead 200 cavalrymen and 462 infantrymen.

In January, Reeve fought one important combat where twelve Spaniards lost their lives. His men sniped at forts, intercepted a supply convoy, and torched sugarcane plantations that were the property of the Montejo mill.

As rebel strategists had foreseen, once Gómez moved west the Spanish high command began transferring regiments deployed in Oriente and Camagüey to Las Villas and Matanzas. The units that remained in the eastern territories withdrew to towns and villages. In Camagüey, the Magarabomba and Corralito forts were abandoned, the countryside relinquished to Reeve's men and to a few Spanish units that included Cubans who fought with Spain. Military operations declined significantly and no major victories were achieved.

In February and March only skirmishes took place. On April 18, in the evening, as Reeve, his security detail, and five adjuncts bivouacked at the Alacranes pasture ground, a Cuban

farmer came to tell them that a Spanish squadron on the hunt
for El Inglesito had pitched camp a league away. Early next
morning, a fleeing sentinel warned that more than a hundred
enemy cavalrymen were less than two hundred varas away.
Reeve managed to mount his horse in time to escape. In hot
pursuit followed the "Twelve Apostles," a dozen deserters from
the Liberation Army thus dubbed, who rode with the Spanish
squadron.

"Fall back. Fall back as agreed," Quesada barked to Reeve's
four escorts.

Antonio and Modesto, the adjunct, galloped alongside
Reeve, not firing, looking back every few yards. Pascual and
Nicolás followed them for a hundred yards or so while Quesada and a soldier named Otilio Varona fired to cover the retreat. Soon after, Pascual and Nicolás reined in their horses,
turned, and opened fire to permit Quesada and Varona to back
off. The general and his two escorts kept going. Reeve's security detail repeated this twice and felled two of the Apostles.
The second time, Varona fell from his horse, was captured, and
executed by firing squad that same day. But Reeve and all the
others escaped unharmed.

In May, El Inglesito learned that in the Department of Oriente disgruntled rebel officers led by Gen. Vicente García
wanted to depose President Cisneros, modify the constitution,
and reform the government.

"But Battle, they deposed President Céspedes less than two
years ago," complained Reeve to his friend. "Now they want
to depose Cisneros? For the love of God! Having a falling-out
every year or so, we won't defeat the Spaniards."

Reeve had learned the euphemistic oath from Anunciación—
por el amor de Dios in Spanish—and, finding it not in the
least offensive, had adopted it. On the first few occasions that

Battle heard his friend swearing like a señorita, he suppressed smiles. Reeve refused to say the other euphemism most men utilized, *Me cago en diez*—literally, "I shit on ten"—not to say *Me cago en Dios*"—literally, "I shit on God"—*diez* substituting for *Dios*. This time, however, Battle was so incensed he overlooked the feminine oath.

"I don't know what they think, Henry. I just don't know. These men are not stupid; they've been risking their lives for Cuba Libre for years. They must have a reason."

All week long, Reeve had ridden with Battle's company, his old squadron. Since his appointment as chief of the regiment, he hadn't spent time with his favorite unit for two reasons: Others might think he was giving it preferential treatment; and where his friend was in charge, supervision was unnecessary. In the daytime, veterans had eagerly—and unsuccessfully— searched for the enemy, hoping to be led into combat by the man they admired most. In the evenings, after supper, anecdotes were recounted. Illuminated by swarms of fireflies and several smoldering stogies, between forty and fifty men surrounded El Inglesito, Battle, and the longest-serving officers and soldiers. They would listen to the old hands recounting amusing stories, pointing at one another, slapping their thighs and doubling over, or growing serious and silent when the name of a fallen brother in arms was mentioned. Reeve's visit had another purpose: to promote Battle to lieutenant colonel, an advancement long overdue.

This Sunday afternoon was cloudless and all around flowers in bloom, fluttering butterflies, chirping birds, and courting quadrupeds signaled that spring was at its peak. Battle was sitting in his hammock, Reeve in his very special *taburete*.

"The Major told me once," Reeve said to Battle, "'In war,

you shelve things like democracy and politics. You postpone disagreements concerning governance, justice, taxes, and so forth and so on. Those things are discussed after total victory is achieved.' You people haven't understood that."

"Hey, hey, hold on. What do you mean 'you people'?"

"You Cubans."

Battle looked around, making sure no one could overhear, then said in English, "Henry, I'll be dad shamed if that ain't the cussedest thing you've ever said."

"What?"

"'You Cubans.'"

"Well, all those disgruntled officers you mentioned are Cubans: Miguel Bravo, General Vicente García, and . . . others I don't know, but their last names sound Cuban."

"You are no less Cuban than they are, Henry," Battle scolded, reverting to his mother tongue. "You keep trying to distance yourself: 'You Cubans'; 'I'm a foreigner'; 'I wash my hands'— that kind of crap. Everybody here considers you a true-blue Cuban. The Major told you once that you are more Cuban than others born here who love Spain and deride Cuba. You were born in the United States; you love the United States. That's fine by me. But you have two nationalities now, whether you like it or not."

Reeve rolled his eyes and crossed his left leg over his right. Battle puffed his cigar.

"All right, I'm Cuban, all right. But that's not the point," Reeve said. "The point is, right now we need to stand united. There are Cuban rebels who think about the whole island as a nation, like the Major, like you, like Maceo. But to the east, it seems, others want to found the Republic of Oriente. Since the Major's death, some here in Camagüey seem to be having similar thoughts: Republic of Camagüey. Rebels in Las Villas refuse to be led by officers from other provinces. What the hell is the matter with you folks—I mean, with us?"

Once again, Battle proved to be an invaluable source of information as, for almost half an hour, he sketched the social and economic distinctions between eastern and western Cuba. The flourishing west, he expounded, produced and exported 95 percent of the sugar and grew all the high-quality tobacco leaves for rolling the famous *puros*. La Habana, seat of the Spanish governor-general, had the busiest port, the only university, and the main branches of all major banks. Matanzas was the richest province. Most of the homegrown talent—engineers, physicians, lawyers, musicians, and writers—had been educated in western Cuba, Spain, or the United States Most of those who were born and raised in the eastern territories, once they returned home, moved to La Habana or Matanzas at the first opportunity.

In eastern Cuba, Battle went on, raising cattle was dominant; all sugar mills were small and bankrupt. For reasons not quite clear—perhaps climate and soil—the quality of tobacco was inferior; its coffee beans, in contrast, were the finest. All in all, Battle said, the majority of the wealthiest families in eastern Cuba had grown envious of the Western Department; they seemed unwilling to modernize their businesses, seek new trading partners, educate the middle class, and diversify. Their construct of euphoric patriotism consisted in arguing that in eastern Cuba the sky was bluest, the mountains higher, the plains immense, the rivers longer and wider, the forests gigantic, the women prettier, and the men braver. They wanted to be independent of Spain . . . and from its collaborators to the west.

"So, what can you, sorry, what can *we* do to make these people see they have to postpone all that . . . how you call it?"

"Regionalism."

". . . regionalism until we kick the *gallegos* out?

"Nothing, Henry. We can do nothing. Regionalism has developed over a century, maybe two. Every Cuban child born in Oriente learns it from the cradle. Remember Brigadier Figueredo?"

"Of course I remember him."

"He's that kind of man. Figueredo wants Cuba to become independent so he can buy all the herds of fleeing Spanish cattlemen and be the richest cattleman in Cuba. He will never leave his land and his mistress to fight the war here, or in Las Villas, or in Matanzas. And I hate to admit this, but there are many Figueredos in Oriente."

Reeve stared at his friend for a few moments. "Jordan saw it coming," he said at last.

"The American general?"

"Yep. You never met him, right?"

"No, I didn't."

"Shrewd man. Except for *sí* and *no*, he didn't understand a word in Spanish, but in staff meetings, just judging by voice tones and expressions, he grasped that *orientales* despised *camagüeyanos*, and vice versa. Now, I know *villareños* hate the guts of both their eastern neighbors."

"He told you?"

"Yeah, and he thought it would be one of the reasons you, I mean, *we* wouldn't win the war."

Battle took a deep breath and exhaled. Then he dragged on his cigar, found it had gone dead, clicked his tongue in disgust, and dropped the stub to the ground. "I reckon Jordan was some pumpkins. What other reasons did he give you?"

"Well, he said we were short on men and weapons, inexperienced and unwilling to learn from the experienced—meaning himself, of course. He also believed our, I mean, *their* neutrality agreement . . . Oh, for the love of God, Battle. Is it *our* neutrality agreement or *their* neutrality agreement?"

Battle doubled over with laughter, and eventually Reeve chortled gleefully. Not far away, Antonio chuckled.

After a minute, Battle wiped tears from his cheeks and said, "Go on, go on. You were referring to the neutrality agreement."

"Jordan believed strict enforcement of the neutrality agreement would sever our main supply line. And he was right. Now expeditions come from Jamaica, like Ryan's."

They remained silent for a minute or so, looking without seeing, hearing without listening, absorbed in their thoughts.

"Are we going to lose this war, Henry?"

"Only if regionalists get the upper hand. In the morning, I'll promote you to lieutenant colonel. Then you'll ride to this place—what's its name?"

"What place?"

"The place where General Vicente García is bivouacking."

"Lagunas de Varona."

"Ride there as fast as greased lightning and give our views as the views of the acting commander of the Liberation Army in Camagüey."

"At your service, General," Battle mumbled, more stunned by the daunting mission he had been given than by a promotion he felt he deserved.

"Take a six-man escort. Your second in command will head the company until you come back."

"Yes, sir."

"Go, pardner, go and do what you have to do to get ready. I have to take a dump. Damn okra. Antonioooo!"

★　★　★

Even though the rebel government asked Gen. Máximo Gómez to return to Oriente and mediate (which entailed retracing his path and crossing the Trocha, then traversing it again to return to Las Villas), despite long negotiations between Gómez and García, and regardless of the impassioned appeals for unity made by Battle and others who feared factionalism, the regionalists got the upper hand and President Cisneros had to resign.

One reason that peeved the dissenters was the modification of the island's territorial division. The Eastern Department began at Punta de Maisí and ended at the Jobabo River. The rest of the island—roughly 60 percent of the total area, two-thirds of its total length, and where around 80 percent of the invested capital resided—was the Western Department. But in March, the government of President Cisneros had passed the creation of three Departments: Eastern, Central, and Western. The Central Department included the jurisdictions of Tunas, Nuevitas, and Puerto Príncipe—originally part of the Eastern Department.

The ensuing army reorganization provoked additional resistance. Three corps were formed: the First, Second, and Third, under Gen. Manuel Calvar, Gen. Vicente García, and Gen. Máximo Gómez, respectively. Albeit other factors were in play, such as bad blood between generals and personal ambitions, in Battle's opinion regionalists believed that both changes proved the government was too western-minded and had to be deposed.

Reeve had wanted to be part of the thrust to the west since its inception, but factionalism sickened him to the point that he obsessed with joining Máximo Gómez in Las Villas. He believed the war had to be won before further dissension made internecine conflict probable. If that happened, he thought, the rebellion would self-defeat itself.

In September, Vicente García nominally assumed command of the rebel army's Second Corps. In reality, the government asked Reeve to keep the position of acting commander in Camagüey so that García wouldn't have to leave the combat zone that he knew like the back of his hand. Reeve was understandably offended.

"I won't do it, Battle," he said to his confidant after making up his mind, "for two reasons. First, I fear I may not get along with General García; I don't approve of what he did to President Cisneros and I'm not good at pretense. Sooner or later, we would clash. Second, this gives me the perfect reason to irrevocably resign my commission in Camagüey and join General Gómez in Las Villas."

"Can I go with you?"

"I would be honored. But General García must give his authorization."

As things turned out, Gen. Vicente García had listened to so many favorable opinions about Reeve's courage and determination that he admired the man even before they met on September 30 in Peralejo. García was mulling over moving units from Camagüey to Oriente and asked Reeve's opinion. Reeve advised against it and García canceled the idea. That same day, El Inglesito learned that the government had approved his transfer to the Third Corps.

Seventeen days later, he received a letter.

FROM: *The Chiefs and Officers of the Second Corps, First Division.*
TO: *Brigadier General H. M. Reeve.*
General:
    For six years we have witnessed your noble and generous efforts in behalf of the cause that our arms defend.
    We have admired the bravery and self-sacrifice of the

young foreigner who renounced his homeland to fight for ours.

Since June 23, 1874, we have bestowed upon you our respect and obedience because we trusted you implicitly. You have proved deserving of such trust.

Now that you have resolved to serve in Las Villas and shan't lead us any longer, we give you a most friendly farewell and express our sadness for your departure and deep gratitude for your past service.

What comforts us is that down yonder, where so many laurels await our brave brothers, they shall become worthy of your commendation and deserving of your courage. We hope that in the midst of your glory and victories, you will kindly remember this division, so saddened today by your departure.

Oblivion is impossible where gratitude reigns, and our gratitude and admiration will always be with you.

Camp at Los Peralejos, October 17, 1875

Fifty-two men had signed the letter.

On November 3, Henry Reeve, his orderly, adjunct, four-man security detail, six officers, and a guide crossed the Trocha. The dry season had begun, the temperature had dropped somewhat, and Reeve felt physically better and mentally alert. Riding in the daytime, he observed his new surroundings with curiosity. To the untrained eye, vegetation was indistinguishable. He had the impression that similar species of trees, shrubbery, grasslands, flowers, and herbs were to be found throughout the island. Smells and sounds were identical, water tasted the same. It was impossible to tell the fauna apart:

jutías, majáes, nightingales, mockingbirds, *zunzuncitos.* The Escambray range, silhouetted on the horizon, brought to mind the high mountain range to the north of Oriente. Plain folks encountered by chance seemed as destitute as their equals in Camagüey and had an identical racial composition. Maybe they even shared legends and superstitions—such as a belief in the *guije,* a naughty gnome (an old black man or a black boy, depending on who told the story) who enjoyed playing tricks on people; circling the trunk of a *ceiba* three times for luck; crossing one's shoes beneath the bed to sleep better; seeing mysterious lights on roads and trails at night; and many other notions.

They joined Gen. Máximo Gómez two days later, near Sancti Spiritus. That night, at Arroyo Grande, in pitch-darkness, both generals conferred.

"I want you to assume command of the Second Division; it has two cavalry squadrons and three hundred infantrymen," Gómez said, getting right to the heart of the matter. "I recommend you appoint Colonel Cecilio González chief of the infantry. He has been operating all this year near the Zapata marshland and knows the region very well."

"Good. When do you want me to start operating, Major General?"

"Yesterday."

Reeve smiled, shook his head, and clucked his tongue. Reeve's body language made Gómez think El Inglesito had gone totally native. "I am ready, and the men who came with me are ready, but our horses aren't," Reeve said. "We covered forty leagues in three days. Can you give us fresh mounts?"

"I'm short on horses."

"Then I will assume command, but I need to rest our crow baits."

"I understand. Take your time."

"Any tactical suggestions, sir?"

Involuntarily, Gómez gave a nod of approval. El Inglesito had not gone totally native. Cubans seldom asked for suggestions; most acted as though they knew all the answers.

"You know our goal: Take the war to the plains of Colón and Matanzas, the heartland of sugar production," the major general began. "The more we cripple the sugar industry, the less tax money goes to the enemy's coffers. But right now we are short on men, weapons, and supplies. The government has promised to send me reinforcements, but until they do, I avoid confronting large enemy formations, so as not to come out at the little end of the horn. The plantations and sugar mills around Cienfuegos are a one-horse industry compared with those in Matanzas, but they are within our reach. So, what I have been doing . . . Did Agramonte ever mention what the Spaniards did after Napoleon occupied their country?"

"He did, yes."

"It's what I've been doing—establishing small, highly mobile flying squads led by a lieutenant and local dispatch riders—folks who know nearly every nook and cranny around here—so I may order them to regroup at certain spots if an important action is to take place. I keep a squadron with me, along with my security detail and as many messengers as the number of platoons operating. I move from one platoon to the next, or reinforce the one being hunted down, or that which is closer to a big enemy unit."

"Seems the wise thing to do."

"Not what General Jordan would've done."

Reeve nodded twice. "I know. But under the circumstances, I think your tactics more appropriate. The enemy can send battalions here much faster than to Camagüey or Oriente. So it's prudent to make them believe there're just a couple of small rebel parties operating here."

"They may reach another conclusion."

"What do you mean, sir?"

"We hit them simultaneously at a dozen places, they may overestimate our force."

"So?"

"It's a risk we have to assume."

Reeve's division started operating four days later. He dispatched platoons to eight districts, under orders to snipe at forts and sugar mills, torch warehouses and sugarcane plantations. On December 7, an infantry unit under Colonel González captured a launch, burned it down, and executed the Spanish lieutenant Francisco Cantero, who had participated in the execution of a Cuban colonel. Two days later, González attacked and occupied the town of Jagüey Grande and set on fire ten stores, the army barracks, the church, and a number of houses.

All in all, in December the Second Division engaged the enemy at eighteen locations, set fire to nine sugarcane plantations, sniped at mills, and derailed a train. To celebrate New Year's Eve, Reeve attacked the Jagua fortress, occupied the house where the governor of the fortress lived (the governor died in combat), and pillaged and burned two stores.

The Spanish general headquarters judged the threat serious enough to reorganize, mobilize units to Las Villas, and try to prevent the rebels from spilling over into Matanzas.

SEVEN

1876

★

The rebel offensive went full steam ahead in January. While Máximo Gómez devoted his main efforts to stocking up on weapons and ammunition, recruiting volunteers, and pressing the rebel government for the additional troops he had been promised, Reeve torched eleven sugarcane plantations and sniped at the Spanish units guarding the mills proper. He lost three men and twenty horses attacking a Spanish unit at La Larga, but during the remaining weeks he set fire to a sugar warehouse, a distillery, and several stores. He sank a small steamer a few days later. On January 24, he assaulted the Pasalodo mill, which resulted in seven fatalities among its defense force.

The newly appointed governor-general, Joaquín Jovellar, rose to the challenge. He regrouped 152,000 men in four divisions—one deployed in Oriente, another in Camagüey, and two in Las Villas. He partitioned the new theater of operations into twenty-seven military zones. The division under Brigadier

General Armiñan would deal with El Inglesito. That under Brigadier General Baile would contend with Máximo Gómez. Jovellar also added a brigade based in the town of Colón commanded by Brigadier General Rivero.

After struggling for months, the rebel government managed to send two hundred cavalrymen led by Gen. Manuel Calvar to Las Villas. On February 23, Gómez and four hundred riders bivouacking at Manicaragua started getting ready to head for the plains of Cienfuegos and reinforce Reeve.

The new governor-general either figured out by himself or learned from spies that Gómez was organizing his cavalry to intensify the push westward. Jovellar, a strong-willed front-line military man, decided that enough was enough and resolved to lead the combined operations personally. He told his general staff that their paramount goal had to be to quash the rebellion in Las Villas and kill Gómez, Cecilio González, El Inglesito, and as many other rebel officers as possible; those who surrendered or were captured wounded were to be executed by firing squad.

In his heart of hearts, though, Jovellar would have contented himself with thwarting rebel attempts to invade Matanzas.

Reeve persevered in his tactic of harassing the enemy, avoiding combat, gaining time, and waiting for the much-needed reinforcements. He marched, countermarched, and kept torching sugarcane plantations and warehouses.

Gómez was still at Manicaragua on February 26 when scouts reported that less than half a league away, three infantry battalions and five hundred cavalrymen—about two thousand men—with several pieces of field artillery were hunting them down. The Dominican retreated fast, but one hour later he clashed with the enemy cavalry. The combat, one of the bloodiest ever waged in Las Villas, had been going on for two hours when news that the enemy infantry and artillery were getting close reached Gómez. Again he had to flee. The Spaniards suffered almost a hundred casualties; eight rebels died and twenty-two were wounded.

On February 29, with Jovellar in hot pursuit, the Dominican realized that linking up with Reeve would be impossible. To do so, he would have to march and countermarch about twenty leagues, but the horses were exhausted after covering many leagues in three days along terrain unsuitable for cavalcades. Compounding the problem was the fact that the animals had little to eat because most pastures had been torched. Gómez decided to call it quits and retreated to Sancti Spiritus.

Spain had about sixty thousand regular soldiers and volunteers in Las Villas. Slews of units were interposed between Cienfuegos and Sancti Spiritus, effectively keeping Reeve and his men within the confines of Cienfuegos and Colón. At no time had the threat of being encircled and annihilated been greater for El Inglesito and his subordinates.

"What the hell is the matter?" said Reeve, bitterly complaining to Battle on February 29. "Promises, promises, all I get are promises. Damn it, promises don't fire guns or brandish machetes."

Battle raised his eyebrows, pulled down the corners of his mouth, and turned up the palms of his hands in incomprehension. "The letter Gómez sent said he would be here in a couple of days. It was dated the twenty-fourth. What's keeping him?"

"No, no, I don't mean that. Gómez may have been forced to countermarch or engage in combat. What I mean is, in September the government started promising reinforcements. Five months later, they send two hundred men. They must know we are outnumbered ten to one, maybe twenty to one, thirty to one. I haven't the faintest idea how many men this damn Jovellar has moved to Las Villas, but it seems we have a *gallego* per square yard, blast the cursed old imp! And we get two hundred men. I can't believe this."

"Well, right now you know who the biggest toad in the puddle is. What goes on in Las Villas or Matanzas is not his funeral."

"You mean Vicente García?"

"Who else?"

Reeve mulled this over. "Let me tell you. I know he is opposed to extending the war to the west. But I believe he won't oppose sending more men if he learns we are in a bad fix."

This time, Battle only pulled down the corners of his mouth to signal he doubted Reeve's judgment.

"You don't think so?" Cuban body language no longer held secrets for Reeve.

"I don't know, Henry. The man's a mystery to me."

It was the final private conversation the two friends had. The next day, March 1, Reeve and twenty-two cavalrymen engaged the enemy at Perico. A .54-caliber bullet perforated Battle's left cheek and exited through his upper neck, killing him instantly. After a moment of disbelief, Reeve ordered Nicolás and Pascual to recover the body, then retreated in haste.

Reeve had gradually become inured to seeing rebels die, and he had come to accept death in combat as the price of sovereignty. Mystified by the mild sadness he had felt following the deaths of Agramonte and Ryan, he believed he had become unresponsive to the loss of life. But Battle's death made him experience the most profound, almost incapacitating grief of his life. The distinction, he suddenly comprehended, lay in not having had the possibility of staring at the dead bodies of the Major and the Canadian.

Watching Battle's glassy eyes as the corpse was lowered into the three-foot-deep grave, he confronted a gigantic doubt. Anunciación's voice whispered in his ear: *Why do men fight so much? Couldn't you resolve your differences in courts of law? Are wars inevitable?*

Was the price of sovereignty too steep? Reeve wondered. How many noble, intelligent, and kind men had abandoned the women they loved and the children they adored, forgone their professions, relinquished the comfort and security of normal life . . . to end like this? At the bottom of a hole in the middle of nowhere as other men who called themselves patriots bitterly disagreed over politics, territory, and power?

With watery eyes, he watched as exhausted men took turns shoveling the earth back in with their only spade, carried around for that chore. He had been present at dozens of internments, but when clumps of the reddish, wet clay started hitting the face of his friend, he had to avert his gaze. Once Pascual finished tapping the top of the grave with the back of the shovel, he addressed Reeve.

"You pray, Genral."

"No, Pascual. If God watches over us as we think He does, this man doesn't need prayers. He is already in heaven. Thank you all. Let's mount and get out of here."

The daily report, which he dictated at sundown, concluded:

We lost Lt. Col. Emilio Battle in this confrontation. Words can't properly express the profound admiration I felt for this man, nor the extraordinary sacrifices he made for Cuba Libre. I shall write a letter to the government, asking them to notify his wife, and to promote him posthumously to the rank of full colonel.

★   ★   ★

In early March, Reeve sent orders to several flying squads to regroup, and by the thirteenth he had raised a full cavalry company. On the fifteenth he burned three mills to the ground. The next day, he torched the railway station and telegraph station at Retamar and set fire to the sugarcane plantations of three other mills. On March 18, after repelling a Spanish unit that surprised them at their bivouac, the company retreated in an orderly fashion, crossed the main railroad line, ransacked a store, and set fire to a mill and its plantation. Next he ravaged a village, burned fifty houses, and killed a captain and two soldiers from the Corps of Volunteers.

That evening, Modesto, his adjunct, asked permission to speak.

"Granted."

"I want to tell you something, General."

"Go ahead."

"I think it unfair to burn down the homes of civilians."

Reeve nodded twice and folded his arms. He clearly remembered having expressed that opinion to Agramonte the night of the optical-tower fiasco.

"You think it unfair. Interesting. Let me see. Hmm. Yes, it may be unfair to some."

"Then, sir, why do you order homes burned?"

"Because I can't distinguish the innocent from the guilty. Can you?"

Modesto lifted his gaze to the treetops, pondering his answer. "Sir, I believe all civilians are innocent, regardless of whether they are Spaniards, Cubans who side with Spain, or Cubans who are for Cuba Libre."

"Well, Modesto, I take exception to that. Spanish subjects and Cuban traitors do all they can to see us defeated. They pay taxes to the Spanish Crown, fully knowing that with their money the scalawag king pays off the soldiers shooting at *us*, and buys the weapons to shoot at *us* with. The traitors dine and wine Spanish officers at their homes, hoping their daughters will marry Spaniards. They join the accursed Volunteers Corps. Now, how can I fucking find out which are the houses of those who stand for Cuba Libre? Should I politely ask them to raise their hands?"

"General, I didn't mean to get you in a huff."

"I'm not in a huff. Tell me. Should I politely ask those who sympathize with us to raise their hands?"

"Of course not, General."

"All right. Then how am I going to separate the patriots from the traitors?"

"There's no way."

"Let's assume there is a way. What would happen to the patriots after we go away? We would've singled them out as patriots."

"If we didn't burn any home at all, nobody would be singled out."

Reeve snorted and averted his eyes, knowing Modesto was right.

"General, I have to be frank with you. I have no qualms about torching sugarcane plantations, mills, stores, railroad depots, whatever. But I am against torching the homes of civilians. You are my commanding officer and I am supposed neither to question your orders nor to disobey you. Therefore, I respectfully request to be discharged."

This took Reeve by surprise. Rebel soldiers either asked permission to visit the family or deserted. To his knowledge, nobody had ever asked to be relieved from service.

"You request to be discharged?"

"Respectfully. Yes, sir."

"Well, give me some time to consider that."

From that day on, Reeve abstained from burning houses. Modesto never raised again the matter of his discharge.

On March 20, Reeve set an ambush before attacking and reducing to ashes the Reparador sugar mill. The Spanish cavalry unit chasing the arsonists fell into the ambush and eighteen of its riders perished before the survivors took flight. Rebel Lt. Col. Maximiliano Ramos was sent to a field hospital after being badly wounded.

A few days later, the arrival of a dispatch rider made Reeve chuckle for the first time since Battle's death. The man, clad as a Franciscan friar, had an ample girth and rode a burro, like Sancho Panza, Don Quixote's attendant. The news the man brought was not funny, though. El Inglesito had been relieved as commander of the Second Division; the new commander was Maj. Gen. Manuel Calvar. Even so, Reeve had been appointed the division's chief of operations. The dispatch rider also delivered a letter from Maj. Gen. Máximo Gómez. It said that Julio Sanguily had resigned his position as commander of the First Division because the rebels in Las Villas strongly opposed him. The Dominican assured El Inglesito that as soon as his horses were back in shape and he had recruited good guides, he would join him.

It seemed prudent to disperse, so Reeve reassembled the flying squads and kept with him merely twenty men. On April 4, he ransacked and torched the store of the Manacas mill, then burned the store and railway station at Caimito. On April 9, he repelled the attack of an enemy unit; the next day, he burned the Zacatecas mill to the ground; the day after, the San Juan mill went up in flames.

One week later, five leagues to the east of Colón, he set fire to the Santa Bárbara mill, ransacked its store, and seized ten rifles, five hundred cartridges, and ten horses. In the next few days, six other mills and their stores suffered identical fate. In the last two weeks of April, he sniped at other towns and mills.

The rainy season started in early May and displayed its whole gamut, from drizzles to torrential downpours. Horses floundered and tired much sooner because they sank in mud to their knees and hocks, and to their forearms and gaskins on bad days. The sucking sound their legs made when they pulled themselves out and the swelled streams and rivers rumbling day and night were two of the season's typical sounds.

With each passing day, Reeve's old wounds and right hip hurt more and more; his right leg had shortened and was thinner than his left. He consumed the remaining salicylic acid to little avail and frequent nosebleeds. When mounting and dismounting, he ground his teeth to avoid screaming in pain, but once he was strapped to the saddle, the suffering was bearable and he could ride for hours on end.

He missed Anunciación enormously and wrote her letters every time he had an hour to himself. After the execution of Acosta, however, in the letter where he had made clear why he wouldn't visit her again for a long time, he had asked his fiancée not to write back. He did this knowing that the few dispatch riders who infrequently delivered correspondence to the field hospital were under orders to take for delivery only letters penned by Dr. Luaces and by recovering patients writing to their spouses or parents. She wasn't a recovering patient, and even though he felt sure Luaces could arrange it, he believed rank or friendship should not be sources of privilege.

On May eleventh, while bivouacking at Aguacate, Reeve was so feeble that he sent Gabino Quesada, the chief of his security detail, to raze the El Escorial mill. On the twenty-first, feeling better, Reeve successfully led the attack against a Spanish column near Cienfuegos. Other flying squads under El Inglesito sniped or charged at Spanish columns at six sites.

Again, Reeve ordered flying squads to regroup and assembled two squadrons. On June 8, he ransacked the store of the Victoria mill. The defending garrison fought valiantly and six rebels were wounded, Nicolás among them. He died a few hours later.

"What do you mean, he had no last name?" Reeve asked Antonio with a quivering voice, getting ready to say a prayer by the grave.

"No last name, Genral."

"He must have had."

"He said he want forget last name. He last name his owner last name."

Reeve nodded, harrumphed, bowed his head, and closed his eyes. Those in attendance imitated him. He was silent for so long that other rebels partially opened their eyes and stole looks at him. Finally, he prayed.

"Oh Lord, please, I beg you, receive the soul of this man. You know how much he suffered. I don't understand why you permitted his parents to be abducted from Africa, or why you made him a slave. Whatever reasons you had escape my understanding. But he was noble, he was kind, and, above all, he was a brave man. In his ignorance, he worshiped African gods, but if it's true that blessed are the poor in spirit and that you lift up the meek, I beg you to admit him in your kingdom, for he was poor in spirit and meek. In the name of the Father, the Son, and the Holy Spirit. Amen."

Poor discipline and petty internal squabbles in Las Villas kept weakening the rebel forces and making the situation Reeve and his men faced even more difficult. Suspecting he wouldn't get reinforcements or supplies anytime soon, and to stock up and make a show of strength, Reeve ordered his flying squads to head for and disperse around the cities of Colón, Cárdenas, and Matanzas. But it was raining buckets and no important actions took place in the rest of June or in the first two weeks of July, so he countermarched.

On July 21, while resting at Cocodrilo, a Spanish cavalry unit surprised the Cubans. As Antonio bridled and saddled up Reeve's horse, the rest of the squadron charged. By the time El Inglesito joined his subordinates, the enemy was in full retreat. This time, it was Pascual who took a bullet below the sternum and expired before Reeve got to him. That night, Antonio was scared to death when he spied the son of Ogún muttering to himself and hobbling around his hammock, which was, as always, spread on the ground.

"Damn, damn, damn. What am I doing wrong? Why am I losing the bravest, the most faithful? Why don't I get reinforcements? I need reinforcements. There's a limit to what you can do when you are so short of men and weapons. I need more men. I need more rifles and cartridges. We are half-hiding near this marshland, getting eaten alive by mosquitoes and gnats. But what can I do? Damn Spaniards. And damn *villareños*, damn *orientales*, damn *camagüeyanos*. Why don't these people stop their stupid squabbling? Maybe I should try to communicate with patriots in Matanzas and La Habana. Maybe they would join me. Oh God, are you trying my heart? Because, I tell you, I'm no Job, and I'm starting to doubt you. Yes, dear Lord, I'm seriously starting to doubt you, so I think you should lend a hand, right here and right now."

Three days later, Reeve ordered Lieutenant Agüero to take by assault the watchtower at Galdós. All ten Spaniards defending it died; the building was torched. Jovellar, the governor-general, was infuriated. He summoned his general staff and peremptorily ordered—whatever it took, no expense spared—to get El Inglesito, dead or alive. All the territory where Reeve was known to operate was placed under siege. To encircle Reeve's men, troops stationed at urban nuclei were deployed to the countryside. Seeing the defenses of six towns debilitated, rebels from the First Division successfully attacked them.

On August 1, Reeve moved out of the marshland and bivouacked with his men at Las Grietas, a league away from the village of Yaguaramas, among the oldest on the island. He hadn't received news in the last two weeks, but he imagined there was nothing to report, not that his line of communication had been effectively cut by two enemy infantry battalions, Baza and Tarragona, and two cavalry regiments, Regimiento del Príncipe and Regimiento del Rey.

On August 3, he learned that an enemy unit was near. After consultation with staff officers, he decided to ambush it and do what he had done a hundred times: snipe, charge, and flee. Accordingly, the next morning he left the savanna near Yaguaramas and took the road to the town. The sky was clear and by midmorning the sun was mercilessly beating down on men and horses. But intense sunshine lowered the humidity, easing somewhat Reeve's permanent suffering. A gentle breeze flew from the east. Nightingales exchanged trills, butterflies flitted around, and buzzards flew overhead.

He made a brief stop at Cayo Inglés, half a league before the town's limits, to regroup and send his vanguard ahead. He followed closely, too closely. Soon after he heard shots; his scouts had clashed with the enemy. He raced ahead and encountered the Spanish vanguard. Customarily, colonial regiments sent a squad to explore, so when Reeve saw twenty-odd riders, he supposed he was confronting the whole unit chasing him. This time, though, the enemy commander had sent a full platoon to reconnoiter. Reeve drew his machete and charged. He was flanked by Antonio and Gabino Quesada, the chief of his decimated security detail, and followed by Modesto, his adjunct. Soon they found themselves at the center of the Spanish regiment.

A hand-to-hand battle ensued. Reeve stopped the saber blow that a Spanish sergeant aimed at him, swerved, and struck back. His blade cut into his adversary's right thigh; the man grunted and blood gushed. Reeve eyed a Spanish captain and spurred his crow bait in the man's direction; Antonio followed him. The wounded sergeant, however, pulled out his revolver and fired at Gabino Quesada, who took the bullet in the stomach, fell from his horse, and was finished off by a mounted corporal, who fired his Remington carbine at Quesada's face.

Reeve reached his chosen adversary and swung at him. The officer stopped the blow with his saber, then aimed and fired the Colt revolver he held in his left hand at the same instant that his horse bucked. The slug went into Reeve's groin. The Spaniard fired again, but this time, rather than hitting Reeve, the bullet went through the head of his horse. The animal's legs buckled and it fell to the ground. Reeve got his good leg caught under the dying mount.

"*A salvar al general, carajo, que se cayó del caballo*," Modesto shouted at the top of his lungs.

In the din of battle, few rebels heard him, but those who did and saw El Inglesito under his horse, about ten riders, pushed on with such impetus that the Spaniards closer to Reeve shrank away. Antonio dismounted, ran toward the son of Ogún, and started trying to unfasten the harness.

"Run, Antonio, save yourself," Reeve yelled as he pulled his carbine from the saddle holster. Pain engulfed him. Antonio kept trying to untie the harness.

Protected by the horse, Reeve started firing. The animal's spasms of death and the awkward position he found himself in made his aim terrible. Antonio managed to free Reeve from the harness.

"Genral, come."

Reeve tried to get out from under the animal. He had no idea a crow bait could be so heavy.

"I can't."

Antonio strove to lift the animal somewhat but failed. He stood, grabbed the saddle's pommel, and again tried to lift the horse a bit. A Spanish bullet broke his lower jaw and perforated his left carotid artery. Half-choked by a torrent of blood, the orderly fell over the spasmodic animal.

"Antoniooo!" Reeve yelled.

On all fours, Modesto reached El Inglesito. "General, I'll get you out," he said as he grabbed Reeve by the shoulders and ineffectively tugged.

The Spaniards were returning. The horse had died and was immobile, but Antonio was still convulsing. Reeve emptied his Spencer and downed an enemy rider.

"Modesto, run," he yelled, pulling out his revolver. "Tell others what happened. That's an order, Modesto. Run, *co-jones*, hurry."

The adjunct got to his feet and ran as fast as he could. He was ten yards away from a horse when he was cut down.

Enemy riders were closing in on Reeve.

"One," he said when he fired his Colt's first round.

"Two," he counted as galloping Spaniards drew closer. "Three, four, five."

He took the gun's hot muzzle to his right temple. "Six."

Thoughts and images flooded his mind: Mom in a bonnet and her go-to-meeting clothes, taking him and his sisters to St. Paul's on Sunday morning; Agramonte chatting with artisans at a Najasa workshop; a smiling Ramona riding him, watching him closely; traveling aboard a ferry from Brooklyn to Manhattan, a bitterly cold arctic wind blowing; Anunciación on her knees, sobbing, asking him to not go back to the squadron; General Jordan addressing exiled Cubans at Delmonico's; Dr. Luaces putting the awful reeking mask on his face; Anunciación kissing him passionately; his father, preaching; the smiling Ryan wanting to know whether he had a cherry in Havana; embarrassedly feeling the hands of Rosa la Bayamesa wiping his anus clean; why couldn't he move?; the sky was so blue; Máximo Gómez planning the assault on Santa Cruz del Sur; Acosta, hanging by the neck, feet kicking; the Spanish execution squad opening fire on the captured members of the *Perrit*'s expedition; Mr. Saunders, his fifth-grade teacher, recounting the first Thanksgiving.

Anunciación began whispering in his ear.

I love you with all my heart, mind, and each and every bone in my body. I love you too, dear. *I love you since I was born and until I die.* I am dying now, sweetheart. *I love you because of how you are; I love you despite how you are.* I love you because you are perfect, sublime. *I love you because loving you is the greatest of pleasures and the most heartbreaking of sufferings.* There is no suffering in loving you, dearest. *As I love you, I become part of you; I disappear in you.* I will disappear now, but not in you; dust returning to the earth, spirit returning unto God? *As I love you, I grow old and retract to childhood at the same time.* Please, child, grow old for me, live to see Cuba Libre. *I love you because my only reason to live is to love you.* Forgive me, Anunciación. I failed you. God, protect her.

The colonialists recovered Reeve's body and transported it to Cienfuegos.

AFTERWORD

★

I attest: That under number 10, folio 199, number 627, of the Registry of Deaths, the note that literally follows has been entered. This document is issued in accordance with the constitution of the Republic.

In the Parish Ascensión de la Purísima Concepción, village of Cienfuegos, on August six, eighteen seventy-six, I, the Presbyter, Licenciado Don Aureliano Avello, appointed deputy priest by the very illustrious governor of the bishopric, and since the presbyter, Don Francisco Javier de Piñera, interim parish priest and judge ecco, is absent, proceeded to perform the funeral service for the body of Don Enrique Reeve, dubbed "El Inglesito," rebel leader who, according to an official letter issued by the lieutenant colonel governor of this

*village, was killed by the army yesterday near the village of Yaguara-
mas. Said body was taken to this parish's General Cemetery and interred ecca.*

For the record I sign below.

Aureliano Avello

Camagüey, November 26, 1876
Mrs. A.M. Reeve
Madam:

 The undersigned—brothers in arms, friends, and subalterns of
the lamented Brig. Gen. H.M. Reeve, your illustrious son—perform
the sad duty of conveying to you, in their name and in the name
of the whole army, their great sadness at the loss of the leader who,
on August 4 of the current year, tragic day that our homeland will
inscribe in its calendar of ill-fated dates, chose to commit heroic
suicide rather than to be taken prisoner by the Spaniards.

 Your suffering must be intense, madam, but [illegible, possibly
"the Motherland"] is saddened and in mourning as you—fate
denies her the consolation of paying homage to her best champi-
ons, of digging the graves of those who, to break her shackles,
defied the wrath of the tyrant and serenely faced the vagaries of
Destiny.

 From his country of birth he heard the clamor of this unfortunate people, appealing to all free Americans to lend a hand. His
impulsive generosity made him land on our shores, a young and
impetuous legionary of liberty—lacking qualifications other than
his fervent enthusiasm and his strong resolve to fight for the independence of Cuba, a country that he adopted and loved as his own.
Totally devoted to the social and political rebirth of this nation, our

countryside witnessed his heroic feats. At the vanguard of the revo-
lution, the savannas of Colón admired the fantastic rider who—
disabled but indefatigable—appeared to be the avenging angel of
freedom and justice.

He fought incessantly for almost eight years [illegible]. After
conquering the love, gratitude, and admiration of his colleagues
and brothers, when he fell in Yaguaramas like a gladiator in the Ro-
man circus, all those with a sensitive heart simultaneously cried and
applauded. A quotation from Schakespeare could sum up his life:
"Danger and I are two lions born on the same day; but I am the
firstborn."

That is his story. And if something in this world may take com-
fort to the heart of a grieving mother and alleviate the saddest of
her afflictions, it is [illegible] has been sacrificed for the redemption
of a race debased by the stigma of slavery, and for the betterment,
the dignity, and the happiness of a people suffering under the yoke
of despotism.

Cuba safeguards in its heart and mind, as the most precious of
jewels, the efforts, physical sufferings, and heroic deeds of the re-
nowned leader. Despite our anguish, with fortitude we raise our
bloodied banner, fully resolved to conquer our independence and
liberty, which is the best way to honor virtue and heroism.

We hope you understand the distress of our homeland [illegible]
also a mother who has lost a beloved son at the point in time when
his services were most needed. Never forget that all of us, like you,
shed tears over the sacred, magnificent, and supreme sacrifice of
his life.

Accept, madam, our heartfelt condolences and the respectful
regards that from this heroic and unfortunate island send you all
those who, like you, cry disconsolately over the tragedy.

[Twenty-four signatures appear at the end of the letter.]

HENRY REEVE—RECORD OF SERVICE
Promotions

Soldier	May 4, 1869
Sergeant	June 13, 1869
Lieutenant	October 2, 1869
Captain	April 16, 1870
Commander	January 16, 1872
Lieutenant Colonel	March 3, 1873
Colonel	July 27, 1873
Brigadier General	December 10, 1873

Wounds Sustained At	*Date*
El Ramón	May 16, 1869
Las Calabazas	May 27, 1869
La Jagua	November 18, 1870
Hato Potrero	May 28, 1871
Sitio Potrero	November 27, 1871
El Carmen	November 29, 1871
Santa Cruz del Sur	September 28, 1873
Camujiro	July 4, 1874
Río Hanábana	July 25, 1876
Yaguaramas	August 4, 1876
Time served	Seven years and three months

AUTHOR'S NOTE

★

This novel's primary historical source is *Reeve, el Inglesito,* by Gilberto Toste Ballart (Cuban edition, 1973).

All the quotations from historical documents were taken from said work, as was Reeve's record of service, which includes the dates and battles where he was wounded and his term of service. I translated these documents into English. I did not correct certain errors, such as Schakespeare instead of Shakespeare and the inexact quote from *Julius Caesar,* considering that probably the writer(s) quoted from memory during the extremely complex conditions prevailing near the end of the Ten Years War. (The exact quotation from the play is: "We are two lions litter'd in one day. And I the elder and more terrible.")

Sadly, the efforts made to research Reeve's life in Brooklyn from his birth to the day he sailed for Cuba were unsuccessful.